Meredith,

I hope you enjoyed
reading it as much as I
enjoyed writing it.

MY AWFULLY WEDDED HUSBAND

xoxo;

Xavier Stewart

MINERVA STEWART

Novel Lane Books

2018

My Awfully Wedded Husband

Novel Lane Books

PO Box 750402

Las Vegas, NV 89131

Printed in the United States of America

First Printing, 2018

(print)ISBN-978-1732109414

(ePub)ISBN-978-1732109421

(mobi)ISBN-978-1732109407

Library of Congress Control Number: 2018904553

Cover Design

Minerva Stewart @ MinervaStewart.com

Photographer

Emanuel Stewart @ EricEmanuelPhotography.com

for my husband
who made me believe

PROLOGUE

1998

It's midnight. Jocelyn, Mariah, Vanessa and Toni are wearing identical white dresses, their hair plaited into pigtails with their hands rigidly at their sides like they're standing at attention. Aside from their height, weight and complexion, they look exactly the same. And, that's the point. These four are now one.

The pledges stand in a middle of a circle, surrounded by their big sisters of Alpha Delta Zeta. Leona Ellis, the president and dean of pledges, steps forward and ceremoniously opens a Tiffany box revealing four platinum eternity rings.

Jocelyn, radiating confidence, tilts her head even higher as Leona places the ring on her pinkie finger. "The bond of sisterhood is eternal," Leona proclaims.

"This ring represents our strength and our intelligence. Our pledge to remain dignified at all times under all circumstances." Leona continues as she stands before Mariah, the studious one wearing thick black glasses. Mariah nods to Leona as the coveted ring slides onto her finger.

Vanessa, the pretty bombshell and future Ms. California, shimmies with excitement, squealing as she accepts her ring. "Our femininity and grace exude class and good standing in our community." Leona reminds Vanessa.

"And above all, the ring of Alpha Delta Zeta is a symbol of our collective ability to improve the lives of all women, everywhere." Toni, the voracious eater, glances at the dessert table. Leona forces the ring onto Toni's plump pinkie.

"Welcome sisters, to Alpha Delta Zeta Sorority Incorporated!" The circle of sisters toss pink and yellow rose petals over the newly initiated ADZs.

Jocelyn quickly throws her arms around her line sisters and squeezes them. "Let's swear that no matter how rich and successful we will obviously become, we'll always be there for each other."

The ladies raise their pinkies and unanimously swear, "Promise!" A camera flash immortalizes the ladies, pinkies raised and oath taken.

ONE

JOCELYN the SOCIAL CLIMBER

My husband gave me herpes. On purpose. He wasn't my husband at the time. He was Big Brother Herschel Harris of the Martha's Vineyard Harrises. That's how he introduced himself to me, like I knew where Martha's Vineyard was or that I should be impressed. I never heard anyone be so proud of their family name. Maybe this is how students talk about where they're from at the University of Santa Barbara (USB). My family wasn't anything other than working poor who never took vacations, let alone knew about Martha's Vineyard, the summer home for the Black elite. But Herschel didn't know that and I wasn't going to tell him. So I decided, without really knowing I had decided, to reinvent myself right then and there.

Those life-defining moments come out of nowhere, don't they? Suddenly you just decide to shed your past. Here I was, attending a university, far, far away from home. I could be anybody I wanted to be. And I wanted to be like them, the Black elite. They moved with an ease, like they were never late and if they were late, they knew everybody would wait until they showed up. They didn't step out of the way or say 'excuse me' or 'sorry' when they bumped into someone. They expected you to move. They commanded the right of way on the bike path, in the hall, even on the quad. I wanted that kind of respect.

I gave it right back to Big Brother Herschel with my head tilted like his and the same tone as his and I said I was Jocelyn Downes of the Vallejo Downes. He looked at me like he couldn't tell if I was serious, joking, or making fun of him. That was awkward. When his smile started to fade, I did what I read about in the book I stole from the library, *How To Win Friends and Influence People;* I complimented him on his teeth. Hey, it's 1998. I'm eighteen. I'm not a genius. I'm winging it and Herschel did have good teeth. White. Perfectly aligned. No chips. No stains. Colgate teeth. A Crest mouth raised on fluoride. I've always been a mouth snob. If you didn't have nice teeth, I couldn't date you 'cause I couldn't kiss you, and bad, yellow stained teeth spoke volumes about your hygiene and habits. Herpes, on the other hand, I didn't have any previous association with the simplex. I only knew you couldn't get rid of it. Gargling with Listerine was no match for the virus. I was stuck. But as dear ole' drunken dad used to say during a blurry-eyed moment of clarity, 'Don't be stuck down, be stuck up.' So I made another decision that would change my life. I decided herpes would be the best thing to ever happen to me. I was right. Until I was very wrong.

My future ex-husband, Herschel, was a sophomore at USB. I was a freshman when I caught his roving eye. Me. Jocelyn Downes. The first in my family to go to college. Daughter of a truck driver father and telemarketer mother. Big Brother Herschel of Kappa Omega Fraternity Incorporated was everything a Kappa Omega man ought to be. Handsome. Tall. Persuasive. Smart. And supremely confident. But because God saw fit not to give anyone too much good stuff, Herschel also had a cleft lip that had been reconstructed when he as a child but

3

the scar was still visible and his nostrils were slightly twisted. He also had a slight lisp. But you couldn't tell Herschel that he wasn't fine. He knew he was and he made others believe it too. That's what confidence can do. It can make others believe what isn't there. And if he ever felt self-conscious about his Picasso appearance, his upbringing straightened him out. Herschel hailed from the Harris family, which I quickly learned was an established Black political family with ties to Congress. His uncle was the current senator from Alabama. His aunt on his father's side was the mayor of a town in Arkansas and contemplating a bid for governor. His father was a corporate lawyer on Wall Street and his mother, Martha, attended only the important fundraisers for high profile diseases. All this was heady stuff for a girl from Vallejo, a place you pass on your way to somewhere else. My family's claim of distinction was having goats and chickens in our backyard and a father who taught his kids how to drive an 18-wheeler. By the time I entered the university, I could double shift gears without touching the clutch. A subject that never came up during freshmen ice cream socials. What I lacked in a reputable family name, I made up for in resourcefulness and moxie.

At the time, I believed getting infected with herpes was an act of love. An act of God. Divine intervention. I had to believe something. All the self-help books told me that everything happens for a reason. I was not going to be infected with an STD for nothing. I had to believe

Herschel was my destiny and the simplex virus would be an incurable bond that would unite us forever. Can you believe that crap? I was young, dumb, and full of… delusion. If I believed anything else, like the reality of the situation, I'd be suicidal. There I was, eighteen and tainted. That's how we sealed our courtship. Not with flowers but with a sexually transmitted disease.

When Herschel told me he gave me herpes he expected me to throw a fit and curse him out. If I were any other girl, I would have told him to f*&k himself and lament my dilemma. So he did what any guy would do who wants to protect himself, he told me in the most public way possible, during finals week in study hall.

"There she is," Herschel announced, disrupting the silence of my Economics study group, grinning wide enough to show all thirty-two perfectly white teeth. Before I could tear off my lopsided glasses, he planted a wet kiss on my lips.

"Hey. What are you doing here? I thought you went to the leadership conference in L.A." He stood behind my chair, kissed me on top of my head, smiling at the freshmen girls across the table. They gushed and giggled back at him. Herschel was also an incurable flirt.

"I need you," he whispered.

"Now? Herschel, I look a mess," I said, smoothing down my frizzy bangs.

"You're just the way I like you. C'mon." He said this loud enough for the girls to hear. They practically swooned.

Herschel pulled out my chair and helped me stand. My knees popped with indignation. I'd been sitting for two hours studying Econ for my final on Wednesday. I hoped I didn't smell. Did I put on deodorant? I did a discreet smell check as he led me to the patio. The patio. That was when I knew something was wrong. He was putting me on display. The patio is brightly lit so anyone walking by or even across the quad, not to mention inside the library's first floor, can see us. The patio was known as the fishbowl. I was in full view of my study group. He didn't want to make out in the Black Studies section like I thought. Herschel was breaking up with me! The fucker even backed me up against the railing, so I was facing everyone in the library.

"I have something to tell you. But before I do, I want you to know that I love you."

He loves me? He never told me that before. Not even post-coital when we were covered in sweat and my hair was a poufy afro even though I had just flat ironed and hot combed it into straight submission. He loves me. Am I supposed to say it back? I didn't know what to do or say, so I just blinked.

"I have..." he looked around and whispered, "herpes. And I'm pretty sure you have it too." He waited for my response. I didn't move. I stopped blinking. "Well, say something."

"Well, I mean. First, you tell me you love me and then you tell me you gave me herpes. Which came first? The herpes or the love?"

"I don't know. It's jumbled together. I thought I was in remission."

"Remission?"

"I haven't had a flare-up in years."

"Years!"

"Lower your voice," Herschel hissed.

I looked over his shoulder. My study group was whispering and watching us. By the look on my face, they assumed he was breaking up with me. Probably wondering how long before they can knock on his door or 'bump' into him. What would Emily Post advise on the appropriate time to wait for sloppy seconds? Herschel gripped my hand, pulling me closer, forcing me to focus on him.

"Yeah so, I thought I was fine. But after the last time with you, I noticed something. And now I'm dealing with it."

"You gave me a disease. On purpose. You knew and you infected me."

"Don't make it sound bad. You're making it sound like I gave you cancer."

"I'm sorry. Educate me. Is there a cure for herpes?"

"Ssssh! Stop saying that word." He looked around the empty patio. "Hey, you're the one who didn't want to use a condom."

"You said you were clean! I'd never been with anyone else. I asked you…" I took a breath, lowered my voice. "…I asked you if you had anything. And you know what, if you try to blame this on me, I will raise my voice. I'll shout from the bell tower Herschel Harris is diseased and dangerous."

"You want to ruin me, is that it?"

"You don't get to play the victim. That's my role. You're the perp. Remember that. You did this. This is your doing."

"I said I love you, baby. The way I see it. Look, we both got it. So…nothing's changed. We can still kick it sometime. It's not the end of the world. Everybody's got something. Nobody's a hundred percent clean no more. Look at all the stuff they put in the water. I mean, what's in the meat we eat? Nothing's organic. We all got a little pesticide in us."

He had the nerve to flirt with me! The smirk. The oily smile. I was disgusted but not undone.

"Uh huh."

Herschel released his grip on my hand and his eyes flickered as he calculated my worth. It was the first time I saw him weigh the consequences of his actions. It wouldn't be the last. "I'll take you to my family doctor. You can get your prescription from him instead of the university med center. You know, so nobody'll know. And as far as you having sex with other people, well, that's on you. I'm not going to tell you to do something I'm not going to do."

Again, I fell into silence and blinked. This jerk doesn't know what it's like to be poor with nothing to lose. The only difference between him and me, is that I fucked up. I didn't fuck down.

"We can still be cool but we don't need to be exclusive," he continued.

I overlooked the insult and blinked.

He grabbed me again. This time, pleading with me. "No one knows about my condition. Not even my family. Look, what do you want from me? Jo-Jo, I'm really sorry. I'll give you money. I know you don't have much."

My dad may have been a truck driver instead of a senator, but Ike didn't raise no fool. I was a woman determined to rise and Herschel Harris's pride and shame were my gateway to a better life. Staring at Herschel, his desperation felt thick and gooey like quicksand. He was sinking and I was his lifeline. For the first time in my life, I had the upper hand over a man. This was a defining moment. When you grow up with farm animals, you learn how to turn shit into fertilizer. I shushed him and kissed his cheeks.

"I didn't realize until this moment how much you mean to me. Maybe it was an accident or maybe you did it on purpose, but I'm yours now. I can't be with anyone else. You made sure of that, didn't you? Don't worry. This will be our secret." He looked relieved.

"I promise I'll make this up to you. Just tell me what you want me to do."

That's it. That's what I was waiting for. I wanted him in my good graces. I had him. "I want to meet your family."

He looked perplexed. "Okay." He sounded hesitant. "You know what, no. I'll give you money or something but there's no reason for you to meet my family. Forget it."

*****

A month later, I was at Martha's Vineyard to meet his family. It was my first time on the Vineyard and I was worried my clothes would look shabby against the New England backdrop. Every house looked straight out of a Norman Rockwell painting. Perfect lawns. White picket fences. Pastel Victorian homes. And this was the Black section! I learned Oak Bluffs was where Black people have been vacationing for generations. Well no one told my family. We never went anywhere except to barbecue at the local park.

Herschel's mother looked like Lena Horne. Timeless. Ageless. Elegant. She didn't walk so much as glide across the room. I'd never met a Black woman like her. I'd never met any woman like her. And by the way, his mother's name was Martha. I don't know how it escaped my mouth but it did, "Oh, I get it. Martha's Vineyard." She looked at me. Her eyes laughed before she howled. In fact, the whole family burst out laughing.

"That's flattering, but no dear, this isn't my vineyard although I act like it is."

I. Died. Inside. I was mortified. I knew the vineyard wasn't named after her, I mean I'm not an idiot. I had a 4.0 G.P.A. I was just associating her name with the vineyard so I wouldn't forget it. Well, it was too late to explain myself. I looked at Herschel for help. He knew I was terrible at remembering names but all he did was laugh along with them. I think his mother saw how red my cheeks were so she hugged me.

"I needed that laugh. Whew! You are funny. Herschel, show Jocelyn to her room. She's staying in the Magnolia."

I followed Herschel through the house, or cottage, as they called it. Apparently, people on Martha's Vineyard live in cottages even if the house is as big as a mansion. The Harris' cottage in Oak Bluffs was a two-story, classic shingle style Victorian home with a wraparound porch shaded by mature oak trees. And yes, there was a white picket fence. The house, sorry, the cottage, had been handed down through the generations and impeccably maintained.

The cottage was their summer home, used for family gatherings throughout the year, and on this occasion, the gathering was for Herschel's spring break. I marveled at the oddest things, like the pale blonde wood floors with wide planks. That struck me as very chic. Pale wood floors. And not a speck of dirt? I guess dirt ain't allowed in Martha's cottage in Martha's Vineyard. The library was magnificent. It wasn't huge or anything, but bookshelves filled with real books covered the walls. And not paperbacks. Hardcovers. Serious books with titles like Torts, Constitution, and such. No romance novels here. His father, Mr. Hezekiel Harris, was scheduled to arrive on the Friday night daddy boat. He was known as HH to family and old friends. Herschel called him Sir. I made a promise to come back to the library and inspect the reading selection before Sir HH arrived. The library smelled like tobacco and flowers. Their very own library! A room dedicated to reading and thinking. How rich are these people?

Martha kept fresh cut flowers in the house. So the rooms smelled like lavender or rose or lilies, depending on which room you were in. The Magnolia room was aptly named. The sweet, heady fragrance met me at the door. Herschel balked at the overpowering scent before opening the window but I loved it. I leaned over the fresh flowers on my nightstand and inhaled. Deeply. I wanted all of my senses to imprint this moment into my being. A watercolor painting of magnolia flowers hung above my headboard. Yes, my headboard. I claimed this room as my own. The buttercream paint matched the yellow bud in the middle of the magnolia flower. And the magnolia motif continued on the Egyptian cotton sheets and plush towels. Martha opened the door and watched me take in everything.

"Is it too strong? Some people don't like the scent," she said, looking at Herschel opening all three windows.

"Of course it's too strong. You make everything too strong," he said as he kissed his mother's cheek.

"Well aren't you lucky I made you?" she asked, grazing her thumb over his chin, pleased with herself.

"I'm gonna take a shower," he said to me before disappearing, leaving me alone with his mother. "If there are any plants in the shower, I'm throwing them out," he called out.

"Leave the peonies in the bathtub!"

She returned her attention to me, watching me unpack my pitiful selection of clothing. I felt as thinly exposed as my second-hand sweater from Goodwill. I carefully lifted my clothes out of my borrowed weekender bag and quickly placed them in the dresser drawer. I must have been frowning while doing this because she asked if I liked the room. If not, there were three other guest rooms to choose from. Four guest rooms! How. Rich. Are. These. People? I grew up in a three-bedroom house, no hallway, and one bathroom for the five of us. When my older brother came back from the Army, he slept on the couch until his PTSD kicked in and we woke up one morning to find him standing naked in the front yard. After that, my parents made me sleep in their room.

"The room is beautiful, ma'am. It's the prettiest room I've ever been in. I love magnolias." She stood there waiting for me to continue. Or maybe not. But she had this amused look on her face and I suddenly saw a gnat fly across my forehead. I tried not to swipe at it. Gnats are drawn to me.

"You do? You love magnolias?" she asked, sitting on the overstuffed striped armchair, prompting me to continue.

"Yes, ma'am. They're not afraid to be what they are. They're big and bold. They stand out and make their presence known. They're not a fearful flower."

"I don't think I've ever met a fearful flower and I know my flora. I've come across wallflowers on occasion. But never fearful flowers."

And again, I felt like a fool. I can't say nothing right. "No, I meant ... they're not shrinking violets."

Martha looked at me like I was an idiot savant and let out another deep rich laugh. She laughed like she was in the great outdoors. Her mouth opened so wide I could see her tonsils and all her teeth popped against her bright red lipstick. I laughed too.

"HH is going to love you. Feel free to rest or freshen up. We're having the neighbors over. Dinner's at five. Are you allergic to anything?"

"No, ma'am. I eat everything. Thank you again for having me here. This is the most beautiful house I've ever seen."

"Call me Martha."

"Yes, ma'am."

After she closed the door, I collapsed on the bed. I must have died of bliss 'cause Herschel had to shake me awake.

"Hurry up and get dressed. Everyone's arrived." He kissed me and looked at me. And smiled.

I smiled back. He pulled back the covers. I was in a USB t-shirt and panties. When he reached for my thong, I playfully slapped his hand away.

"Your mother thinks I'm an idiot."

"She told me she likes you. You're different."

"Different? Is that good?"

"She said you were a delightful rube."

"Like a hick, a bumpkin?"

"Focus on the word delightful. Repeat after me," he said as he worked his way into my panties. "Delightful."

"Delightful," I whispered.

It was the best ten-minute sex we've ever had. Not counting the fifteen-minute sex we had when he gave me herpes. He held my hand as we walked outside onto the porch. Or, the veranda as they called it. The view was spectacular. And I'm not talking about the bay view with sailboats bobbing on the water or the dozens of Black kids skimming the water on jet skis like motorized mosquitoes. The view that struck me was these distinguished Black people having drinks, smoking cigars and lounging, bathed in the glow of the setting sun. I walked into an Essence editorial.

The Mitchells, the Llewellyns, the Halls, and me. The women had easy laughs. Again, I noted the relaxed manner of the rich. The men smoked cigars on the veranda overlooking the bay. For some reason, I thought of my mother who always looked stressed and tight. On occasion, I'd hear her laugh, usually while on the phone, clenching a Benson & Hedges cigarette between her fingers. One thing I learned about being poor is that it keeps you tight. Your mind and your body. Stress and anxiety were frenemies of mine. But here on Martha's Vineyard, I could relax too.

I'd never been around Black people who could drink whiskey and scotch without inevitably getting drunk and the evening end when the police show up in response to a domestic disturbance. But not these people. Here they were, drinking high balls and wine spritzers and the occasional imported beer and everybody was getting along, actually enjoying each other's company even more as the day wore on.

The Black folks on Martha's Vineyard were what WEB DuBois proclaimed as the Talented Tenth. They were the leaders of Black America. They were the descendants of slaves turned domestic help turned teachers turned doctors and lawyers turned politicians. The men carried themselves like Harry Belafonte. You know, dignified and graceful. My pop would call them smooth. They talked about politics, art, religion, the latest news stories, books, the vineyard but they never talked about their jobs. I knew they had important jobs to be able to afford a summer home but I couldn't tell who was a doctor, lawyer or politician. And the women joined in on their conversations. They interrupted the men! These women had space to voice their opinions and to actually disagree with their husbands. Another unimaginable act from where I'm from. My father's word was law and if you didn't agree you learned to keep it to yourself. But like I said, not these people.

These enlightened, educated folks expected their children to join the conversation. There wasn't the unspoken rule that adults and kids didn't mix. At Martha's house on Martha's Vineyard, kids were encouraged to have an opinion. When the conversation turned to the misogynistic lyrics of hip-hop, Martha prompted Courtney, the Hall's thirteen-year-old daughter, to voice her thoughts.

"I like the music but I don't take it seriously. It's for dancing not discussing. No one takes it seriously. It's music," Courtney said.

"So you don't care that you're singing bitch this and ho that and my nigga?" Courtney's father, Mr. Hall, asked her.

"Everyone else is! Dang daddy. It's a song!" Courtney exclaimed.

"That's how they have you fooled. The message is in the medium. This whole west coast east coast contention is fueled by the record company to drive sales with violence and misogyny." Mr. Hall continued. "How many rappers have died? Besides that one from New York?"

"You mean Biggie?" Herschel asked.

"See what I mean? These boys don't even have names. They have aliases."

"Dad, it's not like you have street cred," Courtney said to her father.

"Street cred!" Sir HH interrupted, setting down his drink. "Let me tell you about street cred or 'keeping it real' as you young folks say. I had a paper route at six years old, got up every morning before sunrise and biked through the county delivering papers to the KKK."

"The KKK?" Mr. Hall asked, laughing.

"Yeah man, I was fast in those days. That's how I got that football scholarship. Fast on my feet and could throw." Sir HH added. "And there weren't neighborhoods with street lights and paved roads neither. Dirt roads. Dark, dirt roads and dogs. I was paid seventy-five cents a day."

"I had a paper route too," Mr. Mitchell said. His first interjection into the conversation. All the while he talked, he had the most serene look on his face, watching his wife play badminton with the Llewellyns.

I would later learn that the Mitchells opened the first advertising agency on Madison Ave and the Llewellyns owned a bank in Harlem.

"All these rappers talking about representing their hood, don't none of them own nothing in their community." Sir HH puffed on his Monte Cristo cigar. I was surprised to hear the double, triple negatives coming out of Sir HH's mouth. But it's not like he was addressing the court. I guess you can let it all hang out when you're in the company of your own.

"They keep the jewelers in business," Mr. Hall added.

"Those gold ropes look like chains to me," Mr. Mitchell said, frowning.

"I saw a young man with N-I-G-G-A tattooed on the back of his arm in big, bold letters. Right here, down his arm. Tattooed! I couldn't believe he did that to himself," Mrs. Hall said.

"It's the music they listen to. Glorifying ignorance and self-hatred," Martha added. "And the way they talk about women! I didn't know so many words rhymed with bitch."

"It's just music!" Courtney exclaimed. "I'm sure Nat King Cole was controversial in your day."

"Wrong generation, sweetheart," Her father said. "In our day it was Rick James and the Funkadelics, Slave, Parliament, Prince!"

"Ohio Players. *Skin Tight* was my song," Mr. Mitchell recalled. "You a real fine lady…though your walk a little shady…"

"Back when musicians could play instruments and sing." Martha joined in, humming a song I couldn't place. "Remember HH? The first song we ever danced to?"

He pulled her onto his lap. "Would you mind, if I touched if I kissed if I held you tight in the morning light...." She kissed her husband on his forehead. "Love has found its way in my heart tonight."

"These young folks don't know nothing about that," Courtney's father said, smiling at his daughter.

"The point is, music is art. Besides, it's a scientific fact that the more you say a word the less power the word has. Eventually, it'll lose all its stigma. Right, Herschel?" Courtney said, taking it upon herself to defend her generation.

I'd been watching Herschel keep quiet. He was reading the room. Deciding how to address the issue. Playing the politician even now. He never wanted to be on the wrong side of his father, who didn't believe rap music had any redeeming qualities. Herschel loved Tupac. Called him an innovator. The mastermind of the rap game. Before Herschel could speak up, HH took over.

"I bet you a Black professor didn't tell you that. Anyone who is socially, historically, culturally, even politically aware knows the brutality attached to that word. Whether you say it with an A or an R, they know that word reduces Black people to non-human status. Words may become obsolete but that word, the word nigga, has too much blood attached to it to ever lose its stigma," Sir HH said.

"That's different. I didn't say that. That's outside the context of music, Uncle H," Courtney said.

"But that is what you said. By your theory, your professor has to keep calling you nigga for you to be okay with it. Let me ask you something, why are they still singing nigga but they're not singing honkey or cracker?" Courtney's father asked. "Who do you think is controlling the record industry in the first place? It isn't the rappers, honey."

"What do you think, Jocelyn?" Martha swiveled in her chair, sipping a Vodka Gimlet. "Do you agree with Courtney that the more you use that disgusting word the less hurtful it is?"

Everyone waited for my answer. "I think it perpetuates and glamorizes ignorance. It caters to the lowest common denominator. I like rap. The beat. The flow. Even some of the lyrics. Public Enemy raps about hypocrisy. PM Dawn sings about love in a hippie kind of way. But in terms of gangsta rappers, I have to say I understand the anger and frustration. I'm not over slavery either but I don't agree that the more you hear a negative word, the less power it has. The more you hear it, the more desensitized you become to other slights."

"She gets it!" Mr. Hall winked at me. "There's still hope for the next generation. Ha! Not over slavery. That's right."

"Wait, wait, wait. What do you mean you're not over slavery? What does that mean?" Martha pressed.

"I mean my ancestors were Black, poor, and marginalized, and it wasn't that long ago. I'm like one generation removed from Alabama where my father's from. He grew up on a farm, sharecropping and picking cotton. He saw what whiteys could do."

Everyone on the veranda got quiet until Sir HH blew out a cloud of cigar smoke, and said, "Whiteys."

"What Jocelyn means is," Herschel said, jumping on my bandwagon, "nigga is a violent, volatile word that demeans and dehumanizes people of African descent. And when we call each other and ourselves nigga, we're perpetuating the slave masters' grand design. Nigga is drenched in blood. Nigga is hanging from a tree. Nigga is raped while pregnant. Nigga is not me. That's what she means."

The room nodded in agreement. I didn't need Herschel to speak for me. I was doing fine on my own.

"Well said, son."

"And you best believe whiteys aren't over it either. That's why the prison population is filled with our brothers," Herschel continued.

"Don't say whiteys, son," Sir HH instructed.

"Speaking of prisons, did anyone read Cornel West's book *Black Robes, White Justice*?" Martha asked. "I slipped it in your bookbag, the last time you were here, Herschel."

22

That's how the conversation continued into the evening. One lively, informed debate after the next. I learned that these parents were grooming their children to have a place in society. Teaching them to speak up, by debating with them in the living room, they were preparing them for the courtroom or the boardroom. Confidence doesn't just happen. It's groomed, encouraged and nurtured.

Throughout Spring Break, I was captivated by Martha. She was the perfect hostess. Her fingers lightly clasped her throat when she laughed. Her clothes were deceptively simple but tailored to nip just so at the waist. She was chic. She was also my unofficial mentor. When I learned she was an Alpha Delta Zeta, I vowed to pledge the same sorority. If you want success, you have to mirror success, right? These people were my people. Vallejo, who? Vallejo, what? Please. Jocelyn Downes from Vallejo was dead. I had finally found my tribe. I was home. From then on, I only associated with people who came from somewhere and from somebody.

When Herschel and I returned to USB, we were the perfect couple. The first in our group of university friends to be in a committed relationship. Aside from the daily medication to treat the virus, which I taped to the back of the communal toilet so my dorm mates wouldn't find out, herpes was the best thing that ever happened to me. Whenever a fresh crop of Alpha Delta Zeta pledges caused Herschel to linger too long at the student lounge, I only had to mention I was running low on meds. That set him straight. By the time I graduated from USB, I was planning our wedding. My sorority sisters never figured out how I was able to keep Herschel, the notorious pussy hound, from straying.

TWO

VANESSA the BEAUTY QUEEN

"The hardest thing I ever had to do was visit my father in prison and tell him I committed my mother to a home for Alzheimer's patients. How's that for a buzzkill?" I answered the interview question with a bit more honesty and transparency than the pledge committee of Alpha Delta Zeta was used to hearing. But so what?

I'm Vanessa Noisette. I have nothing to be ashamed of.

Big sister Leona Ellis, known on campus as Miss ADZ cleared her throat and made a note on her scorecard. Toni, one of the other girls interested in pledging, almost fell out of her seat. Only Jocelyn chuckled. I had a feeling she started at the bottom too.

"Your mother's listed as an Alpha. Where did she pledge?" Leona continued the sorority interview.

"Mother pledged Chi Omega chapter at Northern Tennessee. But please, don't accept me because I'm a legacy candidate. I have my own accomplishments."

"Go on."

"I'm a young woman who knows who she is and what she wants out of life."

"And who refers to herself in the third person," Leona noted. The other girls giggled.

"My goal is to have my own skin care line and I'm active in Alzheimer charity organizations. And if that doesn't convince you. I'm a reigning beauty queen." I did the pageant wave. "Plus, I know all the tricks of the trade. Like, Vaseline on the teeth to prevent embarrassing lipstick smears." I tap my teeth and point to one of the sorority girls who has red lipstick on her front teeth. "And hairspray on your pantyhose to prevent static cling."

"Please tell us how your pageant experience has shaped you," Leona asked.

"I'm the reigning Ms. Teen San Diego, and I won a four-year scholarship, which got me to where I am now, a freshman at the University of Santa Barbara and in front of you, the ladies of Alpha Delta Zeta. I've been in pageants since I was a child and I'm good at it. I like pageants. I like the camaraderie with the girls. I'm not catty and I believe in female empowerment. So I'm sure I'll love being in your sorority. I'm more than a pretty face. My mother used to say, a pretty face may get you a seat at the table but you better have something interesting to say. Although having a pretty face has gotten me pretty far." I chuckled. No one else did.

"Not that I'm bragging. I got into pageantry to support my family. As I said, father went away when I was young, leaving my mother and me to take care of ourselves. I won a bunch of pageants throughout my life because I had to. Oh, you know I never thought about that before.

I'm a winner because I have to be. That makes sense though, doesn't it? I probably won over one hundred and fifty pageants. I was able to buy my mother a house and a car. Like I said earlier, she lives in a different home and she doesn't drive anymore, so I have the car. But you know, if anyone needs a ride..." No takers. "I promise to bring all my pageantry knowledge as well as my poise and diction to elevate the image of ADZ because let's face it, image is the first thing we're judged on. Am I right, ladies? A little refinement never hurt anyone."

"What's your talent?" Leona asked, sitting erect in a pink and yellow sweater set. I bet Miss Leona is also called Little Miss Perfect behind her back. I bet she can rattle off the founding mothers and all nineteen commandments they instituted. Wouldn't be surprised if she's studying to be a lawyer and likes to practice her cross-examinations on wanna be pledges during rush week.

"Beauty pageants rate talent as well as beauty. You've demonstrated how beautiful you are, Ms. Noisette. Can you demonstrate your talent to us?"

"I'm happy you asked," I answered.

"But before you do, I have one nagging question," Leona interrupted me.

I knew she wasn't going to make it easy. I knew what she wanted to ask. The insecure ones always ask the same thing.

"Don't you feel parading around in a bathing suit is demeaning to women because you're essentially walking around in a bikini or is it a one-piece? I'm sure it's a difficult choice," Leona scoffed.

"It's an individual choice," I said.

"And you choose…"

"A bikini."

"Parading around in a bikini and heels being judged by a panel of men on what exactly?"

"Poise."

"Poise? In a bikini," she continued, then looked dubiously at her fellow sisters.

"Is there a question?" I asked. Oh, she didn't like that. Her eyes narrowed and her mouth tensed. But I had to let her know she didn't scare me.

"My question is, how do you reconcile the sexist construct of beauty pageants with being a feminist? Assuming you are a feminist. Are you feminist, Ms. Noisette?"

I didn't peg Ms. Perfectly ADZ as a hater. She thought she'd said something profound to embarrass me but it was nothing I hadn't heard before. "Is it demeaning for Japanese geishas to practice the ancient art of the fan dance or to pour tea for businessmen? Is it demeaning for your mother to remove your father's shoes? Girls who enter pageants do so because they're realistic about the role of women in society."

"Which is?" Leona asked me, leaning in, practically ready to pounce on whatever I said. Wow, she looked like a wolverine.

"The innate ability to disarm and charm," I said, smiling with my eyes. Smizing. "Men fight wars, men work to earn money for power and prestige and they do it to impress women. We don't have to compete with them. Let them duel it out to win our affection."

"That's offensive and simplistic."

"That's the real world. And the world isn't that complicated," I replied.

Someone from the back of the room muttered, "Says the beauty queen." A few of the ladies giggled. I saw Leona suppress a smirk.

"So women are supposed to wait for a man to take care of them? You believe we're the weaker sex." The sorority screening committee waited to hear my answer.

"We're the smarter sex." For a moment, Leona looked baffled.

Toni came to my defense and interjected, "The Bible says man cannot live alone so God created woman." That was sweet of her but completely unnecessary.

"Let Vanessa answer the question. According to your theory, Ms. Noisette, a woman is wasting her time studying to become a lawyer when she can just marry one instead. I mean, it's practically the same thing," Leona said, addressing the group.

"I am only saying women have a feminine mystique that men don't have, and we need not become masculine to achieve our goals. I am a feminist and I'm proud to be a Black woman. I won Ms. Teen San Diego, not Ms. Black Teen San Diego. There's only a handful of Black women competing on my level. And I'm very proud to represent us. I bring up my race because as Black women we have to be careful not to be labeled as 'Angry or Masculine'. Women forget there's power in our femininity. Let me ask you a question. When you're on a date, do you open his door or drive him to the restaurant?"

Some of the women were mumbling to themselves and nodding. Leona said, "I don't open his door but I do drive sometimes and sometimes I even pay."

"Well, stop. Men like praise. And the only thing they like more than praise, is earning our praise. The next time you go out with your boyfriend, let him be the man. Praise him when he does something you like. And when he doesn't, don't say a word. Ignore him. He'll fall over himself to get your approval and be your hero."

The room was silent. No one giggled or looked at me sideways anymore.

"We're modern women. This isn't the 1950s. We, at Alpha Delta Zeta, believe in gender equality," Leona asserted. "Don't we ladies?" Only a few of the ladies nodded.

I responded, "Why on Earth would you want to be equal to a man? Without our gentle, nurturing nature men would be animals. We bring them back to their humanity." The room nodded in agreement. I positioned my violin against my chin to begin the talent portion of the interview.

"That won't be necessary."

"I'd like to hear her play." Sweet Bible thumper Toni spoke up. The wannabe pledges clapped for me to play. I may like these girls after all.

"What a load of crap," Mariah asserted. "You're not buying this, are you? Not all of us can win beauty pageants for a living. Some of us wouldn't be caught dead in a bikini or a one-piece even if we were a size two. Some of us will have to work and earn our own way."

"Some of us, Mariah, are more feminine than others," I countered.

"What's that supposed to mean?" Mariah asked, with a slight edge in her voice.

"I don't apologize for being a successful beauty queen and making enough money to take care of my family. Clearly, I didn't earn it the way you think I should have, but I'm not on financial aid. I had a full scholarship to any university of my choosing. I chose this one because it's close to my parents. And all the money I earned, all $250,000 of it, is accruing compound interest. The ladies who enter pageants are of all faiths who love their country and value education. And when we say we want world peace, we actually do. I use my femininity and my brain to get what I want and here I am, right here, next to you. My professors are just as hard on me as they are on you. And I have a 3.8 G.P.A."

Mariah flicked lint off her pants.

"It takes brains to achieve anything no matter what you look like," I added.

"I'd like to hear you play," Toni said, easing the tension. "Is that okay? Can we hear her play?" Toni looked around, asking the group. Before Leona could give her approval, I picked up my violin and gave these ladies Mendelssohn's Violin Concerto in E minor because it was twenty-five minutes long and I wanted them to remember this moment and think twice before challenging me again.

*****

The first time I met my husband was at the university's taping of The Dating Game. I was Bachelorette Number One, representing Alpha Delta Zeta, along with Ms. Phi Omega, a super sweet Latina who later became Ms. World, and Ms. Tri Delta, a White girl who overdosed on Oxycontin a few years later. The bachelor was Fred 'The Freezer' Jones, a third-round NFL draft pick for the Raiders.

The Freezer was known for dating college girls. He was the typical eligible player, a love 'em and leave 'em type, only The Freezer would ice your wrist when he left you. Tiffany tennis bracelets were his parting gift. His father owned a string of barbershops in South Central so he didn't grow up poor but he did grow up without his mother. I never found out what happened. He didn't talk about her and I wouldn't have dared ask his father, Farley.

Farley Jones did a number on his son's attitude about women. According to Farley, 'The Numbskull Jones, all women were gold diggers who couldn't be trusted. So not only did Fred's mother abandon him under mysterious circumstances when he was young, but his father had a rotation of women in and out of Fred's life ever since. And the recurring reason why the relationships didn't work out was, 'She's a gold digger and can't be trusted.' That was what I knew about him going into the dating game and I knew enough to know I didn't want to know any more. I didn't care if he picked me or not so I just had fun with his questions.

"Bachelorette Number One, I love playing games on and off the field. What new games can you teach me to play?" he asked.

"I'd teach you to play house because being in a relationship is just a game to you."

"Do we know each other?"

"Your reputation precedes you."

I looked out at the audience to see my sorority sisters looking at me like, 'what are you doing?' I gestured that I got this.

"Oh, okay. Feisty Number One. Let me ask you something else. If we were alone on a deserted island and there was one thing you could have, what would that one thing be?"

"I'm alone with you, right?"

"Yeah. Me."

"Well, then the one thing I'd want is a rescue plane." I saw Jocelyn hit her forehead and shake her head.

"Bachelorette Number Two, the same question, and you can't say rescue plane."

Ms. Phi Omega replied, "If you were with me, I'd have everything I could want."

He chose her. When he came around the partition, I winked at him to let him know it was all in good fun. He looked confused. I don't think he'd ever been rejected before.

The second time I met my husband was in prison. We were both stuck in the waiting area next to the security station. I was waiting to visit my father. He was there to see his twin brother, Frank. Fred and Frank are identical twins but as different as night and day.

Fred, for all his childish ways, is a saint while his brother Frank is doing life for drug trafficking and a double homicide. Frank gave Fred the nickname, Freezer. When they were kids, Fred climbed into a freezer to hide from Frank in a game of hide and seek. Fortunately, Frank found him before he suffocated and Fred became 'The Freezer' Jones.

When you visit a super-maximum-security prison, you spend more time waiting than you do visiting, so you have to be prepared to be patient. You wait in line to fill out the visitor's security log. You wait in the reception area to be called to go through security, where you wait until they bring in the inmate. There are a good two hours wasted just waiting to get into the visitors' area.

I never got used to the plastic chairs or the smell of body odor mixed with Lysol. But there was one indulgence I allowed myself, Nutter Butters from the vending machine. I only ate them there, and for some reason I never had any luck with the vending machines. Especially this one machine. The candy always got stuck and took my money. Every time! So I stood there staring at my one treat for the day, trapped between the glass and the spiral thingy. I was out of quarters when this guy walked up and said, "You have to know how to handle it." He put in three quarters and bought the Vanilla Wafers right above my wedged cookies, knocking the Nutter Butters down to the drop.

"You did it!" I was surprised.

"If your snack is stuck, don't buy the same thing. Get something just above it and it'll knock your snack down." He stood up, holding out my cookies. "You!" he said. "You're the girl from the show. I shouldn't give you this. You busted my balls."

"I was getting you back for busting my lip."

"Whoa. You got me confused."

"My dad used to get his hair cut at your dad's barbershop. The one on Crenshaw. You and your brother were playing catch and you

Minerva Stewart

knocked me out the way and I hit my mouth on the radiator. See this scar, right at the top of my lip? That's you."

He leaned closer to me, staring at my face. "The only thing I see is your mustache."

"Anyway! May I have my Nutter Butters?"

"Take 'em both. I don't eat sweets."

"Appreciate it." I walked away and sat across the room next to a young mom dressed in a tight black dress with her baby in a white communion gown.

Fred sat next to me, and for the next two hours, we talked. Maybe it was the surroundings or that we'd met before, but he was easy company. We talked about a lot of things, not just football and pageants. I thought he was going to be a meathead but he was funny and personable. Smarter than I gave him credit for and surprisingly open and honest.

"My father says all women are gold diggers," he said.

The baby next to me had hiccups so I didn't quite hear what he said. "Goal diggers? Like we have hopes and dreams?"

"No, Gold, gold diggers. Like women are conniving. They present themselves one way, get you hooked, then take you for what you got."

"Can't you tell the difference between a gold digger and a good woman?"

"Yeah, I can."

36

"Then don't worry about it. You're from South Central. Nobody's going to get anything from you that you don't want them to have. So, when's your brother getting out?"

"He's not."

Silence.

"What about your father?"

"Yeah, no. He killed a cop. It wasn't his fault. He was protecting my mom."

"Your mom passed?"

"Yeah, sort of. Her mind is gone, her body just doesn't know it yet." I didn't say anything else because I can't talk about my mom without getting sad. I was startled when Fred squeezed my hand and held it. I looked down at his hand clasped around mine.

"Is this okay?" he asked.

I nod. And after a moment, I remembered something and smiled at him.

"What?"

"I was thinking about the dating game. The question you asked, if we were on a deserted island what's the one thing I'd want?"

"Rescue plane is a good answer."

"The other thing I'd want is someone to hold my hand."

I think we caused a little scene because in a sea of unhappiness and uncertainty we were basically on the best first date ever.

*****

Phone calls led to visits, which led to dates, and we became known as the glamour couple on campus. Whenever Fred came to visit me, everyone wanted his autograph, including my professors. They took pictures with him, asked for tickets to the games. I have to admit, classes became easier. And then I got pregnant. For the record, we used a condom. I insisted. I wasn't trying to trap him. I didn't see him as my meal ticket. I figured if one football player was attracted to me, I could attract plenty more. I didn't need Fred to save me.

I was in my junior year when I learned I was pregnant. I knew I had to tell him but I didn't know what was going to happen after that. I didn't know if we were going to break up, the most likely scenario. Or, if he was going to accuse me of trapping him before we broke up. Or, the most unlikely scenario, if we were going to get married. The only thing I knew for sure was that I wasn't going to get an abortion. I'm not a pro-lifer. I do believe in a woman's right to choose. But my mother didn't choose to get an abortion when she was nineteen and pregnant with me. And I'm not going to either. If Fred's response is 'What are you going to do about it?' then I'll know we're through. Before I could tell him my news, he had news for me.

He walked in looking good. Freshly showered with a new fade and his beard trimmed. The Freezer stays camera ready. Someone always wants to take a picture with him. But today, he wasn't his usual jokey self. Before he sat down, he cut to the chase.

"Things aren't going so good with the Raiders. They have some concerns about my knee."

"Isn't that what pre-season's for? To work out the kinks? You just need to build up and strengthen your body."

"I got traded. The doctor said my knee's a liability" He pulled out a Saints hat. "I'm going to New Orleans. And I want you to go with me." He put the hat on me.

"New Orleans? I can't go to New Orleans. I have school. You know I can't leave my parents."

"They'll understand. Your father will. He wants you to move on. And your mother isn't getting better. When was the last time she recognized you? I don't know why you put yourself through the pain."

"Because she's my mother. It's important for the staff to know someone cares. I'm her advocate."

"Right. Right. I didn't mean to upset you. I'm just saying, you can't live your life for them."

I took off the Saints hat and retreated into the kitchen to clear my head. I busied myself with putting water in the tea kettle.

"What do you say? You want to live in N'awlins?" Smiling, he leaned against the wall, watching me shuffling around the tiny apartment kitchen. "Eat crawfish and étouffée. Live in one of those old, haunted mansions. Get bitten up by mosquitoes in the summer. You want to do that with me?"

"What are you offering me to go?" I blurt out without thinking.

"Whoa. Oh, it's like that? You need an incentive to be with me?"

"I need a reason. We're not talking about going away on vacation. You want me to leave my life, my school, my friends, my family. What are you offering in return?" I looked him in the eye, waiting for an answer.

He stepped back into the living room, easing closer to the front door, and I knew his father's warnings about women were running through his head. Just like my father's warnings about men were running through mine. "When a man loves you, he'll move heaven and earth for you. And you make sure he does before you trust him with your heart," my father would say.

"Don't run away. It's a fair question. What are you offering?" I asked again. The tea kettle was gathering heat.

"I'm giving you a place to live, V."

"I have a place to live, Fred," I said, gesturing to my off-campus apartment.

"Okay. Let's put the cards on the table." He sat back down at the little kitchen table. "You won't have to work. You can do whatever you want till I get home. How's that?"

I shook my head. That wasn't good enough. "No."

"No? What do you mean no."

"You want me to commit to you. I want you to commit to me."

"That's what I'm doing. I said I'd take care of you."

"And then what?"

"What, what? That's it."

"Fred. I'm not going to move across the country to play house. You expect me to meet the coaches and the players and their wives without a ring on my finger ... like a groupie."

"Ah! Now you're getting to it. You want me to marry you, Vanessa? Why didn't you say so? Go ahead. You can ask me to marry you."

"I'm serious."

He got up and pulled me to close to him. "Come with me. Be my girl. And the rest will work itself out."

"I'm a woman. I'm not a girl."

"You're about to talk yourself out of a situation."

"Then I'm talking to the wrong man. Do you want chamomile or mint?"

"Why you making this so hard?"

"Don't you know what you want?" I say, holding up the tea bags.

"Uh huh. Mint. You know I like mint."

I made his mint tea and realized I wasn't even angry with him. This was our first hard conversation and I was glad I didn't tell him I was pregnant. He didn't need to know that my life and my baby's life and all our future choices were being decided right then.

"Anybody else offering you a home, money, cars? You know how many women would jump on this gravy train."

"You're not asking them. You're asking me. And you're not a gravy train." I carried the tea and Nutter Butters into the living room. It took a while for him to come out of the kitchen.

"You want me to pay you to be with me, is that it? You want financial security until we work out all the rest?"

"I have money, Fred. You know that."

"Then why don't you ever pay for anything?" He grumbled and flopped on the sofa. "I hear what you're saying. I'll think about it. Now that's all I can say for now. Take it or leave it."

We sipped our tea in silence. He kept glancing over at me as I stared into my teacup.

"You're making this difficult and it don't have to be," he said.

"You're right. It doesn't have to be." I got up and walked into the bedroom and returned with his shirt.

"I replaced the button and reinforced the others so they won't pop off."

"Thanks. My favorite shirt," he grumbled.

"I know." I opened the front door.

"You gotta get the white picket fence." He got up, shaking his leg out to loosen up his right knee, all the while looking at me to see if I was going to give in.

I looked back at him, blinking. I learned that from Jocelyn. She'd say every question doesn't need an answer. When men start acting ridiculous, just blink at them. It'll bring them back to their senses. I quietly stood by the door and I let him work it out.

"All or nothing, huh? You got some balls to walk away from all this."

"I've already had nothing, Fred. I deserve it all. I can't be your groupie."

"I never treated you like that."

I cupped his face in my hands and did my best to sincerely wish him well so he could walk through the door. The last thing I want is to force anyone to do anything they don't want to do. "You're going to do well with The Saints. They're getting the best offensive lineman in the history of the NFL. You're going to love New Orleans. Don't eat too much jambalaya, too much spice upsets your stomach the next day. Stay in touch."

He searched my face. "I don't want to stay in touch."

"What do you want?"

Fred didn't react. He just stood in the doorway. One foot out, one foot in.

43

"What do you want, Fred?"

"A prenup."

THREE

MARIAH the MILITARY BRAT

"Why would I ever want to get married when there's so much good dick in the world." The screening committee of Alpha Delta Zeta nearly fell over. Everyone's mouth dropped open except for the one dressed like a sister-wife. Her body clenched. "I don't apologize for being an equal opportunity sexual being. I like sex. I like men. And yes, I'm a feminist. I'm also very much a lady. What I'm not, is a slut so you can't slut-shame me. I don't understand why a woman has to pretend she isn't a sexual being who enjoys an orgasm. What's that about? We are of the flesh. God created us to have a physical experience, am I right, sister?" I direct my question to the one wearing the name tag 'Toni.' She's got repressed sexual desires written all over. Repressed laughter, repressed independent thought, the only thing not repressed is probably her appetite. She gives in to that urge with full abandon. To my surprise, Humpty looked up and said, "That's one way of telling it." So she's got some spunk under her layers of clothing.

"Just so you get the right impression of me, I am Mariah Stewart. I'm an Air Force brat. I've lived all over Europe and Asia and a bunch of US bases. When I was ten, I could speak German, Italian, and Japanese. The only words I can say now are the basics: hello, how are you, thank you and see you later in three languages, four including

English. My favorite curse word is *scheisse*, which is German for shit. I'm a germaphobe. My pet peeve is strangers hugging me. Give me a minute to know you before coming at me. Announcing, 'I'm a hugger!' does not make it okay. I hate being forced into non-consensual contact. I don't hear pedophiles approaching kids saying, 'I'm a pedophile!'."

The ladies shifted uncomfortably. I'm losing my audience. "That came out wrong."

"Ummm…. Military brats are a different breed. Any brats in the audience?"

No hands.

"Really? No one?"

More blank stares.

"Usually, there's… okay so being in the military means you move around a lot, like a lot a lot, and you learn everything is temporary. That's why we say, see you later instead of goodbye. You learn your family is the only stabilizing force in your life. And everyone has their specialty. Mother's specialty was keeping our family together, and mother didn't play. To begin with, she insisted we call her mother. Not mommy or ma, always mother. When we were alone, we could call her Miss Ellie, short for Eleanor. Mother's from Louisiana. Who dat! Anyone? Saints fans? No? Okay, well, Poppa Joe is a Master Sergeant in the Air Force. His specialty is Air Traffic Control, so Poppa Joe controls the air and mother controls the home. Like I was saying, everyone has a specialty. My parents have a great relationship. They're equal partners. There aren't many men who claim to be feminists but Poppa Joe is one. After I'm done sowing my oats, I hope to marry a feminist like Poppa Joe. And... I know I'm rambling, I get diarrhea of the mouth when I'm nervous. There was something else I wanted to tell you."

I don't feel too bad about losing my train of thought. The Vanessa girl did drone on about femininity and men's roles and women's roles and I drifted off thinking I never wanted to be married. She can have those societal constructs. More power to her. I'm sure she'll find a Mr. Man who's the captain of some shiny industry. All her talk about being an entrepreneur and majoring in business is BS. That girl is majoring in MRS. I wouldn't waste a fantasy on a Black knight riding a white horse. The whole idea is ridiculous. No one is going to save you, girl. Save yourself! Spoiler alert: there's no Black knight. There's no level playing field. Some people rise by sin and others fall by virtue. I read that somewhere. I could tell the girl next to me, Jocelyn, was hell bent on rising and the other one, Toni, Ms. Virtuous Sanctimonious Goody Two Shoes, was going to let her virtue be her downfall.

"Where did you graduate from high school?" Jocelyn asked.

"I'm glad you asked. I graduated from high school in Las Vegas. Vegas has a weird reputation for being Sin City, the adult playground where you let your freak flag fly, but it's really family oriented. I graduated valedictorian. My graduation speech focused on being true to yourself. My goal in life is to do just that, be true to me and without apologies. I'm direct, and a lot of us women are not. We spend way too much time not saying what we mean. And apologizing! My father, Poppa Joe, taught me to say what you mean and that everything is in the delivery. I want you to know that I have integrity. I was raised to be a leader and though I may falter, I will never fail. Oh! I have three older brothers, all in the Air Force. I come from three generations of blue shirts, can you believe it? Well… ahem, I'm the black sheep. I'm not in the Academy. But I'm an over-achiever. I have a quick wit, and my ADHD kicks in when I'm nervous. I think I said that already. So yea, I believe the best investment is in yourself and real success is being your own boss. And like all of you ladies, I am a woman determined to rise and if you choose me to join your esteemed sorority, which I hope you do, I will be honored to be an asset to Alpha Delta Zeta Sorority Incorporated."

And with that, I sat down, confident that I had covered all pertinent parts of my life. Then Big Sister Leona hit me with my least favorite question.

"Where are you from?" Big Sister Leona asked.

Ugh! This question again. I stood up.

"I'm still trying to figure that one out. Everywhere. Nowhere. Officially, I was born in Guam and moved when I was four months old to Japan." I recite all the reassignments in chronological order, all ten of them. I'm doing my best to appear normal but I'm still learning how to interact with civilians. "Not being on a military base still freaks me out. So unofficially, I'm from the Air Force. I still wake up at 0600 expecting to hear reveille, and every time I see the American flag on campus, I hear TAPS playing in my head. The only reason, well, there are two reasons I'm not at the Academy. The first reason is because there are enough Stewarts in the Air Force, my father, his father and now my brothers like I said before, and the second reason is I want to experience college life as a civilian. I know I'm a civilian, kind of, but I'm also part of the silent ranks so I'm not in the military but I was raised in the military so I am *of* the military. That's a convoluted answer but it's the only answer I have."

"Next question. What's the hardest thing you ever had to do and how has it made you stronger?" Big Sister Leona asked me like she asked the other girls.

"Here's the thing about living on a military base, everyone's watching you. Everything you do is judged and if you do anything wrong, or bad, or just normal teenage stuff, it'll get back to your parents and the last thing you want is for your parents to be called into the commanding officer's office. Being a military family, a Black military family living around the world, you're always making a new impression. So we were under a lot of scrutinies. We couldn't wild out.

We couldn't swear, which is why, *scheisse!* is my favorite word. We couldn't even get our school clothes dirty. We stayed on our Ps and Qs. All. The. Time. Do you know how exhausting that is? It's no fun, I'll tell you that. And like I said, under no circumstances did mother want Poppa Joe to be called into the commanding officer's office to discuss something we'd done. But boys will be boys and one day, he was called in. My brothers did something, I don't know what happened, I never got the official story but it had to do with a jeep and live rounds of ammo. Anyway, when Poppa Joe finally brought Joe Junior, James, and Joshua home, my brothers looked like all the shenanigans had been snatched out of their teenage souls. After eighteen years of growing up with rules and regulations, I need to wild out like no one is watching."

The committee seemed satisfied with my answer. When I heard Big Sister Leona ask the other two girls the same question, I had my response teed up. To be honest, the full, complete answer is nobody's business. I wasn't going to stand up there and tell them the hardest thing I had to do was witness my parents' attempt to murder my brothers. After Poppa Joe and my brothers came back from the CO's office, Poppa Joe went into the garage to drink. Like I said, everyone watches everyone so drinking in the garage was his only private place. So he was there, drinking, arguing with himself, getting worked up over what happened with the CO until he finally came in and woke us all up. He made my brothers get down on their knees and he tied their hands behind their backs and stood behind them with a Bowie knife. He made them tell him everything that happened with the jeep and the ammo. He forced a confession out of them like he was a CIA agent and his sons were domestic terrorists. I'll never forget mother sitting there smoking a Virginia Slim cigarette, watching the whole thing with no expression. I thought she was in shock, traumatized by the sight of her husband about to gut her sons. But she didn't say a thing. Just smoked and watched. At the end, when Poppa Joe was sure he had heard everything exactly the way it happened, mother told me to untie my brothers and go to bed. Nobody ever spoke about that night. But Poppa Joe was never called into the CO's office again. So the hardest thing I ever had to do was witness what my parents were capable of doing if we didn't toe the line. I don't know if the realization made me stronger but it made me decide that I didn't want to stay in the military. I couldn't risk becoming Poppa Joe or marrying someone like him.

*****

I met my husband at a sex club. I was there with a fun buddy I was dating, which for anyone else would be unconventional but for me made perfect sense. I was known for doing things my way. I was twenty-eight, living my life and enjoying doing whatever with whomever, however and whenever. I was having the time of my life, living on my own, making my own money, and paying my bills. After putting in sixty hours a week as a producer for a demanding advertising agency, I hosted parties in my downtown loft, bought art, and kicked it with whomever I had on rotation.

On this particular Thursday night, my buddy and I decided to go to a sex club. It was called Forty Deuce, down the street from my loft building. This was before the gentrification of downtown Los Angeles. Back when you had to scrape the drunks and prostitutes off the hood of your car in the morning. So my cuddle buddy and I walked over to Forty Deuce in our grown and sexy costumes. I had on a black leather bustier, red feather mask and red thigh high boots. He had on chaps with the ass out, no shirt and cowboy boots and hat.

The first thing we did upon entering Forty Deuce was meet the owners, a lesbian couple who told us the two rules of the club. No men were allowed *in* the club unless accompanied by a woman. No men were allowed *anywhere* in the club unless accompanied by a woman. The last thing they wanted was a group of guys roaming around making women feel uncomfortable. After getting the rules for the establishment, we took in the lay of the land.

The club was a giant warehouse with themed rooms. The dungeon. The jail cell. The doctor's office, with an examination table. That was popular. We saw a woman with her feet in stirrups and couples wearing latex gloves examining her to an orgasm. We wandered over to the dollhouse, just large enough for a couple to have missionary sex while the neighbors watched through the windows and roof. The X room had multiple cushioned platforms in the shape of Xs. The good vibrations room had every imaginable dildo and vibrator. And there were condoms and lubricants everywhere. No excuse for unsafe sex. There was even a clothing boutique in case you wanted to change your costume. Oh, and the price of entry to this cornucopia of copulation was steep, $150 for the guys. Girls got in free. It isn't a sex club if there aren't any women, unless you were looking for a sausage fest and this wasn't that kind of club. For the price of admission, guests could also enjoy a dance club with free top-shelf liquor, aged wines and a surf and turf buffet. Forty Deuce was more than a sex club. It was a sensual extravaganza that catered to all appetites.

At one point, my bed buddy and a raven-haired sex kitten hooked up in the dungeon, leaving me to amuse myself. The only room I hadn't explored was the Black Room. I'm terrified of the dark. I slept with the night light on until I left home. Mother called it the eternal flame because I never turned it off, not even in the daytime. I suffered from night terrors after the bowie knife incident. But tonight, I could handle the abyss. I had on my power bustier and kick-ass boots. I was armed and ready to enter the dreaded darkness, plus I was tipsy off the Patron.

The Black Room was not a euphemism. It was pitch black. It was so black. I couldn't see my hand in front of my face. No light at all. And I loved it! Soon as I was enveloped in darkness, all my other senses were on high alert. I was instantly sober. With outstretched hands, I felt my way along the wall. The wall would be my guide. I planned to stick to the wall and eventually make my way out of the room. I cautiously waded deeper into the cavernous space. There were so many moans and groans and giggles, I didn't know what my fingers would find. Eventually, I came across skin, hair, and possibly a nipple? A nose? Whoever I touched, gasped and pulled me closer to him? Or her? Turns out, both. A couple was making out against the wall. One of them held me, inviting me to join them. He or she caressed my back. I wasn't ready for anonymous monsters-in-the-dark sex so I politely rubbed whatever body part my fingers were touching and stepped away from the wall. Why did I do that? I was adrift in the abyss. No wall to anchor me. I didn't know which way to turn so I slid to the left and miraculously didn't crash into anyone. I slid forward and felt strangely free. No one could see me. No one could judge me. We were all equal in the dark.

"Oooops. Trying to get out," a man's voice said.

"I'm caught on your… is that you I'm caught on?" I said.

"You're on my shirt."

"Don't pull. I'm stuck on you."

"Which way is out?" he asked.

"You're making it worse," I replied.

Right behind me, someone was quietly orgasming. I could tell because she gripped my arm with a strength that only comes from toe-curling sex. While I didn't mind being someone's bedpost, I did mind being stuck to this guy with the deep voice. Someone else was moaning nearby. It sounded like everyone was moaning. I was swept up in orgy tidal wave. The guy I was attached to pulled away.

"Owww. My hair."

"Follow me."

"No shit, Sherlock."

"Hey, I'm trying to help."

"Wait. I'm … are you touching me?"

"I swear, I'm not. My hands are right where I can't see them." He chuckled. "I don't know what I'm touching but it's not you."

"Get me out of here."

"Yeah, well. I'm trying."

"Ouch! You're pulling me."

"I'm going to feel for your hand. Don't freak out."

We finally emerged into the light. My hair was caught on his Swarovski crystal-studded shirt collar. We looked like conjoined twins. I was bent over and my head was facing his hairy neck so I still couldn't see his face. He tried to untangle my hair for a few excruciating seconds before giving up.

"Hold on. I might need scissors."

"You're not cutting my hair! Take your shirt off so you can see what you're doing."

"I'm not taking my shirt off."

"Half the people in here are naked. What difference does it make?"

He took his shirt off. The weight of the crystals yanked my neck down. "How many Swarovski crystals are on this thing?"

"A lot. And I don't want to lose any."

"I feel the same way about my hair."

"Stop moving."

He finally untwisted my hair, leaving a fistful of strands attached to his collar. Rubbing the tension in my neck, I looked at my hair, stuck to his stupid collar. Then looked at him. He was wearing a Swarovski multi-colored crystal suit.

"You're welcome," he said, buttoning up his shirt. He was short and pudgy. I didn't like him. Or, maybe it was the crushing headache. I couldn't distinguish between the two.

"It's the least you could do. Your outfit is a danger to women and animals," I said.

"It's Gucci."

"It's ridiculous. You look like you're going to perform in front of 50,000 people."

I lifted my shoulders up and down to help ease the cramp in my neck when he placed his palms on my shoulders and gently rolled the tension away.

"You have a lot of stress in your neck, he said. "Sit down."

I sat on the bench next to a bowl of cherry flavored condoms.

"How's that?"

"You have nice hands. Are you a pianist?"

"Stop referring to me as Elton John."

"I didn't call you Elton John."

"Yeah, you did. That 50,000 people quip. The crystal suit. I know who you meant."

I smiled to myself. "Well, what's your name?" I asked.

"Clifton Ash. Nice to meet you. And you are?"

"Missing a fistful of hair."

"Do you ever stop being tough? It was dark. I didn't see you. I'm falling on my sword here, massaging your neck trying to make amends."

I looked up at him. "You have nice eyes."

"That's better. Do you want to get a drink?"

I saw my fun buddy down the hall talking to a dominatrix. "My ride is here. I have to go."

"Who? The ass-less cowboy? He doesn't look ready to saddle up."

"Awkward bumping into you, Clifton Ash. Thanks for the massage." I rolled my head forward. "The pain is gone. You really do have nice hands and kind eyes."

"Wait a minute. What's your name?"

I don't know why I didn't want to tell him. "You're reflecting light like a disco ball. I have to look away before my headache comes back."

"Here, here's my card if you ever want to meet again under normal circumstances."

I read his card. "You produce porn soundtracks? Sorry. I'm never going to call you."

"I make a living. What do you do that's so great?"

"I produce commercials."

"We're both producers! We can get together and talk shop. Or not. No pressure. Do me a favor? Don't throw the card away in the club. I don't want the owners to think I'm soliciting."

I walked away from Clifton Ash thinking I can't remember the last time I felt so at ease with someone. When he massaged me there was something about his hands that felt capable and reassuring. His hands reminded me of Poppa Joe. I never let strangers touch me without a grace period. The thought of his touch and his kind eyes stayed with me for a month before I called him. We were married a year later.

FOUR

TONI is GOD'S DAUGHTER

Good morning God, thank you so much for waking me up. All honor and glory goes to you. With you I am everything, without you I am nothing. I pray for all your children; my family immediate and extended, my enemies, my friends, strangers, young and old, babies, rich, poor, sick, dying and suffering, alcoholics and addicts, homeless, starving, missing, disappeared, kidnapped and hostage, runaways, even those with the tainted minds to do harm to your children. I pray that you wrap your loving shield of armor and wings of protection around them and guide them and lead them down your path of righteousness so they may better do your will, thy will be done. In your name Jesus. Amen.

*****

With Jocelyn as my dorm mate, I was in the habit of waiting before I climbed out of the top bunk. More times than I cared to remember, I found Herschel sleeping with her in the bottom bed. I learned to listen for snoring, or any other noises coming from below. I didn't hear anything, so I peered over the bunk. The coast was clear. They must have slept in his dorm room last night.

Riffling through my underwear drawer, every panty, every bra has my name on it. My mama made sure she labeled everything with Antoinette Trammell. Even my towels are labeled. "Your clothes may get mixed up in the laundry," she reasoned. The sight of seeing my name written on everything felt like a burden. I know my name! I don't need a constant reminder. Maybe mama did it to remind me of who I am so I won't get caught up in…. in what exactly? College life? Sex, drugs, all night study sessions? A couple of freshmen did approach me for a hookup, they weren't even subtle. I guess seeing me and my baby fat as papa calls it, made me easy prey to the roving jackals. But I'm God's daughter and I don't play that. I don't think I play that. Found it! I snatched the mini Snickers bar from under my folded 36DD bra.

I'm busty and I'm fat. Always have been. Have come to accept I always will be. When I was in the 5th grade, my breasts were bigger than my belly which made me self-conscious, so I started eating more to draw attention away from my boobs. In the 7th grade, kids were calling me 'bootydo', which meant my belly stuck out more than my booty do. That didn't end until I punched Marcus Scott in his bootydo. It felt good to punch him and I kept punching him till he had two black eyes and a broken nose. That day Marcus learned that big girls are strong girls. Papa made me apologize to Marcus and to the Lord but the Lord knew I wasn't sorry.

I'm the daughter of a Pentecostal preacher. I had rules and restrictions that the other kids didn't have so I was an easy target. But after I beat up Marcus, papa and mama pulled me out of school and home-schooled me. They didn't have to. The other kids left me alone after that. At least when they teased me, I had some interaction. Being at home, all the time, I thought I'd go crazy. But I studied hard and learned not only the Lord's way, but also Einstein's theory of relativity, the great ancient civilizations of Africa, and how to cook.

I loved baking, and my reward for doing well was learning how to bake homemade cornbread, monkey bread, dumplings, and my favorite red velvet cake. I wanted to go to Cordon Bleu, the famous cooking school in Paris, but papa wouldn't have his only daughter so far away. So the University of Santa Barbara was the compromise. It was only an hour away from Ojai. I had to promise to attend his church every Sunday and help mama cook the buffet. They bought me a new 1998 Toyota Corolla to make the drive. I thought my car would be my chariot to freedom but it was a long leash to keep me tied to home.

Late in the afternoon, I was done studying and ready to sit with my Bible when Jocelyn burst in, pulling the sheets off her bed. She asked me to go to an Alpha Delta Zeta toga party with her. That was a surprise. She never invited me to anything before. I didn't think she liked me. Jocelyn was up to something. I carefully placed the bookmark in my Bible and got down from my bunk. Ever since she came back from spring break, she had been different. Uppity, my mama would say. I caught her more than once practice-laughing in the mirror, holding her neck like a high society rich white woman. She didn't even eat like a normal person. She'd put granola in her hand and peck at it like a pigeon. I guess that should have influenced me to stop eating but why would I starve myself? I'm short and round. My mama's short and round. The Trammell women are short and round. We cook. We eat. And we fear the Lord. Praise Jesus.

"You're thinking about pledging Alpha Delta Zeta?" I asked, putting my Bible on the desk.

"Yeah. It'll be fun," she said. "You should pledge too."

"You shouldn't make fun of me."

"Hey, I'm just being nice. I thought you'd want to get out of your Bible and get a social life. Aren't you lonely?"

At 5'2" and tipping the scale at 140 pounds, I wasn't exactly sorority material, especially the Alpha Delta Zeta sorority. They are the most prestigious Black sorority in America and super strict on who they let in. They were known for maintaining a coterie of well-bred young women who would married well to maintained good breeding in the Black community. There was even a hair and skin test one had to pass but that was generations ago, back when my grandmama pledged, before she married grandpapa and became a devout Pentecostal. If I did decide to pledge ADZ, they couldn't refuse me. I had legacy status.

I watched Jocelyn throw her blue sheet back on her bunk. She shifted through her dirty laundry and held up a dingy white sheet. "Oh, by the way, Herschel's coming over tonight," she said without turning around.

"It's Friday night. You usually go to his dorm on Fridays."

"Well, tonight he's coming to mine."

"Ours," I corrected her. "He's coming to our room."

Jocelyn turned entirely around to face me and studied me for a moment. "You know Antoinette, if you had your own social life, or a boyfriend, or even friends, you would have something to do on Friday night instead of keeping track of me and my man." And with that, she flipped her head around and turned her back to me.

"You're mean!" I blurted out.

"You're weird and boring and you act like you're a hundred years old!"

We were silent for a while. I looked out our 6th-floor window to see the sun setting and students walking around in togas. They looked like they were having fun.

Jocelyn broke the silence. "I know one of your relatives is an Alpha. I saw the pearl pin in your drawer."

"You went through my drawer?"

"The point is, I can't go to their toga party unless I go with a Greek or a legacy. You're a legacy. So be my roomie and go with me. It'll be fun. Don't you want to have fun?" she said, holding the dingy sheet against her body.

"But why do we have to wear sheets?"

"It's not a sheet. It's a toga. Here, I'll show you." She ripped my white sheet off my bed, releasing a confetti of candy wrappers. "We're gonna have ants if you keep eating in bed." She stepped out of her clothes, unsnapped her bra and twisted my sheet around her waist, tying a knot over her shoulder. "See? Cute, right? Here. Let's do you." She wrapped the fitted sheet around me. Unlike Jocelyn, I kept my bra on. I have too much bosom to let loose. "I think you look cute."

I looked in the mirror. "I don't know. I have a test on Monday."

"You're a legacy, Toni. You have to come with me." This was the first time Jocelyn had shown any interest in me. "I'll do your make up."

"I don't wear make-up. It's against my religion."

"I won't tell if you won't." Jocelyn opened her make up kit and smiled at me.

I actually contemplated forsaking my teachings. I shook my head. "My parents might call."

"Tell them you were out having fun," she continued.

"Fun? Oh no. I'm here to get an education. The church gave me a scholarship. I owe them. I'm not supposed to squander my time having fun. This is an opportunity and a privilege."

Jocelyn stared at me blinking. "I think you're having a nervous breakdown."

I looked at myself in the full-length mirror and saw my mama staring back at me. Same disapproving frown. Hair pulled into a tight bun, two ringlets coiled near my temples. I felt a panic attack coming on. Jocelyn snapped the make-up kit closed and dropped all pretense of caring about me. I was clearly a lost cause.

"Fine. Can I use your sheet or is sharing against your religion too?"

Herschel knocked. Jocelyn brightened and swung the door open. He wore a gold crown on his head and gold sandals on his feet and the whitest sheet I've ever seen. "Cleopatra."

"Caesar," Jocelyn replied and mock bowed. "You changed your mind."

"I aim to please." He stepped over the sheet on the floor and looked at me finally noticing I was in the room. "Studying tonight or Bible study?"

"My parents might call so …"

Jocelyn cleared her throat. "Toni, will you give us a minute. I need to talk to Herschel real quick." She smiled at me. Her mouth was smiling but her eyes told me to beat it.

"How much time do you need? I'll just take my notebook if you…"

"Take everything. We have a lot to talk about."

"Oh, sure, okay." I left with my backpack and blanket and Bible.

Just as I closed the door I heard Jocelyn laugh and say, "She's so tragic."

I stood by the door and heard them kissing and Jocelyn giggling. She's gonna talk! Ha! If she's not careful, she's gonna get an STD.

Herschel was in our room almost every night, forcing me to agree that it was 'of course fine for me to sleep in the hall lounge. No problem! I'll just take my books, my blanket and my well-thumbed Bible and mosey myself on down the hall. See you in the morning. No, I don't mind dressing in the dark so as not to disturb your precious Herschel's sleep. No problem!' Oh Lord, I'm getting hangry. Think happy thoughts! Think happy thoughts. What's a happy thought? Yes, Jesus loves me. Yes, Jesus loves me. The Bible tells me so....

A group of students wearing togas stumbled down the hall, whooping and hollering out Toga! Toga! Toga! Red beer cups in hand. They stopped laughing when they saw me leaning against the door trying to disappear.

"You know where the toga party's at?" one of 'em asked me.

I shook my head and scuttled to the hall lounge. I stayed in the 6th-floor lounge so often I started getting my mail there. Sure enough, on the table waiting for me was a care package from home. A Pentecostal book of hymns, jellybeans and M&Ms that somehow managed not to melt, and underwear and socks with my name written neatly in small block letter in mama's penmanship. And a note: Daughter, I know our Lord Jesus is looking after all you do. Trust in Him and His will.

After a good while, I returned to my dorm, pressed my ear against the door to make sure they were gone, or at least were decent. I knocked and called out, "Jocelyn?" No answer. My bottom sheet was on the floor where Jocelyn dropped it. I could hear the toga party from across the quad. It was only nine o'clock. The party would last until midnight. I had three hours to wait it out. I reached for my stash between the mattress. Just what I needed. A friendly face. I ripped the wrapper off the bite-size Kitty Kat and made my bed. Humming a hymn to drown out the revelry drifting in from the window, I crawled into bed, feeling exhausted. I wasn't physically tired, I just collapsed from the weight of expectations. The church. My parents. Myself. A Twix bar oughta curb the loneliness.

This is what happens when you're homeschooled. No social skills, I thought. I lay in bed surrounded by an explosion of candy wrappers. The music and the laughter increased. I couldn't escape it. Oh, what the heck!

I put on the sheet, making sure it covered my bra, and looked at myself. I looked like a dumpling. I was about to take it off when Jocelyn walked in. Stopping in her tracks, her mouth dropped open, then she snapped it closed. She didn't say a word, she just picked up a brush and freed my hair from the tight bun. "Tension kills hair. You have to let your hair be free every now and then." She fluffed my hair into an afro and put a sparkly headband on me. She looked at me and smiled a genuine smile. "Ready?" Before I could answer, she took my hand and led me out of the dorm room.

*****

Bright and early Saturday morning, I walked through the quad. It was rush week. All the Greek organizations were out. Some passed out flyers. Others played hacky sack. I slowly made my way down sorority row. Out of curiosity, I walked up to the Beta Sigma table when I caught one of the girls snickering at me. Maybe it was my long plaid skirt and checkered shirt, maybe it was my size or my tight bun but whatever it was, it wasn't very sisterly. I froze and tried to melt into nothingness when one of the seniors from the Alpha Delta Zeta table waved me over. Leona Ellis was the chapter president. Her mama knew some of the women from our congregation. The church contacted her on my behalf and asked Leona to look after me. We'd talked once before and she was nice enough. Usually, when I saw her around campus, she was walking fast to somewhere important. But today, we exchanged a few pleasantries and I gathered my courage to pick up the pencil and sign up as a pledge. I hesitated to see if she would grimace or smirk or give me some sign that I wasn't wanted. She didn't. She just kept talking about Alphas being of service to the community and their long tradition of inclusiveness and sisterhood. I was grateful for her kindness.

Jocelyn bumped into me. "You're pledging?"

I nodded and signed my full name, Antoinette Trammell, in a flourish.

"We're conducting interviews tonight at the house," Leona said to me. "See you at seven." The girls behind the table followed Leona's lead and waved goodbye to me. I noticed they were all dressed in various shades of pink and yellow. And they all wore short skirts, tank tops and thin sweaters. Jocelyn came up next to me as I was walking away. "It doesn't matter what you wear. You're already in. You're legacy, remember?"

"I can get in on my own."

"Oh, you think so?"

"Yeah, I do."

"Well, I heard they're only taking four girls this semester. And look at the line."

There were at least two dozen girls surrounding the ADZ booth. They were all thin.

"Use your 'get in free' card. I would," Jocelyn said.

*****

When I arrived at the sorority house, there were dozens of other girls already seated. My parents called and kept me on the phone for two hours. I barely made it to the ADZ house before seven. Jocelyn saved me a seat next to her, which was nice. But there I was in a full skirt that was sticking to the back of my legs 'cause I biked over. And my peasant blouse, which looked cute in the dorm, now looked disheveled next to the form-fitting sweaters around me. Where do they get these thin sweaters? Sweaters are supposed to be big and bulky.

All the candidates sat in a semi-circle facing the sorority sisters. Leona randomly called each girl to stand up and answer a series of questions. Vanessa just shocked everybody by telling us her papa was in prison and her mama had Alzheimer's. Wow. How honest are we supposed to be? I liked her. She was pretty and gutsy. The rest of the girls were in dresses but this girl, Vanessa, she had on jeans with holes at the knees and she had on flip-flops. Flip flops! Here I am trying not to pull at my pantyhose and she's twirling her flip-flops on her big toe. I guess when you're beautiful you can wear whatever you want. She looked comfortable and carefree. Like one of the girls on the hair relaxer box. Or in the Newport ads. Long hair, laughing with an irreverent cigarette. Ha! Ha! I can smoke while skiing.

That Mariah girl. The blasphemy that came out of her mouth! I can't even repeat what she said. God made us in his likeness and we are spirits having a human experience but she's taking the sex thing too far. I almost admired her for knowing who she is and not apologizing and not giving an H, E, double hockey sticks what anyone else thinks. That seems to be a recurring theme around these girls, not caring what anyone thinks about them. My Lord, they need me more than I thought.

"Toni Trammell, please stand."

I stood up and quickly shook my skirt loose from the back of my sweaty thighs. I wish I'd worn something less… pentecostally. Leona asked the same questions she asked everyone. "What would you like us to know about you?"

"I'm from a devout Pentecostal family which is why I dress like this."

A couple of the girls chuckled.

"I want to join Alpha Delta Zeta to be a part of a sisterhood 'dat performs acts of service while striving for educational excellence. Your sorority is different from the others. You were the only ones nice to me. I'm a good student and I have an agreeable personality. And, well, I'd … I just want to do stuff I've never done before."

"Like what?"

"Everything! I dress like 'dis 'cause Jesus told me to be modest. If I have a problem or crisis, Jesus will handle it. He'll take the wheel. My whole life is dictated by somebody else. I've done what others expect. I cook to help my mama. I sing in the choir to make my papa proud. I've never even had an aspirin. And I get headaches all the time! I don't know why you should choose me when I'm struggling to choose myself. And my struggle is real. But here I am! I'm not hip. I'm not cool. I don't know any rap songs. I can't dance. I've never been to a dance, or a movie or a public swimming pool. I'm Pentecostal. We don't do 'dat. But maybe I do, do 'dat. I might like to do 'dat. I'm ready to try. But I do know every day I'm kinda excited and scared. I'm true and I'm kind. I want to be free. I don't know what 'dat means but I have an idea how it should feel.

I just have 'dis notion that I can learn more about me if I'm surrounded by big sisters like you. So if any of 'dis makes sense then maybe we are sisters?"

I want to wipe the sweat from my armpits. So bad.

"Thank you, Ms. Trammell. Another revealing confessional. Listen, I hope you take this in the way I intend it but whether we choose you as a pledge or not, I want to you to know that you're far too beautiful and intelligent to use the words 'dis and 'dat," Leona said.

I could have died. Someone coughed to disguise a laugh.

"You may sit down."

I sat and knew it was over. I made a fool out of myself. I don't know what I was trying to prove. This was a mistake.

Jocelyn whispers, "Tell them you're legacy."

I shook my head. And wished she'd shut up.

"Is there something else?" Leona asked.

"No, ma'am," I answered.

Jocelyn low whispered in a sing-songy voice, "They're not going to take you…"

I closed my ears to her and waited for them to call the next candidate. I'm not like Jo-Jo. I won't force myself on someone.

"Did you say something, Ms. Downes?"

Jocelyn stood. "Ms. Trammell failed to mention she's a legacy candidate."

"Is that true?" Leona asked.

"Yes'um. Umm…. Yes, ma'am."

"You have to take her, right?" Jocelyn pressed.

Maybe she was trying to do the right thing in her usual wrong way but I wished she would sit her narrow ass down.

"Last year at Nationals we voted against the legacy statute. Now, every candidate is judged on her own merit."

I stared at the floor. I felt everyone's eyes on me. Look at the backward 'bama, biscuit eatin', can't talk good no way, roly poly wanna be somebody special. Oh my Lord. Strike me down! Sweat's runnin' in my eyes! I think I'm making an ass sweat stain on the cloth chair. Papa was right. I should have stayed at home and taught Sunday school.

Two weeks later, the sorority made their selection. The four girls were me, (yay!), Vanessa the beauty queen, Mariah the man-eatin' military brat and my roommate Jocelyn the irritant. What I didn't know then was that these women would become my lifelong friends. We would see each other through weddings, miscarriages, career triumphs and failures. Even when long stretches of time passed without seeing each other, when one of us was in need, the others would come a'runnin. Which is what happened when we heard from Jo-Jo after a ten-year absence.

FIVE

Twenty years later.... 2018

JOCELYN

"The doctor will see you now," says Nurse Gwen. I sip my cucumber water, tighten my Egyptian cotton robe, and follow Nurse Gwen down the hall. Nurse Gwen's booty is mesmerizing. When did women start growing butts like this? I bet Martha would disapprove. She'd call it 'gauche', which is code for 'ghetto.' With a butt like that, I seriously doubt if Nurse Gwen is a trained nurse. She's probably a wanna be model turned plastic surgery junkie. No one can have a body like that and still work for a living. She turns around as if to comment on my thoughts but instead asks if this is my first time with Dr. Kiss.

"Yes. I flew in from the East Coast."

"How did you hear about us?"

"A sorority sister recommended him. She had a facelift a couple of months ago and looks great."

"Ever since we started posting our operations on social media, we've become so busy. We get clients from all over the world. Mostly Japan. And of course A-list celebrities. You must have an influential friend to get an appointment so quickly."

Nurse Gwen looks Jamaican but speaks with a British accent. I doubt if that's real either. She turns back around.

"You look so familiar. I know I've seen you but I can't place where."

"I was married to Senator Harris."

"Oh! That's right. I'm so sorry."

I don't respond. What am I supposed to say to a stranger's pity? We finally walk through the double doors to Dr. Kiss' opulent office.

"Come in, Mrs. Harris," Dr. Kiss says in a thick Hungarian accent, beckoning me to sit across from him. His office could rival Louis XIV's Versailles. Nurse Gwen pours a flute of Cristal for me.

"Relax. You're in God's hands," she says.

"Gwendolyn flatters me. I'm not God. But I do correct his mistakes." Dr. Kiss takes Nurse Gwen by her delicate wrist and slowly turns her around, pointing out her ample booty and slim waist.

I thought she had work done but her whole body? I have to ask, "Do you mind if I...?" Nurse Gwen nods and I feel Nurse Gwen's breasts and booty.

"He did me. All of me. Save yourself a second and third appointment. Get The Works."

"I'm impressed. You look incredible but you must have been gorgeous before."

"I don't live in before. Now is all that matters." Nurse Gwen sashays over to the side of the room and waits.

"Who do you want to be, Mrs. Harris?"

I pull out my wedding photo, taken on Martha's Vineyard. It's a picture of my sorority sisters helping me get dressed. Mariah's attaching my veil. Vanessa's fluffing my hair. And Toni's trying to get me to eat an orange so I won't faint from hunger. And in the middle of all the fuss, I'm completely serene, staring into the mirror. I wonder if Dr. Kiss can fix my friendships along with my ass. Say, doctor, can you lift my friendships back up where they belong?

"This was the happiest time of my life. I want to feel like this again."

Dr. Kiss holds the photo up to the light.

"When was this taken?"

"Eighteen years ago."

I got married in the summer of 2000 but I'm wearing Martha's 1972 high neck lace dress with long poufy sleeves and cathedral veil. It didn't matter that the dress was two sizes too small and I had to eat oranges and yogurt for six months and run two miles a day to squeeze into it. It didn't even matter that I didn't particularly like the dress. Herschel wanted me to wear it as a tribute to his mother so I did. He was happy so I was happy. Only Martha thought I was doing too much to please her son. During the reception, she pulled me aside to say, "Don't give a man everything. They'll only want more. Save some part of you for yourself". I told her the only thing that mattered was Herschel's happiness. She never gave me advice again.

"Are you and the senator still married?"

"No," I say, choking on the champagne.

"The time to come in is when you first have suspicions. When you also have access to the accounts and the financial resources are unlimited."

"I was awarded a generous settlement."

Dr. Kiss offers a reassuring smile and hands over the photo. "When I'm done, he'll leave the home-wrecker and crawl back to you on his hands and knees. But you will not take him back."

"I won't?"

"You will have many, many suitors, you will reject him and he will die of shame."

My face lights up. "Give me The Works."

Dr. Kiss cracks his knuckles. Uncaps his red marker. "Let's begin." Nurse Gwen wheels a full-length mirror to the middle of the room. I toss back the last of the champagne and remove my robe. Nurse Gwen refills my glass with more bubbly as Dr. Kiss marks up my body.

"Lipo. Lots of lipo. Breast implants. And a lift. Is the senator a butt man?"

"Yes."

Dr. Kiss turns me around.

"One Brazilian butt. Knee lift. Both knees."

Nurse Gwen takes notes, then gasps, "Oh no."

"What is it?" I ask, looking down at the lumps and sags that is the landscape of my life.

Dr. Kiss and Nurse Gwen sigh, "Cankles."

I lean over, past my belly and hips to inspect my ankles. "They don't look that bad."

Dr. Kiss lifts Nurse Gwen's perfect leg. "You've seen the senator's girlfriend?"

I toss back more of the champagne. The fizz hits the back of my brain. I wrinkle up my nose, trying to push down the image of Herschel and whats-her-name in the laundry room. "She was my maid."

Nurse Gwen shakes her head, checks off cankles. I look in the mirror at my marked up body. "You weren't kidding when you said The Works."

"Now, the face." Dr. Kiss slips on a magnifying shield. He pulls at my face, stretching the skin, making my reflection deformed.

"Lift here. And here. Contour there."

"Yes. Restylane. Juvederm," Nurse Gwen adds, checking off her list.

"And a chemical peel."

"Of course." Nurse Gwen nods and explains, "We'll just burn off the top layer and expose the fresh skin underneath."

He taps my full lips with his marker.

"She has collagen."

"That's not collagen. It's collard greens and Coltrane," I say. "Some of my original parts are worth keeping." The booze has kicked in. I'm getting angry.

Dr. Kiss swings me back toward the mirror. "Voila!" My face and body are completely covered with a road map of red markings. The wind is knocked out of me. I can't breathe from the shock of seeing me naked and carved up. Dr. Kiss and Nurse Gwen stand on either side of me, grinning. Dr. Kiss asks, "How will you be paying?"

*****

Part of the perk of getting plastic surgery in Los Angeles is recovering at Oasis. It is literally a zen oasis in the midst of Santa Monica. It's the perfect place to convalesce. My penthouse suite is an open floor plan that resembles a loft more than an apartment. There are no walls, only sections. I guess it's to help reduce the feeling of isolation. There is, however, a sheer curtain that circles the bed, much like the blue curtains that envelope a hospital bed. The entire west wall of the suite has floor to ceiling views of the Pacific Ocean. Theoretically, I can enjoy warm breezes, the walk-in tub, and the fully stocked organic pantry and kitchen. In the morning, I watch surfers bob on their surfboards like seals waiting for a school of fish. I retained Nurse Gwen's services as my private in-house nurse. She's been through this healing process so she knows what I'm experiencing and she is a real nurse and a rather accomplished physical therapist as well.

I'm not on solid foods yet but she makes a delicious coconut pineapple guava smoothie that I take with a handful of pain meds. Everything hurts. My ears hurt. My eyelashes hurt. I'm a wound wrapped in a cocoon of bandages. Nurse Gwen reassures me I'll emerge a beautiful butterfly but until I do, I'm a slug.

At the moment, Nurse Gwen is holding up two lipsticks. I wink with my left eye to choose the Dior in Rouge Favori. It's the right pop of color against the white bandages. She gently applies lipstick on me and takes a couple of pictures for Dr. Kiss' Instagram feed. Apparently, everyone including plastic surgeons, post their work on 'the gram.' I don't mind being seen like this. No one's made a fuss over me since the last time I was in the hospital with a hernia.

The hotel lobby rings to announce my first visitor. Mariah. Little man-eater Mariah married a music man and now the former military brat is a budding media mogul. I never thought she'd marry any man. I hope she didn't bring him. Cliff is nice enough on his own, but the two of them, together? They don't bring out the best in each other. They remind me of chocolate wine. Chocolate tastes great. And wine tastes great but they should be enjoyed separately. You have a sip of wine followed up by a piece of chocolate. One, two. One, two. Like a dance. Combining the two may sounds like a good idea but in reality, chocolate wine is an abomination. And that's the marriage of Mariah and Cliff, makes sense in theory but in reality they should be enjoyed separately. A few minutes later Mrs. Mariah Stewart Ash, owner of Oyster Music, arrives accompanied by a bellman and thankfully without her husband. That's the rule on the recovery floor. Everyone who is not a patient gets an escort. No photos. No wandering around by looky-loos. Only discretion. Mariah tips the young man and he calls her ma'am. I see her cringe at the sound of ma'am. He didn't have to say ma'am. Just because she's nearing forty doesn't mean she's middle-aged. Youngsters think they're being polite when they're actually rubbing their youth in your face. I know Mariah wanted to say, I'm Mariah Ash, badass bitch. But instead, she turns her back on the offender and freezes him out. I watch her zero in on my bed. She can't see me. I'm too far away and the sheer curtains obstruct me. But I can see her.

"Jo-Jo? Are you over there?"

Before I can grunt an answer, the lobby calls again. Nurse Gwen gestures for Mariah to wait in the living room.

"Just a moment, ma'am," Nurse Gwen says to Mariah. "Please have a seat until the rest of your party arrives."

"My party?" Mariah says. "Who else are we waiting for?" Mariah looks in my direction for an answer then quickly looks away. I forgot how weakness makes her squeamish. She checks her phone. Busy, busy Mariah. I should be grateful she came at all. She's kept her figure. Still boyish. No boobs. No booty. No nonsense Mariah. I remember she used to be a runner back in the day and would frown when she was running like someone was chasing her. By the looks of her expensive bag, she successfully outran her debts. Mariah sits on the Eames chair facing the door. Always watch your back, Mariah.

Toni waddles in carrying a large pink box. She's just like I remember her only much, much plumper and much more radiant.

"Mariah! Girl, you look just the same. Don't lie and tell me I do too 'cause I know I don't."

"Wow. Look at you."

"I'm sweaty, my thighs are sticking together and I'm a size nineteen that's how I look."

Self-deprecating Toni. Stick it to yourself before they can zing you. I wonder if she has diabetes. Is she carrying a dessert box? I can't remember the last time I had a donut or one of Toni's famous pies. I really should stop by her pie shop one day soon.

"You know what they say, as you get older you either lose the badunkadunk or lose the face. I decided to keep both."

Toni drops the box on the coffee table and advances on Mariah with open arms. "Come on over here. You know I'm a hugger." Mariah doesn't move. "Oh, c'mon Mariah. Everybody needs a hug. Even you." Reluctantly, Mariah stands and Toni grabs her. Didn't she say her thighs are sticky? Images of maple syrup running down Toni's thighs enter my head. I can't shake it. A river of butter coursing through her veins. She's so jolly. I'm jealous. She's a hundred pounds heavier than I am and she's happy. She owns a bakery. She surrounds herself with sugar and spice and everything nice. Her life is a fairy tale and it isn't fair. I feel the pain meds kicking in.

Nurse Gwen keeps the door open. "Where's the other guest?"

"The beauty queen had to freshen up." Toni announces, and in walks Vanessa wearing sunglasses and a fur.

Vanessa tips the bellman. "Thank you, Miss," the bellman says, slightly bowing.

"Vanessa." Mariah says. "I haven't seen you since Fred's retirement party." Vanessa air kisses Mariah. Toni rolls her eyes.

"Breanna's cotillion's at the end of the month. Can you believe it? My baby's a debutante."

"No! She's sixteen already? Time truly does fly," Mariah says. It is uncanny how Vanessa can pull off a fur coat in summer. And she's barely aged at all. I guess when you don't have a job, you have the luxury of pampering yourself. Even when she did have a job, Vanessa would call in sick on days when work disrupted her beauty routine. Quite a few times I had to step in and take her place at the university library because she had an inconvenient pimple. I wonder if she does Zumba. I need a new workout routine.

"As hot as it is, she's wearing a fur," Toni says.

"It's a summer fur. And I'm quite comfortable."

"Follow me, ladies, Mrs. Harris will receive you now. She's a little nervous to see all of you. So please, keep the mood light. If you feel sick, there's a loo by the front door." Nurse Gwen leads them to me. For some strange reason, I feel like a spider awaiting my dinner.

"I got a bad feeling," Toni whispers to Mariah.

Nurse Gwen slides back the curtains to reveal me, bound in fresh bandages. My lips ruby rouge. Wires and solutions and monitors are hooked up to me. Toni clutches the pastry box. Mariah steps back. Only Vanessa bravely picks up the bottle of water with a straw to offer me a sip. "You have to hydrate, Jocelyn," Vanessa says. "Helps the swelling go down."

Toni sways the opened box of pastries in front of my bandaged face. "I made these for you! They're organic! And gluten free!" Toni yells.

"She can't eat them. She can barely open her mouth," Vanessa says.

"Oh," Toni says. "I have peach tarts, lemon meringue, bear claws! I made them myself. At my pie shop. Remember, my pie shop?" Toni yells.

I moan something that's affirmative.

Toni turns to Vanessa, "You think she heard me?"

"She's wrapped like a mummy and moaning in pain as she regains consciousness but yes, I'm sure she heard you say you own a pie shop," Vanessa replies.

Mariah still stands by the window, staring at me. "She has a pedicure," Mariah says.

"Nice color," Vanessa adds. "She always had a talent for choosing the right shade. Oh. There's a chip."

"I can't believe she did this to herself," Mariah says, keeping her distance.

Toni touches the IV drip as Nurse Gwen enters with a new bag of fluids.

"Feeding time!" Nurse Gwen brightly announces.

"She needs real food," Toni says.

"Food got her into this situation," Vanessa says.

"Her husband got her into this situation," Mariah counters.

"Doesn't she look great?" Nurse Gwen ignores the comments and replaces my IV bag. She smiles at me. "You look great!" she yells.

I moan.

Satisfied, Nurse Gwen slowly straightens her nurse uniform and sashays out the room. Vanessa gently tugs at her face.

"I knew she was getting some work done, but not The Works."

"In college, she was so confident. And smart. I don't understand why she'd do this to herself," Toni says, biting into a tart while staring at the IV flowing into my arm.

"Her husband was cheating on her! What's not to understand?" Mariah says, finally taking a step closer to my bed.

I moan.

"Did you hear he got engaged less than a month after their divorce?" Vanessa asks.

I moan louder to get them to change the subject.

"Which means he was cheating during their marriage," Mariah says.

"Remember their wedding on Martha's Vineyard? And her vintage dress?" Toni says. "I thought they were the perfect couple. They looked so glamorous."

"Looks can be deceiving," Vanessa adds, rubbing lotion into her hands.

I moan again to get their attention. The ladies lean in.

"She's trying to say something," Toni says. Vanessa presses her lips together, forcing herself not to say something rude to Toni. "What is it, Jo-Jo? This is like charades! Is it Mariah?" Toni places her hand on Mariah. I moan, no. I move my eyes to the right, then down.

"Maybe she needs the nurse," Vanessa decides.

"Do you need the nurse, Jo-Jo?!" Toni asks, louder than necessary.

I look down at the nightstand. Mariah opens the drawer and pulls out a photo of the four of us at USB when we crossed over into the sorority. Pinkie fingers in the air. Pledging to be sisters forever. Mariah gives the photo to Toni. Underneath the photo is an envelope addressed to my three friends.

"Read it Mariah," Vanessa says.

Mariah opens the envelope. My perfect penmanship says:

"To my closest friends and sisters, Mariah, Vanessa and Antoinette. I should be embarrassed calling you my closest friends when I haven't seen you in years. But the truth is the truth and Mariah you were never afraid of the truth. So here goes. My truth to you. I regret being careless with our friendship. There were times I wanted to reach out to each of you but so much time had passed, I didn't know how to say I've been thinking about you. Thank you for coming today. I know it isn't easy to see me like this but change is painful. I'm shedding my old skin and starting a new chapter in my life. Perhaps you think plastic surgery is a pathetic attempt to save my marriage. Mariah, ..."

Mariah stops reading. "Why does she keep saying my name?"

Vanessa takes the letter. "Mariah, I remember you telling me that Herschel was never good enough for me. That relying on a man is a sure way to a broken heart. And Vanessa, you would tell me to forgive and forget. That Herschel will come around because we all return to love. And Toni. Sweet, hopelessly romantic Toni. If I had confided in you, you probably would have baked me a delicious treat and said a prayer for me to find peace and acceptance."

"Jesus, take the wheel," Toni murmurs.

"I'm trying to move on. I'm trying to gather the bits and pieces of myself that I lost over the years. We've always brought out the best in each other. It is my sincere hope that you will share this new chapter in my life as I reclaim my body and my spirit. Your good friend and sister, Jocelyn Downes Harris."

Vanessa stops reading. She looks down at me, wrapped in bandages. She offers the letter to Toni and Mariah. Toni takes it.

"I had no idea she was so alone," Toni says. "Did you know?"

"I reached out to her a few times through the years. Around the holidays I'd get a Christmas card. Or an invitation to a fundraiser for the senator," Mariah says.

"The girl he's engaged to is a few years older than Breanna," Vanessa says.

They shake their heads in unison.

Toni breaks the silence. "So, how are your marriages?"

"Fine." Vanessa and Mariah answer in unison, moving away from my bed.

SIX

VANESSA

I wait in the lobby of the Century Plaza Towers. It's the most expensive office building in Los Angeles, and Fred's divorce attorney's offices are on the 35th floor. The penthouse floor. Figures. I try not to think about how much our lawyers are costing us. How much their fees are eating up our retirement funds. Breanna's college fund is in a trust. Thank God. While I wait, I spritz my favorite perfume on my wrists, Jo Malone fragrance, Pomegranate Noir. It may seem frivolous. Toni would certainly think so but perfume makes me feel better. And this one, the Pomegranate Noir, is Fred's favorite. He surprises me with a different Jo Malone fragrance every Christmas but this dark, tropical scent is his favorite. I wore it when he celebrated his super bowl victory. I wore it when we moved into our forever home. I wore it when we celebrated his retirement from the NFL. This fragrance holds all the good times we've earned. Each whiff is a remembrance of our life together. Here she comes. Ms. Teresita Hawthorne, Esquire, divorce attorney to the stars. For someone who charges $500 an hour, she could at least be punctual.

"I just got off the phone with his attorney. It'll just be a few minutes," she says as she sits across from me and reapplies her lipstick, Mac's Ruby Woo. Great. We're wearing the same color. Thankfully she's four shades darker than me, so it looks like a different color on her. I admit, I'm petty. I'm about to have the most life-defining meeting of my life and all I can think about is comparing my attorney's lipstick to mine.

On Jocelyn's recommendation, I hired Teresita Hawthorne, Esquire because she's a killer divorce attorney. Because of her expertise, Jocelyn is able to maintain the lifestyle to which she'd become accustomed as a senator's wife. For a $250,000 retainer and court fees Jocelyn was awarded over $13 million. I'm hoping for the same results. Why should me and Breanna move out of Lafayette Square because of his infidelity? My bad. Infidelities. Plural to the nth degree. This divorce already cost me four pounds. I'm withering away to nothing. I barely have enough to live on. My savings are depleted. I hope I'm not completely broke before the settlement's awarded. And Bree. My baby won't even speak to me. She had no reaction when I told her we were divorcing. I offered her counseling but she told me to get it for myself. That hurt. Then she said she was fine and wasn't surprised. Most of her friends' parents are on their second and third marriages. And then, she broke my heart by mumbling, "Now I'm from a broken home too."

"Do you want him back?" my lawyer asks.

I snap back to reality. "None of this is my idea. None of it. Fred wants a divorce. He'll get a divorce. He'll get the most painful, costly divorce ever known to the history of divorce. Everything he still owns is because of me. I was the one who established a savings plan, an investment plant and a retirement plan. I paid the bills. I picked out the house we live in. I picked out all the houses we lived in. Shuttling our family from city to city, following him around like a gypsy while he played football. I'll be damned if after seventeen years someone else is stepping into the life I created."

Ms. Hawthorne exhales then repeats the question. "Do you want him back, Mrs. Jones?"

"I have no illusions about the man I married. I love my husband. But love doesn't mean a thing without fidelity and respect. My father taught me that. If I can't have the kind of love my parents had then I don't want him. I want e-v-e-r-y-t-h-i-n-g."

"Mrs. Jones, if you want him back, you'll cave in the hopes that he'll come back to you. You'll deceive yourself into believing that he'll learn his lesson. If you want him back, you're wasting my time and your money. If you don't want him back, prepare yourself. It's going to get nasty."

"Fred isn't vindictive. He'll be fair."

"If he wanted to be fair, I wouldn't be here. You wouldn't need a divorce lawyer, especially one of my caliber. If he were being fair, you'd sit down at the kitchen table and talk it out or hire a mediator to steer the conversation. But you don't have a mediator. You have me. Life isn't fair and neither is divorce. A bit of advice. In every relationship, someone always feels more emotional than the other. And during a divorce, someone feels more vindictive. Your husband isn't going to roll over at the sight of you or the smell of your delightful perfume. He doesn't strike me as the sentimental type so let's go over a few things. Don't get baited by his attorney. He may direct questions at you to get you rattled and make you look bad in front of his client in order to sway your husband from being lenient. Ignore him. Ignore both of them. I'll answer for you. We're here to negotiate assets, not cast blame or get emotional. The time for casting blame was during the marriage."

"Ms. Hawthorne," I lean closer and lower my voice, "the stuff I told you about, his pain management medication, just pretend I never said anything. I shouldn't have told you. It's no one's business but mine and my husband's."

"Ex-husband."

She's about to get on my nerves. "Never the less, it's a sensitive subject. Don't hit below the belt."

We ride the elevator to the 35th floor. The elevator is excruciatingly slow. I'm watching the numbers light up and stewing over her correction, ex-husband. I bet she's not married. I don't see a ring on her finger.

"Only as a last resort," I remind her. She nods while checking her phone. She probably thinks I'm a stupid housewife who knew what I was getting into when I married a professional football player. 6. 7. 8th floor.

Nine months ago, Fred and I separated. He was working at ESPN as a weekend sports commentator when he met Heidi, a twenty-three-year-old red-headed white girl with a black girl's booty. I saw her at a sports function and knew she was nosey and long-eyed. She was way over there looking over at me and mine, wanting everything she could see. She didn't have the decency to disguise her thirst. Bouncing around in no bra. All the wives knew about her and kept their husbands away from her. I didn't see anything special about her other than she was petite, a skank attracted to Black men, and didn't care if they were married. But stupid me, I trusted Fred. I trusted he wouldn't embarrass himself and disrespect our marriage by having an affair with a co-worker, especially, with an intern. I was wrong. 14. 15. 16th floor.

After seventeen years of marriage, you don't see your spouse through new eyes. You see the gray hairs sticking out of his ears. You hear him clearing his throat at six in the morning. Emptying his bowels at six-fifteen. I'm sure he feels the same way about me. Although he never, ever heard me in the bathroom. I made sure of that. I learned to pee quietly. I learned to spray air freshener before pooping. I kept some mystery in our marriage, but after seventeen years, I was as routine as wheat toast mindlessly nibbled on while thinking of the day ahead.

But that ginger child was fresh and sugary sweet like a food court Cinnabon. Looks tasty from the display case but after a couple of bites, your sweet tooth turns into a stomachache. I honestly thought this would blow over. I mean, she's twenty-three! What do they talk about anyway? White women are relentless. They just assume a Black man wants them. We could be walking hand in hand and they'd practically walk through me to get to him! It's a miracle Fred didn't get anyone pregnant. Thank God for his low sperm count. 21. 22. 23rd floor.

I've been getting ready to see Fred since last week. Nails done. Hair done. Working out twice a day. Spin in the morning. Zumba in the afternoon. I stopped drinking. Well, almost. White wine isn't really drinking. When I open my fridge, there are bottles of spring water, coconut water, mineral water, and bottles of Prosecco. I moved my scale out of the master bathroom and into the pantry to remind me not to eat. I dropped another two pounds this morning. I'm down to 125. Thin for my 5'9" frame, even by Los Angeles standards. I can't bring myself to shop for groceries. There's no one to cook for, and cooking for one is just sad. Domesticity is a thankless job. I did everything for my family and they abandoned me. Fred walked out. And Breanna, she's coping but ignoring the situation. Staying with friends. Staying with her father in his new house in Fryman Canyon. If I can't handle my broken spirit, how can I be there for my sixteen-year-old daughter? All the king's horses and all the king's men couldn't put Vanessa back together again.

This morning, I pulled out my best dress. When he sees me, he'll regret leaving. Any twenty-three-year-old wishes she could look like me. He won't be able to take his eyes off me. He'll remember us and what I meant to him. 33. 34. Ready or not. The penthouse floor.

I step out of the elevator. Confident in my appearance as only those who know their looks is their currency can feel. Looking flawless. Feeling invincible. I follow Ms. Hawthorne into the conference room.

I slowly pull out the chair so my husband can take in all of this. Finally, I sit and look at him. Fred, the Freezer, Jones. At forty-one, ten years since his last pro game, he's still fit and handsome. And don't he know it. None of that post-career weight gain. His vanity would never allow it. If it weren't for his trick knee, he'd still be on the field.

Fred's divorce attorney, Mr. Maldonado, young and arrogant, is making a name for himself with sports clients. He pushes a document toward me. "Mrs. Jones, is this your signature?" My lawyer intercedes, pushing the document back. "Please direct your questions to me. Mr. Jones violated the terms of the prenuptial agreement by committing numerous counts of extra-marital affairs and we have documented proof of illegal drug use," she counters.

I told her not to go there!

Fred slams his hand on the table.

Damnit! I don't have to look up to know Fred is staring at me. It's the *I'll die before I quit look. I'm digging in look. I'll destroy you look.*

He leans over to whisper to his attorney. "The prenup only calls into question Mrs. Jones' behavior, not Mr. Jones," Mr. Maldonado says. "And Mr. Jones has reason to believe Mrs. Jones' fidelity is questionable."

"I'm the bad guy? I'm not the bad guy. I never once, threatened to leave you over your many, many groupie trysts. I never 'got even' and slept with anyone else."

"I was your gravy train. You hooked onto me and no matter what I did, you wouldn't let go," Fred sneers.

"And that proves what? That I wanted you for your money?"

"Your words."

"Fred, your father died a long time ago. You don't have to resurrect him."

"Save the psychobabble for your girlfriends. I saw you with my teammates, V. And you slept with at least two of 'em. Two that I know of."

"That's a damn lie! You want to play dirty? You want to drag my name into the mud? Let's do it. The only one who came onto me was your daddy and you know that. That dirty old man felt my ass every chance he could. He was an octopus! Why do you think I stopped having him over to the house?"

My attorney rests her hand on my arm. "There is no evidence to substantiate your claim of infidelity by Mrs. Jones. Now, back to the facts. After seventeen years of marriage, Mrs. Jones deserves fair compensation. According to this, she gets nothing," Ms. Hawthorne says.

"I'll be forced to sell the house," I say to Fred. "Is that what you want, Fred? Me and Breanna living in a shelter?" I reach for the box of tissues on the table. Now I know he's going to leave me with nothing.

"Don't be dramatic. Breanna will be fine."

"And me?"

Fred shrugs.

"You, Mrs. Jones, will get all that you're entitled to," Mr. Maldonado says. He pushes a bag across the table.

This feels bad. "Fred. What's that?" I ask.

"What you entered the marriage with," Fred answers.

I open the bag and unfold a beauty pageant sash.

"Ms. Cali, 2001." Fred smirks.

I stare at the sash in my hand. "Through all the injuries, all the groupies...your weak knee..." My eyes cloud with tears.

"Where were you gonna go?" Fred interrupts. "You were a beauty queen. You brought pageantry to the table. You should be thanking me."

"Thanking you? For what?"

He flicks lint off his sleeve. "For the free ride."

I gasp. This is not turning out right.

"Mrs. Jones was Mr. Jones' sole accountant and secretary. The only reason Mr. Jones has a sizable retirement and investment portfolio is because of Mrs. Jones. She also managed their homes and raised his child. Faithfully, in all regards."

As the lawyers argue, I stop listening. Taking a deep breath to steady my nerves, I inhale my perfume, and my mind is spinning. Memories flood through me. The first time Fred and I went out on a date. His deep laughter. His big, meaty hands on my tiny waist as he lifted me across the threshold of our first home. At the hospital, watching him hold our newborn baby, Breanna, with tears in his eyes. Burying his head in my lap when his awful father died. All these moments are slipping away from me. The promise of growing old together. Gone.

I have thoughts of Jocelyn lying in bed, feeding through an IV with only bandages to hug her tight. Jocelyn in bed. Alone. On the mend. All alone. "I can't end up like Jocelyn," I whisper. I look up at Fred, that stupid smirk etched on his face. Staring at me. Disdain dripping from his dumb hooded eyes. He hates me. He doesn't care what happens to me. What's the opposite of love? Indifference? That's the stupid look in his eyes. I could be hit by a bus and he'd cremate my body. Wouldn't even bother with a funeral. No embalming for Vanessa. That would cost too much. She's not worth the fluids. Just throw her in the oven. Broiler on high. Roast for thirty minutes. Ding! Stick a fork in her. She's dead and done.

I blink back the tears. Then it happens. His phone chimes. It's her. I know it's her. The ESPN intern. The little girl playing dress up. The twenty-three-year-old with red hair, perky boobs, and a high duck booty. Fred takes the call. He turns away, his voice is low, but I can still hear him. Everyone in the room can hear him say, "Get it if you want it. Can't talk now. I'll be home soon."

I'll be home soon reverberates in my body. She's living with him! They live together. The words echo in my brain but they don't make sense. Only my body seems to understand what my mind can't comprehend. I swallow. My spit is thick. My stomach is nauseous. And now, she's texting him. In the middle of our divorce! She's texting him pictures of herself lounging in red lingerie and clear heels. She's sexting him while I sit here losing my life. His neanderthal thumbs punch out a reply, sending smiling faces and stupid emojis. This can't be happening. This is not my beautiful life. I'm ten thousand dollars from the brink of ruin. I can't pay the car note or the health insurance or buy food. I must have been crazy to think if I just held on he'd come home. If I was a good wife, he'd see the error of his philandering ways. He's divorcing me. He ain't coming home. And, he doesn't give a shit. I don't get a gold watch for seventeen years of faithful service. I don't even get a letter of recommendation. I can't breathe. I push back my chair, knocking it over.

"See what I mean?" Fred says.

"Mrs. Jones, please sit down," Ms. Hawthorne whispers.

I stand. Trembling, I grip the edge of the table. I feel like I'm going to throw up. I've been a fool. I promised to love, honor and obey a man who won't stand by me. He doesn't love me. He did. Once. But that was before now and nothing before now matters.

"You should have been an actress instead of a washed-up beauty queen, V."

The room recedes. I take a wobbly step toward the door, and then faint.

"Mrs. Jones!" Ms. Hawthorne scrambles out of her chair and shakes me.

Barely conscious, I open my eyes to see Fred still seated, not bothered.

"Get up, V. You know how much money this is costing me?"

Ms. Hawthorne, God bless her, gives me a sip of water. I'm regaining focus.

"We'll table this discussion until Mrs. Jones is feeling better." Mr. Maldonado ushers Fred out of the room. Ms. Hawthorne checks my pulse, nearly blocking my view of Fred.

"Is he looking? Tell me he's looking."

Ms. Hawthorne drops my hand. "Are you kidding me?"

"Sssh. I can't hear what they're saying."

"I have 9-1-1 on speed dial," Mr. Maldonado assures Fred. "If she doesn't fully regain consciousness, EMT will be here in seven minutes. Nine tops. Unless there's traffic. In either case, I keep smelling salts in my top drawer for these occasions."

"Is she alright?" Fred asks.

"She'll be fine. Give her time to let the shock wear off. Seventeen years of marriage and nothing to show for it can knock anyone on their ass. You wanted me to go hard. This is hard. Plus, I wouldn't put it past her attorney to have set up this whole scenario as a guilt trip."

I watch Mr. Maldonado guide Fred into the elevator. "It's not the first time a wife has fainted in my conference room. I installed a four-inch carpet to soften the landing." The doors close on Fred's concerned face.

"He's gone. You can get up, Mrs. Jones," My lawyer says. She tries to help me stand but I can't move. My life is over.

SEVEN

TONI

My car did the customary shake, rattle and roll, then sputtered to a stop. I gotta get a new car. I say the same thing to myself every time I drive to my bakery in the morning hours. It is 5 a.m. Maybe the engine's cold. My car doesn't act up during the rest of the day, just in the dark, right before dawn. I'm not going to even think about Trey owning a car dealership and how he's never offered to give me a loaner. I shouldn't have to ask. I push the thought away. Nothing is going to upset me this morning, not even myself.

Entering through the back door, I flick on the lights to the kitchen. The lingering aroma of cinnamon and brown sugar greets me and I never get tired of the smell. The scent of sugar and spice is a spiritual cleanser. Some people use sage to clean evil spirits out of a house, but cinnamon and brown sugar clean the bad spirits out of me. Sometimes my kitchen smells like cinnamon and apples, or sugar and lemons, depending on what I baked the night before. But this morning, it's just the two notes that get me in the mood to roll out pie dough and start baking. Today is Friday, which everyone knows is Pie-day. I hope Trey remembers to pick up the crate of fruit I ordered from the market. I called to remind him but he didn't pick up. It's early. I'm sure he remembered.

I grab my apron and tie it around my waist. Humph. The tie's getting short. Fitting a little too snug. Oh well. Who trusts a skinny baker? At the front of the bakery, I do a quick wipe down of the table tops. Ten small tables and one ten-foot-long wooden farm style table set in front of the window with two long benches on either side. None of the furniture matches. I buy tables and chairs from different estate sales then painted them all white and add black cushions, so it's not an eyesore. I saw the design on Pinterest. One of those cute little French cafes in Paris inspired me. Paris. I straighten the photo of Josephine Baker shaking her little rump in a banana skirt. This entire wall is dedicated to Black folks who left America and found their freedom in Paris. James Baldwin is smoking a cigarette and sipping coffee in a cafe. Eartha Kitt's crawling around a stage like an exotic panther. Now my customers post their own Paris photos on the wall. The Sistas Read book club is waving in front of the Eiffel Tower. Chantel and one of her exs are kissing on the famous lock bridge. One day, I'm going to add my picture to the wall. Me and Trey are going to honeymoon in Paris and I'm saving a space right in the middle of the wall. I already hung a gold frame, all I need is the photo.

I flip on the pink and yellow neon sign, *Sweet on Slauson*. It took a long time to come up with a name. My mama wanted to call it Toni's Bakery. Where's the inspiration in that? "You gotta tell people who you are, child, and then you gotta show 'em." I don't know where she came up with that idea. I never saw my mama put herself out there. Far as I know, she always followed papa's lead. Then one day, the spirit moved me, and *Sweet on Slauson* was born. I sell sweets and I'm on Slauson. Bingo. Plus, I like the way it sounds. *Sweet on Slauson*. Every time I say it, it brings a smile to my face. *Sweet on Slauson*, the SOS for your sugar fix. You can't say *Sweet on Slauson* without smiling. That's the secret. Everyone thinks I sell cupcakes, cookies, and pies. I sell smiles. I sell happiness. When you enter *Sweet on Slauson*, you'll leave feeling better than when you came in. You may not feel lighter! But you'll feel better.

There's a saying on the wall next to the cash register. *Happiness is Home Made*. My parents always said, "Find your talent for serving others. And the Lord's will be done." My talent is baking. First, it was eating. I love to be in the kitchen. Life is so much better with a pot of turkey wings and greens boiling on the stove and homemade peach cobbler in the oven. When you walk in the house and that aroma greets you, you can drop your worries at the door. That's what *Sweet on Slauson* means to me. A place to forget your troubles and indulge in the sweetness of homemade goodness.

Speaking of homemade, I don't do none of that gluten-free, soy nonsense. What's the point of having something sweet if it ain't sweet? Jo-Jo suggested I give my health-conscious customers options. To make her happy, I tried it. I made some cakes and things. Nobody ate it. I couldn't give it away. People may buy that stuff in Beverly Hills but over here in Inglewood, they want white sugar, real butter, whole milk, and white flour. Nobody's allergic to gluten over here.

Instead of a tummy tuck, Jocelyn needs a big bowl of red velvet cake with peach ice cream. She doesn't need liposuction; she needs more sweetness in her life. So does Vanessa, and while I'm thinking about it, so does Mariah. Ooooh, I felt a chill. I'm going to have to come up with a special prayer for them.

Lord, please help these girls realize life is too short to skip dessert. Amen.

Jo-Jo was the one who encouraged me to open my own business. She understood having a dream to make a better life for yourself. A few years after she moved to Washington and became a senator's wife, she mailed me a check for $50,000 with a note that said, 'Stop talking about it and start being about it.' I was concerned about paying back that much money but she said it wasn't a loan. All she wanted was a picture of the bakery. I don't know how anyone can be generous and so self-centered but that's the beauty of Jocelyn. When we were pledging, it was me and Jo-Jo who fixed dinner during the all-night study sessions. She could throw down in the kitchen. You can't tell it by looking at her, especially now. There she goes wrapping sheets around her again. First the toga party. Now this plastic surgery shenanigan. When she's healed, I'm going to nurse her back to health 'cause her spirit is in crisis.

Walking into my pantry, I gather twelve apples, just enough for two pies. Glancing at the clock, it's 4:30 a.m. Trey should be here by seven. For the next two hours, I bake sour cream apple pie, traditional apple pie with gingerbread crust, three dozen oatmeal and cran-raisin cookies, three dozen snickerdoodles, three dozen cinnamon fig sweet rolls, three sour cream swirl coffee cakes, three dozen mini pound cakes, three 7up cakes and three maple butter twists. I had some leftover cookie dough so I made my grandmama's icebox cake. People love her icebox cake. By the time I look up, it's 6:48 a.m.

I change out of my dirty apron, go to the front of the bakery and flip the *Open* sign on the door. Trey should be coming any minute. Must be stuck in traffic. In the meantime, I shake out my personalized doormat that mama gave me for the bakery's grand opening. I don't know where she got a Toni doormat but if anyone can find one, it would be her. She stopped writing my name on everything, now she buys things with my name on it. The doormat was part of her attempt to get me to name the bakery after myself.

Right above the door is a little bell that rings whenever the door swings past it. I love that jingle jangle sound. It means company and company means good times which reminds me I have to shine the bell hanging over the door. I asked Trey to do it but I might as well have asked an ant to move a rubber tree plant. No sign of Trey yet. Might as well do a quick sweep.

My Awfully Wedded Husband

The mahogany wood floors were buried underneath layers of paint. It took two weeks to strip the floors to their original magnificence. Backbreaking labor that I will never do again. I wax them once a month to bring out the luster. Trey said I should go ahead and gloss them so they shine but he likes shiny things and I don't. My nails are still brittle from stripping off decades of paint layers to expose the original wood floors. Worth every broken nail. Trey helped. A little. Work at the dealership was busier than usual. Mustapha, my assistant, helped a lot. The dark floors make the white tables and chairs look sharp and clean. The walls are pale, pale blue with giant sepia toned photos of me and the Trammell women in our kitchens. My customers always point out the picture of the fat baby sleeping in a giant mixing bowl, feet and head poking out, mouth smeared with chocolate cake, surrounded by pies on the table. Yep, that's me. Mama had to put me where she could keep an eye on me while baking so she plopped me in a big bowl and I fell asleep eating chocolate cake. The mahogany floors are the same rich, beautiful dark color as the chocolate cake in my baby photo. The same color as papa's casket, mama said when she saw the floors. Papa died four years ago. I figured mama would come and live with me but mama, true to form, she followed papa's lead and stayed in Ojai replacing him as the new pastor of COGIS.

Pulling up the blinds to let the morning sun in, I watch the daybreak over Inglewood. Dawn is my favorite time of day. The world is fresh.

The day is new. And it's quiet. No cars on the street. No people talking loud. Everyone is still and everything is possible.

Humming *Love Lifted Me,* I place freshly baked fruit pies in the display case. Try as I might to remain in a state of grace, I keep thinking back to the girls. They had the nerve to laugh at my engagement to Trey. Seven years is nothing to laugh at! So we're engaged and not married. So what? Our engagement has lasted longer than most marriages. Besides, what did marriage get Mariah and Vanessa? Divorced and deserted. They're no better off than me. They may have more money, expensive clothes, and cars and for all that, they're miserable. Vanessa's clinging to her glory days. And Mariah, poor lost Mariah, sold her soul chasing money a long time ago. I can't believe they had the nerve to criticize my relationship. Mariah looked down her nose at me when I told her Trey and I were practically married. I can still hear her say, 'Nothing's like marriage except marriage'. And so what if I bought my engagement ring... and his. I trust Jesus. And when I prayed for Jesus to send me a good man he sent me Trey. Well, I guess I should have been more specific. Trey may not be the most handsome man or the richest man or even the most considerate man but he is my man. Trey. The light and the way. As he likes to say. I don't know if he's the light and the way but I do know my dark and lonely days are over. As soon as his mama finds her own man, maybe she'll loosen the apron strings and stop using Trey as a surrogate husband. But damn, her grip is tighter than a gnat's behind. He can't even move out her house because of her carpal tunnel disability. That sounds like his car. Yep. That's him. Here comes my baby now. Right on time. Looking up at the clock. 7:45. Well. Close enough.

I watch him from the kitchen. He steps in without the fruit crate. Maybe it's in the car. Trey has a slender frame. He probably needs me to help him carry it in. I put on a fresh apron and see him look down at the doormat and wipe his feet all over my name. He takes a couple of extra swipes, smiling as he does it. It used to bother me, the way he wiped his feet across my doormat but that's why the doormat's there. I've learned to just ignore him.

"Hey, sweetie pie!" Trey calls out.

"Hi, baby. Is the crate in the car?" I ask, placing a sour cream apple pie in the case.

"What? What you talking about now?"

"The fruit crate. You were supposed to pick it up from the farmers market this morning."

"Can I get both feet through the door before you start hounding me? Can a brother get a kiss or somethin'?"

"So you didn't get it." My shoulders automatically stiffen to ward off the disappointment. I glance up at the clock again. 7:50.

"I got held up." Trey gives me a big hug, squeezing my butt. I can smell the stale liquor and fresh marijuana on his clothes.

"The market closes at 8. If I want organic fruit I have to buy retail."

"It costs to be the boss. Handle your business." Trey opens the cash register takes out one hundred dollars in tens, and all the while he's counting out the money, he's telling me how to run my business. I've heard this before, so I'm zoning out on the sign above him that reads, *Happiness is Home Made.*

"Toni. Are you listening to me? I said is this all you got?"

"I have to make change for the customers, Trey."

"If you would have listened to me and called this place Baked like I told you and sold marijuana-laced cookies and cakes, you wouldn't be sweatin' me about a C note." Trey scribbles an IOU and shoves it in the register. "You know I'm good for it."

I don't say anything. It's no use. I'm just glad he stopped by to say good morning.

"What? Am I doing something wrong?" he asks.

"No, Trey." I pick up the dirty doormat and shake it outside the door. His friends loiter around his car. Pookie, Trey's best friend, the one with the permanent scowl on his face, sees me and nods hello.

"Pookie's out, huh?" I say, coming back in the bakery.

"That's what I was trying to tell you. I had to pick him up this morning. I can't be in two places at one time."

Jesus take the wheel. Jesus take the wheel. Jesus take the wheel. I take a deep breath and fix the smile on my face.

"You have to be at work in half an hour. You know how your mama gets when you're late."

"So you're going to get the same way? I don't need this shit."

"I didn't mean anything by it. I was just saying..."

The car horn honks.

"Will I see you later?" I ask.

"You're seeing me now. Once I leave, guess what? You'll be seeing me later." Trey pulls out an apple pie. Smells it.

"What's this?"

"Apple rhubarb."

"With walnuts?"

"No."

Trey scrunches up his face like he's smelling shit instead of a freshly baked pie. For a moment, he looks like he'll drop it on the floor. He looks up at me, grins a wide wicked lopsided grin, sloppily licks two fingers and scoops out a chunk of apple rhubarb pie. He shoves it in his mouth, wipes his hands on of the hanging aprons I have for sale. My stomach churns. This is God testing me to see if I'm ready for marriage.

"I'll take it. Next time, don't forget the walnuts."

Mustapha, my assistant, comes in carrying a crate of apples. Everybody loves him. He's a God-send. Does whatever I ask and apparently what I don't have to ask. I'm not surprised to see him with the fruit. He's dependable like that. I'm hoping some of his qualities will rub off on Trey.

"As-Salaam-Alaikum, my brother," Mustapha says to Trey.

"Apple pies and home fries to you too, Mustapha."

Mustapha ignores him, continues toward the kitchen. He smiles at me. His salt and pepper dreadlocks swinging right below his shoulders. "I stopped by the farmers market. I noticed we're running low on some things."

I don't want to say anything in front of Trey. I just breathe a grateful sigh of relief. I guess that's all Mustapha needs to hear. He nods and disappears into the kitchen.

I wait until I hear running water before reminding Trey about the wedding. "We have an appointment with Reverend Frank to discuss the wedding."

"I can't make it."

"But I haven't told you when it is."

Trey blankly stares at me. "When is it?"

I can only sigh from years of suppressed irritation.

The car horn honks a couple more times. Long, obnoxious what's taking so long honks.

"I told you. Pookie got out, didn't I tell you that?"

Pookie leans on the horn until Trey runs out, holding the pie over his head like a trophy.

"You get the money?" Pookie asks.

"You know me. I keep fresh money."

Trey gives Pookie the pie. "She put nuts in it?"

"Naw."

Pookie scrunches up his face. He looks over at me watching from the door. Then laughs as Trey drives off.

I close the screen door. And look at the doormat with my name on it. All of a sudden, the room feels small. The sun feels too hot and suffocating. Maybe I'm bipolar or going through the change. One minute I'm up and cheery, the next I'm down in the dumps.

Trey wasn't always like this. In the beginning, he was everything I dreamt a man should be. I knew Trey was the one when he insisted we remain celibate until marriage. We met at the grocery store. I was in line in front of him and somehow I left home without my wallet. Luckily, I had ten dollars on me but the groceries cost $10.23 and the cashier was looking at me like I better put something back. Trey stepped up and gave the cashier twenty-three cents. I was so embarrassed, I kept thanking him. He told me it wasn't a problem but if I wanted to make it up to him, I could cook up what I just bought and invite him over. He'd only eat twenty-three cents worth of food. I laughed and he walked me out of the store. He came over for dinner and kept coming over and we've been together ever since. His mama kept calling the first few weeks, asking if he was coming home for dinner but I had already fed him and we would settle in to watch TV. Those were the good days.

The Trammell women have always believed the way to a man's heart is through his stomach. My cooking's kept Trey around for seven years. It kept papa married to mama for forty-two years. Their relationship wasn't perfect. No relationship is but whatever was going on, they had dinner together. They may not have been talking, but they could still fix their mouth to say, "Pass the salt, please, and thank you" Through all the ups and downs, mama was patient and steadfast with her husband and the Lord. Who am I to expect a prince charming? I'm lucky I have Trey. Nobody was beating down my door before we met. The women who come in here, most of 'em come alone; they pick up pies and cupcakes for the week. When they're depressed, they order the red velvet cake. I can tell how they're doing by what they order. The really depressed ones get the Snickers cake. I've seen the side-eyed looks they give me when Trey strolls in and kisses me. And yeah, I feel blessed to have a man. Even a man like Trey.

But sometimes it would have been nice to go out. Oh, what am I thinking? He'd take me out on Monday nights. La Louisiana has a Monday night special during football season, a plate of red beans and rice with two pieces of fried chicken for $2.00. Trey likes the Raiders. And I love not having to cook dinner after baking all day, and their chicken is good. They get a nice scald on the skin. One night, one of the guys at La Louisiana kidded with Trey and told him to take me out on a proper date. Trey told him he knows what his baby likes, and hugged me tightly, kissing me on the cheek. I swelled up with pride. All the other women at the bar were with their friend-girls or sitting alone. I was the only one out with my man. I remember those days of going out alone and I don't want to go back to being single. Single makes me sad. I'm a big girl. I can't be single too.

When I told mama how Trey and I met, she said I bought a man for twenty-three cents. At least she didn't call him my no-good two-bit boyfriend. She didn't have to. I could tell how she felt about him. It's not Trey's fault he doesn't live up to papa's standards. I was holding out for a man like papa but he didn't come, and Trey did. Nobody understands. Not my mama. Not the girls. They have husbands. They've forgotten what it's like to be alone. All. The. Time. Lying awake in bed wondering why you're by yourself. Wondering when you're going to meet your man. Waking up by yourself. Eating in a restaurant. Table for one. Now when I go out, I have a man on my arm. And when he's not with me, my ring says I'm taken, I'm desirable, I'm wanted. I'm not throwing seven years away for nobody. Vanessa and Mariah can disapprove all they want but they can't judge me. Look at Mariah. She's the ultimate businesswoman and her husband doesn't love her. He never loved her! My job is to serve the Lord and my family and my church in that order. I'm working on the family part. Just give me time, Lord.

I stop polishing the bell above the door. It's so shiny I can see my face reflected back at me. I'm frowning.

"Ms. Toni!" Mustapha calls out from the kitchen. "You got a call. Somebody's in the hospital."

EIGHT

MARIAH

Los Angeles is the car status capital of the world. Your whole worth is determined by the car you drive. Your house can be raggedy but as long as you're rolling in a brand new something or other, you can fake it 'til you make it. Fortunately, my house matches my cars. I'm no Jay Leno but I love all types of automobiles. Cliff and I have owned and sold over a dozen vehicles. Right now, we have four cars housed up in our six-car garage. I bought Cliff a Bentley for our fifth anniversary. He always wanted one and I was trying to get him out of the Porsche Roadster. He's too old to climb in and out of a small sports car.

I open the garage and am not surprised to see the Bentley gone. Guess he left early for work. Or for the golf course. There's my baby, sitting patiently in the second row. Shiny and new. I bought myself a silver Maybach for my thirty-fifth birthday. I call her the Silver Goddess because she shields me from chaos. The minute I'm in her, I'm in my own private world. She is well worth the six-figure price tag. I don't usually splurge on expensive items but cars are my weakness. And I earned this car. Next to my sweet silver Maybach is an oldie but a goodie, a 1967 long nose Jaguar, dark green. I love this car. I only drive it on the weekends because I don't trust these cell phone addicted LA drivers. Choosing which car to drive is like Vanessa standing in her closet and choosing which shoes to wear or Toni standing in her kitchen and choosing which baking pan to use. It just depends on how I feel that day.

Today, I feel like my ride or die, the Silver Goddess. She's a classy broad. Smart. Stylish. At first glance she seems conservative, perhaps even boring. But once you're in her, you feel her power and control. I like that. There's more to her than meets the eye. When I couldn't justify buying the Maybach, Jocelyn convinced me to go ahead and get it. She said I deserve the best or nothing. *Das beste oder nichts* is the Mercedes tagline, it could very well be Jocelyn's tagline too.

My dear, dear Jocelyn. Wow. Instead of getting a body makeover she just should have gotten under someone else. How many times have I told her in college never, ever love a man more than he loves you. The minute they know you love them, they know they got you and the relationship as you know it, is *ovah*. And you only have yourself to blame! Cue the orchestra because heartbreak is coming. It's rushing toward you like a runaway freight train. And that whooshing sound you hear, that's your common sense leaving your body, and it's taking your dignity, your morality, and your good name. Whoosh!

If Jocelyn had confided in me, I would have told her to take a long vacation. Go somewhere. Anywhere. You need to find yourself again. Find Jocelyn Downes. She's somewhere under the layers of Harris. Wander around and get lost and I guarantee you, you'll find yourself again. Would I have really said that? Yeah, I would have said it but I would have only half meant it. For Jo-Jo to find herself, she'd have to do the impossible. She'd have to go back to college, back before she met Herschel's family, back before she altered pieces of herself to fit in his world. First, she gave up the way she talked. She used to sing when she spoke. Every sentence had a lilt to it. She spoke softly so we'd have to lean in to hear her. I thought it was a clever tactic to make us pay more attention to her. Either way, it worked, we leaned in like she was E.F. Hutton, but after she came back from Martha's Vineyard, she didn't speak like that anymore. She started speaking like Dominique Deveraux from Dynasty.

Scheisse! I ran a red light. Caution lights flash on my dashboard and my seat vibrates, warning me of my lax in judgment. Luckily the other drivers didn't visit Jocelyn yesterday and are paying closer attention to the road. I better pull over. Get it together, Mariah. Dabbing the sweat on my forehead and chest, I search for my hormone replacement pills. They're supposed to alleviate the hot flashes of menopause. Not only is my internal thermostat out of whack but my emotions are on steroids. I fluctuate between crying fits and fits of rage. Found them. Dry swallowing a capsule, I wait for modern science to chill me out. If these pills don't work, I may switch to medical marijuana. Cliff keeps a stash of edibles in the kitchen cookie jar.

Cliff. Lukewarm, harmless Cliff has been showing his ass. He wasn't always like this. I married him because I thought he was a safe bet. Cliff reminded me of a bowl of oatmeal. Oatmeal isn't fancy. No one wakes up craving oatmeal but it's good for you and it'll improve your quality of life. He was better for me than the random fruit loops I was dating. Cliff also appealed to me because he wasn't a military man. He wasn't domineering. He didn't adhere to gender roles. And most importantly, he didn't compete with me. The disadvantage of being a smart, capable woman is that men don't like us. They say they do, until we start running things and being a boss. *Scheisse*. I thought Cliff was above the fray. There's a saying, 'Be wary of guys who bend over backward for you. Eventually, they stand up.'

I met Cliff when I was twenty-eight and he was thirteen years older than me. We were a good counter-point to each other. He liked my enthusiasm and ideas. I was full of ideas and I needed his calming energy. He had a little music business, which I helped him grow using my innovative ideas. Social media was just starting and I introduced social marketing and branding to him. He let me do whatever I wanted and that fed my entrepreneurial spirit. I was ready to take the reins and shepherd his music company into the 21st century. Neither of us realized how successful our partnership would be.

Together, we formed Oyster Music. We told everyone the name Oyster came from Cliff's favorite saying, The world is your oyster, be the pearl. The truth is one night we were hungry and too tired to go to the store and too broke to order in. We found a can of smoked oysters and a pack of Saltines in the cupboard and two beers in the fridge. As we shared our smorgasbord, Cliff got down on one knee and proposed. I said yes and Oyster Music was born.

People say they want to be a power couple but they have no idea of the toil it takes to stand in the sun and not eclipse your partner. Whoever said familiarity breeds contempt must have been looking at me and Cliff. We were together all the time. At work and at home. The more successful our company became, the more our conversations centered on budgets, recordings, and bookings. We stopped trying to have date nights, dinners, or kids. He used to tell me how much he needed me. He wondered how did he ever get along without me? That was the first two years when we were struggling, when things were slowly coming together and we were seeing real progress building our company.

After our success, he realized he really could not have done it without me and that's when the resentment set in. Artists requested me at the planning meetings. Financiers wanted my input. It's not that Cliff didn't know what he was doing, it's more like he shifted his focus from running our business to tearing me down. He would say anything to make me appear emotionally unstable, usually right before an important meeting. The passive-aggressive comments came first. 'Here you go, boss. Here you go, princess. You're running the show. You don't need me anymore.' Then not so passive and way more aggressive. If I brought something up to discuss, he'd sigh and shake his head like I was wasting his time, like I exasperated him! And he liked to do it in front of people. 'You're so smart. You figure it out. So you don't know everything.' He became downright caustic: 'You wouldn't be here without me. You were nothing when I met you.' He was particularly fond of telling me, at the top of his voice, to go back to where I came from, usually, when he had a new secretary. It was his way of undermining my authority. He was particularly agitated when money was low. He'd panic. Engage in risky behavior. Micromanage. Pace. Prowl. And the needling. He'd needle me until I exploded. He'd pick and pick at something about me. Taunting. Picking. Needling. I couldn't stand it. It was the only thing that would make me lose my temper. The constant criticism. How many times did I tell him, 'Hey I'm on your side' and defer to his judgment. He would come to me for advice and get angry when I wouldn't give my input. Once I told him, he could handle it, he flipped out on me. He fell in love with my strength and business acumen then resented me for them. Damned if I do, damned if I don't.

The pills aren't working. I'm still sweating and I'm still angry. I'm angrier now than I was before. Turning the air conditioning on full blast, I lean back into the leather seat and navigate the congested freeway. How do women deal with this? We run businesses in heels, raise families in heels, and suffer menopause in the same four-inch heels.

There was a news article in the paper covering the women's march, where a woman held up a sign that read, 'Anything you can do, I can do bleeding.' Ha! That's right. And when the bleeding stops, the furnace begins. The fairer sex. Right. There's nothing fair about being a woman. And not for the first time, I wish I'd have been born a man. I'd be a good man.

I call the office. The receptionist answers, "Oyster Music." I don't recognize her voice.

"Who's this?" I ask.

"Renee ma'am. I'm a temp."

"Where's Rose?"

"She called in sick, ma'am."

"Has Mr. Ash arrived?"

"No, ma'am."

"Is he at a meeting?"

"No, ma'am."

"Does anyone know where my husband is?"

"Well ma'am, I mean, if you don't know," she says exasperatedly. I can hear the other lines are ringing. "Hold on, ma'am." Through the phone, I hear the temp ask if anyone has seen Mr. Ash. There was no reply. Radio silence. Cliff doesn't have a secretary. He doesn't like anyone keeping tabs on him anymore. "No one's heard from him, ma'am."

"Do I have any messages?" I know I don't but I just want to keep her on the line a little longer to test her.

"No ma'am."

Did she just suck her teeth? "I'm getting another call." I hang up and click over.

"Hello, Mariah Ash."

"Hello Mrs. Ash, I'm calling from Cedars-Sinai hospital. Vanessa Jones listed you as her contact person. She was admitted an hour ago."

"How is she? What happened?"

Before the nurse can answer, the call drops. I exit the freeway and take the side streets to the hospital. Vanessa is going to let that man drive her crazy. I know Fred has something to do with this. You're just getting a divorce, V. Toughen up. You're not the first wife to divorce a lying, cheating husband and you won't be the last. Speaking of which, let me call Cliff again. He needs to come in and take the meeting with Square Enix, a mobile gaming app company. If I can set up a partnership with them, then we can lay down music tracks for other mobile gaming apps maybe even video games and possibly movies.

Cliff's voice mail picks up. It didn't even ring. Okay, so his phone is off. I am leaving a message when I see a silver Bentley with tinted windows drive past me. The license plate reads Oyster. That's Cliff's car. Where's he going? I'm sweating again. Not from a hot flash. This time I'm radiating pure adrenaline mixed with anxiety and anger, bubbling to the surface of my skin. I pull over half a block away as Cliff parks the car. From the driver's seat emerges a fashionably dressed, young, petite Asian woman. For a moment, I'm confused until she turns around. It's Rose! The receptionist I hired a month ago. Oh hell no. She's driving my car! Calm down, Mariah. Don't let your emotions get the better of you. There's a reasonable explanation for why she's driving the Bentley you gave your husband. I watch her sashay her ass into Tiffany's.

I don't even look both ways as I cut across the traffic. I peer through the tinted windows of the car I gifted to my husband back in the day when he gave a damn. Yep. Cliff's jacket is in the passenger seat and there are shopping bags in the backseat. A lot of shopping bags. Gucci. Versace. Fendi. There's probably $10,000 worth of merchandise in the backseat. My instincts are twitching to go into Tiffany's and pull Rose out the store. But I'm not getting arrested today. Let me go back to my car and wait.

Our marriage has been over for years. I knew it was over when I tripped on a rug and grabbed the mantle to keep from falling and knocked the crystal trophy for Best Commercial Soundtrack to the floor. Of course, the crystal shattered. Cliff was angry. Even when we realized I had broken my toe, he complained on the way to the emergency room that the trophy was irreplaceable. Maybe I could have overlooked the inference that the trophy was more valuable than me but what turned my blood cold was the side-eyed look he gave me. The contempt in his eyes. The sneer on his lips. Wow. I knew he had moments of resentment but I didn't know he despised me. That was it. Our marriage was done.

A month later, we discussed getting a divorce. Nothing concrete. Just broaching the subject and trying to be civil. Two months later, I found a lump in my breast. Boom! Stage two breast cancer. No husband is going to leave a wife diagnosed with stage two breast cancer. Except for the 2008 presidential candidate, John Edwards. I give Cliff a lot of credit. I give us a lot of credit for putting our differences aside. He was there for me through the chemo, the mastectomy, through it all. And, he kept the business afloat. Just when I thought maybe we could make our marriage work, I'd remember that side-eyed look of contempt.

After I survived cancer and a mastectomy, I had to wait a year before reconstructive surgery. I'm no beauty queen but I've gotten used to seeing myself with two breasts. I had half a chest and I felt like half a woman. Even after Dr. Kiss reconstructed my breast and threw in a bonus breast lift to make them both even, I wouldn't let Cliff see me naked, let alone touch me. Neither one of us brought up divorce again and we went back to sleeping in separate bedrooms and staying on our side of the house. We just feel into the ease of it. And now, here I am, flashing through menopause, on a stakeout waiting to catch my husband cheating on me. Yay me! I suck at being a woman.

Fuck this. I get out the car to go drag Rose out of the jewelry store when I see them. My husband, Clifton Nasty Ash and Rose walk out, blissfully unaware there's a shit storm brewing. Rose admires the shiny new bracelet hanging from her wrist and twists the matching necklace. Cliff pulls her closer to him and they walk arm in arm like lovesick teenagers.

Cliff sees me coming from across the street. He tries to duck into a clothing store but it's locked.

"Cliff, no more shopping. I'm hungry," Rose says, still oblivious.

"There's a restaurant back there." Cliff pulls her around, shuffling her away from me.

She turns him back around. "My feet hurt."

"I'll rub your feet when we get there." Clifton keeps an eye on me, waiting for him by the Bentley. I'm fuming. Steam's coming out of my ears. I'm pissed. Then Rose steps away from Cliff and sees me. She waves and walks straight to me.

"Mrs. Ash," Rose says. "I didn't recognize you out of the office."

"You're fired. Don't bother coming back to work."

She laughs. "I won't. I don't need to work." Rose digs into her Prada bag and shakes the car keys to the Bentley.

"Cliff! You let her drive the car!"

Cliff pops the trunk, where there are more designer shopping bags, and tosses the Tiffany bag onto the pile.

"It's my car, Mariah," Cliff responds.

"That I paid for! It was my anniversary present to you, and you let this Chinese -"

"Filipina." Rose is bold enough to interrupt me, standing next to Cliff with a smile on her face. Cliff steps in between us and uses his body to move me away from her.

"Really Cliff? We had a deal. No one from work. No one I know."

"Get in the car. People are watching," Cliff says to Rose.

Rose continues smiling at me. She leisurely gets in the driver's seat. Turns on the radio. Loud.

"Listen, it doesn't matter who I'm with. We're married but we're not in a marriage. You don't respeck me," Cliff tells me.

"It's respecT. With a T."

"Cliffie, I'm hungry," Rose whines.

"I got something for you to chew on."

"She's not the problem, Mariah."

"Oh, I'm the problem?" I press. I follow Cliff around the car. "I wasn't the problem while I built our company."

"When was the last time we had sex? Huh? How many years ago, Mariah?"

"That isn't my fault."

"No, no, it's my fault because you know, nothing is ever your fault. With a T." Cliff gets in the car, slamming the door on me.

"I had breast cancer. I had a mastectomy," I hiss. "What do you want from me?"

Rose drives off, leaving me screaming at the escaping car. "What do you want from me!"

A car horn honks. "Hey, lady! Get out the way!" The car speeds around me. I realize I'm in the middle of Rodeo Drive, acting a damn fool. White people are watching. I broke my family's cardinal rule; I lost control of my emotions and I did it in public. Smoothing out my suit, I walk back to my car with as much dignity as I can muster. A smile curls around my lips. You want a fight, Cliff? I'll give you one. A low down dirty mudslinging, Vaseline on my face bare-knuckle brawl.

On my way to see Vanessa in the hospital, I remembered mother. Before we left the house, she'd check our elbows and ankles to make sure we weren't ashy. Ash was not allowed in the Stewart house. Jokes on me for marrying an Ash, Clifton Ash. *Scheisse*!

NINE

VANESSA

Cedars-Sinai Hospital.

I awake in a hospital bed with IV tubes in my arm. I don't have to look in a mirror to know I'm exhausted, drawn, and pale. But mostly, I'm embarrassed to be in front of Toni and Mariah. Especially judgmental Toni with her holier than thou self. Toni's always carrying a cross on her back. Her cross was so huge back in college she practically walked bent over, shuffling under the weight of her religion. There she is, sitting in the corner, head bowed, praying for my soul. I can hear Mariah in the hall arranging for my release. Dotting I's and crossing Ts. Going over the insurance papers. Good, capable, meticulous Mariah. She's the one to have in your corner. Toni, well, she's good if you need a shoulder to cry on. Or a muffin.

Before Jo-Jo's bedside brought us together, we'd only seen each other a handful of times since graduating from the University of Santa Barbara. Toni reached out but stopped after I canceled a few too many times.

"What happened? Are you okay?" Toni asks, finally noticing I'm awake. She hugs me so tight, I shift my face to avoid being buried in her bosom and discover the scents of cinnamon and nutmeg, which bring up memories of baking cookies on Christmas morning when I was pregnant with Breanna, back when Fred never left my side. I pull away. "You certainly are what you eat," I tell her.

Toni draws back. "Excuse me?"

"You smell like sugar and spice on steroids."

"Oh, thank you." Toni's still unsure that it isn't a dig. "I believe in the power of food. Which you probably need. You're skin and bones, Nessa."

"I'm a perfect size zero."

"Zero isn't a size. Don't nobody want a bone but ..." Toni shakes her head as if she's dry erasing the rest of the phrase.

"Body shaming is beneath you, Toni." Sometimes being around me can try her patience but I'm fine with that.

"I mean zero means nothing. It's nothing. You're skin and bones, Nessa! I know you didn't let Fred reduce you to nothing."

"Well, I certainly am something. I'm a perfect size two."

Toni shakes her head. She makes one last rational attempt. "Nessa, a size isn't perfect. A size is just a number. The only thing that is perfect is God's love. The book of John, chapter two, verse five, whoever keeps his word, in him truly the love of God is perfected."

"Really? Toni. You're doing this now? Can you not quote the Bible to me? Save it for Sunday."

Mariah appears in the doorway. "I got them to not charge you for the last two tests. I saved you a thousand dollars. There's an issue with your insurance coverage but you have forty-five days to resolve it. That should be enough time, don't you think?"

I hear what Mariah's saying but can't muster a response. She saved me a thousand dollars. That means my fainting spell cost over a thousand dollars. How much over? Two thousand. Three? I can't think about it. Mariah, as much as I appreciate you always being a 'boss' in every aspect of your life, I just can't think about it. Pity party. Table for one. Pinot Grigio en masse. No food necessary. Maybe just a morsel to help swallow the pills. Breanna is the only thing keeping me from sweet oblivion.

"Vanessa. Are you listening to me?"

"You know she doesn't like discussing money," Toni answers.

"Well, when you get around to thinking about the bill. I paid it."

I groan. "You shouldn't have done that."

"It's done. Now tell me the truth, did he do this to you?" Mariah asks, still standing in the doorway. Hospitals are not her happy place and she looks particularly down today. Two friends in two hospital beds in two days is too much for her.

"No, no. Nothing like that. I'm dehydrated. The doctor said I need more liquids." I cover my face. "I fainted at the lawyer's office. In front of Fred."

"I knew he had something to do with this," Mariah says.

Defeated, I hold up my arm attached to the IV tap. "Remind you of anybody?"

"You're such a drama queen, V. You don't look anything like Jocelyn," Mariah says.

"No one's forcing you to follow in her footsteps, Nessa," Toni says.

"What is that supposed to mean?" I demand.

Dr. Simon Davis, the emergency room attendant, is preoccupied with referencing my chart when he slams into Mariah, knocking her off balance. Dr. Davis grabs her as Mariah's phone bounces on the floor. They both bend over to pick it up and hit their heads together. I watch as the doctor gestures for Mariah to stand still. Slowly, my doctor picks up Mariah's phone, while checking out Mariah's legs. My doctor's coming onto my friend! Dr. Davis stands. Flashing his stunning signature Idris Elba smile at her, he says, "I hope I didn't hurt it."

"I've dropped my phone so many times. It's indestructible," Mariah says, blushing. Blushing!

"No, not your phone, your noggin. I have a pretty hard Louisiana head. Or so I've been told. Here. Please sit." He pulls out a chair. Dumps my bag at the foot of the bed. He helps her sit down. "Dr. Simon Davis"

"Mariah Ash."

Simon hands Mariah a couple of Tylenols, "Now take two of these and call me in the morning." He pours her a glass of water from my pitcher.

"Yes, go right ahead," I say. "I'm only here because I'm dehydrated."

"There's no reason to make such a fuss. I'm fine, really I am," Mariah says, dry swallowing the aspirins.

"Yes, you are," Simon whispers, bending down, handing her the water. "Drink the water. Dry swallowing is a pet peeve of mine."

Mariah stares up into Simon's big brown Louisiana eyes. And chokes on the pills. She takes a larger gulp of water. Forcing it down.

"Doctor. How are *my* results?" I interrupt.

"Mrs. Jones. It's important that you drink plenty of fluids. We recommend water. No alcohol for a couple of days. And you must eat. Preferably five to six small meals throughout the day. Promise to be good and you're released."

I nod. Sniffle. "And you're sure it wasn't an aneurysm? I've never fainted before. What about medication? I need pain management."

"Your blood sugar is low. From not eating, I assume. But, we've hydrated you and replenished your enzymes." Dr. Davis carefully removes my IV drip.

"You've been very kind. Thank you for your care, doctor." I try batting my eyes at him to get a response. I'm not interested but I can't help competing to be the most desirable girl in the room. The doctor ignores me. Great. I can't sway a handsome doctor's attention away from ho-hum Mariah.

"Will one of you ladies be driving her home?" Dr. Davis asks.

"Yes," Mariah and Toni say in unison.

Mariah's phone rings. "Excuse me." She steps out into the hall.

"Take care, Mrs. Jones." Dr. Davis says to me while following Mariah out.

I sink deeper into the pillow. Further depressed that I'm losing my allure.

"My bag," I say to Toni, pointing to the bottom of the bed.

Toni hands me my limited-edition Gucci shoulder bag. I remove a small vial of hand serum. I squeeze the dropper. A drop of serum balloons into a tiny bubble then retreats into the vial. I sink into the pillows again. "No. More. Serum," I whisper.

Toni pulls out a giant tube of drugstore lotion.

"Raspberry Sensation."

"No thanks."

"Are you sure?" Toni pops open the cap, takes a whiff. She waves the moisturizer under my nose. "Smells yummy."

I turn away. My stomach churns. "I smell chemicals. Cancer-causing chemicals waiting to seep through the pores of my skin and attack my lymph nodes. No thank you."

Toni takes a long look at me. Snaps the cap back on. "Well excuse the hell out of me."

Mariah enters, further flustered. Blushing a deeper shade of crimson.

"Mariah, I think that doctor likes you!" Toni loudly whispers. "Did you tell him you're married?"

"It doesn't matter if she's married or not, she's not interested."

"Why wouldn't I be interested? I was a man-eater once. Just because I work for a living and have responsibilities doesn't mean I don't have needs," Mariah says. "I'm a woman. I'm not a robot. I need love and affection just like anyone else."

"Mariah. Are you okay?" Toni wonders. "Is it the change? The menopause."

"I don't know." Mariah shrugs but under her fluster I can tell something is on her mind besides Dr. Davis. "Anyway. Cliff was on the phone. There's an emergency meeting at work. I'm sorry, V. I have to go."

"Don't worry about it. Toni will take me home."

Toni drops the cancer-causing lotion into her clearance bin Target bag. Mariah hugs me. "Don't let that man drive you crazy."

*****

Outside the hospital, I sit in a wheelchair waiting for Toni. I'm still wearing the power suit I had on this morning. I feign a smile and do a pageant wave as people enter the hospital until Toni's old 1998 Toyota Camry chugs through the parking lot. "Oh, Jesus. Is there no end to my humiliation?" Toni squeezes out the car, all smiles and eager to offer a helping hand until she spots the look on my face. The look I inherited from Fred. The withering stare.

"Nessa. You are getting on my last nerve. Say one more word and I swear before my God, I will leave you at the bus stop."

I screw my lips together and get in the car. Toni slams the car door. Twice. Then hip bumps it for good measure.

On the drive home, I stare out the window. Toni, concerned, keeps looking over at me.

"Everything's going to be okay. Just think happy thoughts."

I look at her like she's crazy. "Think. Happy. Thoughts?"

"Uh huh. Mama used to say it to me when I was feeling down and it turned my frown back up and around." Toni smiles broadly.

I run my finger along the Camry's cracked interior.

"Well, it certainly worked wonders for you."

Toni clenches the steering wheel. "You have no idea how I'm clinging to happy thoughts right now."

I dump the Ms. Cali sash onto my lap and hold it up for Toni to see.

"After seventeen years of marriage, this is my consolation prize."

"I remember when you were crowned. We were so proud of you."

"Are you not hearing me? I'm going to lose my homes, my cars. I'll have to clip coupons and be forced to sell Mary Kay."

"I love Mary Kay! I'll order from you. I remember when I wasn't allowed to wear makeup and I'd see the ladies driving around in pink Cadillacs. Hey, I bet you can earn a pink Cadillac in no time at all. You're good with cosmetics, and with your beauty background. Wow. What a great idea."

"You don't get it. I'm not getting a dime from Fred. No alimony. No nothing. I'm ruined."

"If you say so." She runs over a pothole and nearly derails the car.

"How am I supposed to live with no money?" I whine.

"Earn your own, Nessa. Your beauty is the least of your assets. You're smart. College educated. Resourceful. Very well connected."

I consider Toni's words.

"I remember Vanessa Noisette. And when she wanted something, she got it. That girl had gumption."

"I haven't been Vanessa Noisette for a long time."

"Then it's time you remember who you are."

I roll up the Ms. Cali sash.

"The crown for Ms. California, 2001 goes to…" I take a deep breath, squeeze my opponent's hand. I'm not going to win. Keep smiling. I have a fifty percent chance. I could win. Keep smiling. Why not me? I bet I win. Wow, Ms. Anaheim has a zit on her chin. "… Ms. San Diego, Vanessa Noisette!" The first runner-up gives my hand an extra firm squeeze, digging her nails into my palm. But I don't care. I won! Screaming, I shake Ms. Anaheim's grip off of me. As the crown is pinned onto my mile-high bun, William Shatner, known as Captain Kirk to the Trekkies, hands me a bouquet of roses. He hugs me and whispers, "Welcome to the winner's circle." My eyes shine, tears brimming. I think I'm waving. I'm pretty sure I'm walking. I can't feel my body. But I see my Alpha Delta Zeta sisters in the audience cheering me on. It was the happiest time of my life.

*****

I live in Lafayette Square. A semi-gated community in Mid-City, Los Angeles. Semi-gated because there's one way in and one way out. The way in, is to accrue tons of money. Someone would have to die with no heirs for a house to be on the market. Eight blocks of upper middle-class sanctuary for Black people. Joe Louis used to live in the house next to mine. Most of the residents are television producers and actors. I love it here. Jo-Jo can have Beverly Hills. Lafayette Square is my home and my home is the crowning jewel of this elite enclave. At least on the outside. My neighbors would be shocked to see how I let my home go. I'm depressed and depressed people live like slobs.

Toni's car jerks to a stop in front of my house. She grinds the transmission into reverse. The car sounds like a dying dinosaur. I don't remember much after that. She helped me into my house and I awoke in a robe in my bedroom with a note on Fred's pillow.

Nessa, I cleaned the house. Hope you don't mind! There's monkey bread in the oven. You have a warming oven! Lucky you, I've always wanted one! That's where the bread is. Bread is life. Eat up!

Love you, T.

She cleaned my house? How long have I been asleep? I check my phone. It's 5 am. Wednesday. I met with the attorneys on Monday. I've been sleeping for thirty-six hours. I feel good. Good and hungry. Warm bread sounds nice. My stomach rumbles. I follow the scent of warm bread down the stairs to the kitchen, I notice my house is really clean. Floors swept and mopped. My clothes put away. Even the magazines are stacked neatly on chairs. A wave of warming humility washes over me. Walking through my clean home clears my head. My depression is gone. I feel optimistic. I need to eat. I need a plan. I need to make money. I used to make money modeling. I could do it again. I stop in front of the full-length mirror in the hall and open my robe.

So this is what thirty-seven years looks like. One baby. Two breasts that have been suckled, sucked, kissed, and deserted. Flat stomach with no stretch marks thanks to my mother's advice to use coconut butter day and night, and a little help from Dr. Kiss. Years of yoga. All kinds of yoga: vinyasa, hatha, bikrams. I hated that hotbox of stretching and breathing. The minute I stepped out into the air my muscles seized up. But I went back and I kept going back. I did everything and anything to stay limber and maintain my pageant body. I stayed youthful for Fred.

His vanity wouldn't allow me to look less than perfect. He had me try every fitness trend, every barre class and celebrity cleanse, none of them stuck. The only things that kept me slim were weightloss teas and dipping into Fred's steroid stash. Fred never knew we were both on The Clear. I used to sip it in my tea. I didn't suffer any side effects. No mood swings like he used to have. At least not extreme swings. I had the occasional bouts with depression but we both attributed that to being a woman. Sometimes the stereotype can work in your favor.

Speaking of favor, I'll have to do something to show Toni my appreciation. This monkey bread looks delicious. Sugar and cinnamon pillows oozing sweet vanilla glaze. It smells heavenly. Pulling off a biscuit from the mountain cinnamon roll, I take a deep, deep inhale. I can almost taste it. I can smell the butter, the vanilla paste. I can even see Toni whipping the batter with that smile on her face. She made the biscuits from scratch. Who does that? Does she carry yeast in her purse? Hmph! I'mma about to eat the whole thing and ruin my soon to be perfect size four body.

"Mom!" Breanna slams the front door and runs up the stairs. I smooth down my disheveled hair.

"I'm in the kitchen!"

She runs in and hugs me. She hasn't hugged me since Fred moved out. She smells like lip gloss. At sixteen, Breanna is the spitting image of Fred. She has his fierce, dark eyes and his stoic, pragmatic view of the world. She has my poreless skin and bone but not my body. She's built like a Jones, not a Noisette. She's 5'9 and growing at a healthy weight. When I realized my chubby baby was going to be a chubby girl, I was disappointed. I felt I had done something wrong. But to my credit, I never put her on a diet no matter how much I wanted to! I never put her in dance class. I never forced her to be my version of my daughter. I let her grow into her person even though it became unbearably clear we weren't going to have the mother-daughter relationship that I dreamt of.

Fred always wanted a son, and although Bree is a girl, she might as well have been a boy. I know, I'm selfish. I wish she were a girly girl. I wish we could borrow clothes. I wish she had a glitter and boy band phase but that's not who she is. She's all about sports. She and Fred can watch ESPN for hours and only get up for ham sandwiches and bathroom breaks. If she were a boy, she'd be scouted by the NFL by now. I wouldn't be surprised if she ends up working as a sports analyst. She shadows Fred at work every chance she gets.

Even though Bree's an only child, she's not a brat. A virtue I'm immensely proud of. But lately, she's been an ogre to live with. Moody. Irritable. Demanding. Very demanding. Fred is no help as a mediator, not even now when he's retired from football. I didn't expect much while he was on the field. I knew he'd be an absentee father but there's no excuse for him to be so inept now. Instead of spending quality time and talking with her, guiding her into womanhood, he's buying her affection. But that's Fred. The way to a woman's heart is through his wallet. So I'm not surprised to see her in new clothes and expensive jewelry.

"I just saw your Instagram feed. Why didn't you call me? Are you all right? Do you need me to do something?"

"Honey, I'm fine. I had a dizzy spell and the doctor gave me some water. I'm fine."

"So you're okay?" She looks at me.

"I came home and cleaned the house and baked monkey bread. It's in the warming oven. Go on and get you some. Make me a cup of tea."

She doesn't move. Just keeps looking at me with those critical eyes. "You didn't answer my question."

"Have I ever fainted? You come from stronger stock than that."

"The house does look clean."

"I told you! Pull the monkey bread out of the oven and make some tea. I have to get ready."

"Where are you going?"

"Brett Adams, my old modeling agent called. He wants me to come by. He thinks I can start modeling again."

"You."

"Yes, me. I'm a perfect size two. They say forty is the new twenty."

"I haven't heard that."

"Well, you're not forty."

"Neither are you!"

"But I will be. Breanna. You're going to make me late. Go on and do what I told you to do."

I quickly leave the kitchen. I'm a terrible liar and if Breanna asks anymore questions she'll see through me. I retreat back to my bedroom. Since I said it, I guess I should see Brett. I find my dress, the gold lamé gown I wore when I won the Ms. Cali pageant in 2001. This dress is my good luck charm. It made me a winner before. It can make me a winner again.

TEN

TONI

By the time I returned home, I needed someone to take care of me. Straightening up Vanessa's house was not an easy job but I felt compelled to do it. Cleanliness is next to Godliness and Vanessa needed all the Godliness I could muster.

Soon as I change out of my clothes, I'm going to shower and take a nap. I wish Trey hadn't put a full-length mirror on the bathroom door. It's harder to avoid looking at myself. Let me throw a towel over it. That's better. Jo-Jo is carving up her body, trying to recapture her youth. Vanessa is starving herself to death. What's wrong with their narrow behinds? They both look like toothpicks. I'm chunky. I love my chunky trunk. I just don't like seeing it naked. I'm so grateful today is Monday and the bakery is closed. I have the day to recover and relax. Maybe a little gardening when I get up. I should eat before I go to bed. There's leftover baked chicken, black beans and rice and a little piece of blueberry cobbler in the refrigerator. The blueberry cobbler never sells out and truth be told I'm thankful nobody else likes it 'cause that leaves more for me. My mouth is watering. After my bath, I'll eat the cobbler first, then the chicken. Or should I eat before showering? My stomach is growling. I was hungry at Vanessa's but she doesn't have nothing to eat 'cept rice cakes and champagne. No wonder Breanna is staying with her daddy. Oh, Lord. Vanesa's going to take us through her drama. I already know. This is just the beginning. No, I'mma shower first. Eat. Then sleep. Eating dinner for breakfast and going to sleep at noon. I almost feel like I'm being bad. I turn on the hot water and wait for it to heat up. Just as I step in and wet my hair, the doorbell rings.

Who could this be? Trey's at work. Mustapha comes to mind. No, he wouldn't come to the house. I turn off the water, pull a cotton robe around me and go to the front door where whoever it is keeps ringing the doorbell. "Coming! I'm coming!" This must be an emergency. Maybe it is Mustapha. I hope the bakery's okay. I would have looked through the peephole to see who's raising such a fuss but the person is now banging on the door.

I throw open the door to find Trey's mother standing there, hands stretched out holding a covered dish with oven mittens.

"It's about time you opened the door. Here. This is hot." She shoves the dish at me without giving me the mittens. I wrap an edge of the robe around my burning finger and put the bowl on the table next to the door.

"Ms. Devorah, Trey isn't here," I say, tying my robe closed.

"I know he isn't here. He's been calling me for his lunch after trying to reach you," she says, and walks in uninvited!

"I made him a chicken pot pie. I was going to take it to him at work but I saw your car out front. Girl, you saved me a trip. What are you doing home? You naked under there?" She pulls at my robe to embarrass me. Trey's mother does overly familiar stuff like that. "Don't tell me you got a man up in here. Cheating on my son!" she shouts, knowing there's no one home but also knowing it'll further embarrass me. I might as well close the door; she's walking through my living room. I pick up the casserole and rush to the kitchen. The dish is hot.

"Now Toni, get dressed and go on over to the car dealership before it cools. I'll wait for you to get back. You got HBO right? That movie's coming on … the one with Kevin Hart and Ice Cube. What do you call it?"

I don't answer. I'm running cold water over my burned hands. I'm angry and trying not to show it. Sometimes I wish I weren't Pentecostal. Squeezing my eyes shut against the pain, I stand at the sink until I literally cool down. When I turn around, his mother is standing at the refrigerator, pulling out my leftover chicken. Trey's mother's government name is Ms. Devorah DeVaughn. I never met anyone more judgmental with less reason to be. And I can't stand her. I do everything I can to make this woman like me and she just won't and now she's about to eat my food.

The first time we met, Trey brought me over to his house. Trey lives with his mama so technically it's her house. However, when he brought me over he didn't tell me he lived with his mama, so we were having a romantic dinner at his house, which I was preparing in the kitchen when his mama walked in carrying groceries. There's nothing worse than making yourself at home in someone else's kitchen. Trey didn't say much, he just stuck his head in the refrigerator like an ostrich, just like this heifer is doing now. Only she's not trying to avoid me, she's letting me know she can do whatever she wants in my house. She can ride over me like she rides over Trey. No wonder she can't keep a man. She can't blame it on her weight. I'm a big girl too and Trey loves me. But his mama is mean. And when she drinks, she gets meaner, meaner than a junkyard dog. One time I saw her cuss out the mailman for not bringing her IRS refund check. If you've ever bitten into a sour fruit, that face you make, that's the look his mama keeps on her face. That's her resting face. I don't know who did what to her to make her permanently sour, but I do know she keeps the memory of it alive and close to her heart. The only time that scowl on her face turns right side up is when she's around her precious boy, who is a full-grown man. I want a man who is close to his mother but Lord Almighty, I should have been more specific. I should have prayed for a man who loves his mother but is not a mama's boy.

"You're out of grape soda," Ms. Devorah DeVaughn says, looking at me with that scowl on her face, even more pronounced 'cause she really doesn't like me. She is waiting for me to explain why I'm out of soda and what I'm going to do about it. "You know, Trey loves his grape soda. How do you expect to keep a man in your house if you can't keep grape soda in your refrigerator?"

"You caught me at a bad time, Ms. Devorah. I was in the shower and about to go to sleep."

"Sleep? It's almost noon. What kind of woman sleeps in the middle of the day? Unless you were out all night. You stepping out on my son, Toni?"

"I was helping a friend."

"Well, now that you helped your 'friend' you can help your fiancé and bring him the chicken pot pie I made him. Why weren't you answering his calls?"

"Oh that. My phone died."

"Uh huh." Ms. Devorah DeVaughn sucks her teeth. "Well, he wanted you to make his lunch but since you and your 'friend' were all tied up, he called me. So you owe me one. You know that, right?"

I didn't know what to say. I'm exhausted and frustrated and can't believe this woman is eating my chicken with her fingers!

"Well go on now! Get dressed and get on while his food is hot. And pick up some grape soda on the way. I don't think he has any at work. Bring some back for me too while you're at it. I'll be here. What's that movie with Kevin Hart and Ice Cube?"

"I don't know."

"Well, a lot of good you are. Good thing I was there for my baby while you were out with your 'friend.' You better not tell Trey you were out all night. Well, that's up to you. I don't want to tell you how to handle your business." Ms. DeVaughn's head is back in my refrigerator. "Hmmm. Cobbler. Peach? Oh, damn, what the hell is this? Blueberry? I guess I'll eat it. What you got against peach cobbler?"

"I don't know," I mumble, walking out.

*****

I knock on the door of the car dealership, holding Trey's lunch wrapped in foil. I should never have started making and delivering his lunch but it's been going on too long for me to stop now. It was a fun thing to do in the beginning but now, he doesn't even say thank you. He doesn't even tell me if he orders food. More than a few times, I found my meals piled up in the office refrigerator. You'd think he wouldn't put up a fuss when I'm too busy to make his lunch but Lord, he throws a fit. 'You're not taking care of me. My mama told me about you but I didn't want to believe her.' My God, it's better to just to go ahead and get it over with. It's like putting something new on the menu to see how people respond to it and they end up liking it and the next thing you know they're asking for it all the time and what was supposed to be a specialty item served every once in a while is now a staple that you're known for and you're stuck serving it even though the novelty wore off for you a long time ago. Truth be told, there's a lot of things I would have never started with Trey. At least this time I'm only delivering.

The CLOSED sign hangs on the door. Closed at one p.m.? I peer through the glass doors. No one's inside. I walk to the side of the building. Yep. His car's there. I walk back to the front door. I try the doorknob. It's unlocked. I should have tried this first.

Except for the floor models, the dealership is empty. No signs of life. Trey's had this dealership since his mother signed it over to him. Somebody left it to her in a will. Or so the story goes. It's mostly low-end commuter cars for people in the neighborhood to get back and forth to work. Most of the cars have 100,000 miles already on them. Trey makes most of his money in the service department. He hired a couple of neighborhood mechanics to work part-time, just to be on call if and eventually when something goes wrong with the cars. He sells them cheap so customers know what they're getting. The only thing is he doesn't sell cars often. I suggested he turn the dealership into a motorcycle dealership. Motorcycles are smaller and cheaper than cars and they appeal to a younger more flamboyant buyer. Trey said he'd think about it but never did anything about it. Thinking doesn't lead to doing in Trey's mind. I made a couple of other suggestions that Trey thought about. Now I've given up all hope of ever getting back the money that I loaned him for 'operating costs' as he put it. $250,000 down the drain. My intentions were good. I'm not a complete doormat. I thought a woman was supposed to stand by her man, help him and encourage him to grow. I thought we're in this together. I had visions of us becoming a power couple. Not the Obama level of power but two small business owners servicing the community and having more than enough to meet our needs. Maybe if his mama wasn't always talking against me, things could work out between us.

"Hello?" I call out. "Anybody home?' I smell the faint odor of marijuana. "Trey?" I follow my nose to the back office. Now, I hear muffled sounds. "You whooo! Trey?" I open the outer door and peek in to see Trey sitting at his desk, inhaling a blunt. Thick smoke hovers near the ceiling. I'm about to enter when the sight of Pookie stops me.

"That's one dumb, fat, bitch but she can cook," Pookie says, taking the blunt from Trey. "I don't know how you do it, though."

"You know me. Trey. The light and the way. But for real. Fat chicks be so damn thirsty, they just be pulling on a brother. Throwing money at me. Begging," Trey says. "Low self-esteem chicks. That's the way to go. Put it on 'em. They do anything for you. Any. Thang."

"You gone marry her? Man, I wouldn't put a ring on it," Pookie says. "Hell, ring! You'd need a rope, one of them... what do you call it when you throw a leash around a cow?" Pookie asks.

"A lasso, fool," Trey says.

"Yeah, yeah, a lasso. You gone lasso that cow!" Pookie says.

Trey chokes on smoke and laughter. "She bought her own ring. Bought mine too!" They both crack up. "She about to buy me a house. My mama deserves a new home."

I quietly back away from the door and into a metal chair that clangs against the desk. Oh no. Trey throws open the door. Eyes red. Glassy.

"What you doing here? You spying on me?"

"I-I-I brought you chicken pot pie. For lunch. I thought you might be hungry."

Pookie calls out from the office, "I'm starving! Bring it on in here!" Trey looks back at him, grinning. But when he turns to face me, he's scowling.

"Okay, you brought it. Now leave it."

"You left the door unlocked. You shouldn't be smoking at work. You know your mother doesn't want -"

"I told you, it's medicinal!"

Pookie leans against the wall, smiling like a jackal. He keeps smoking the blunt. Blowing rings in my direction. He's wearing Trey's clothes. He's wearing the shirt I bought Trey for his birthday. Trey looks back at Pookie again, laughing.

"Go ahead! Laugh at the dumb, fat...fatty!" I yell.

"Baby, it's not like that. You know I love your cooking," Trey says.

"Yeah. He's gonna marry you. Any day now," Pookie joins in.

"So I'm a big fat joke? Well, laugh at this!" I throw the foil wrapped chicken pot pie at Trey. Chicken, peas, carrots and dough drip down his stunned face. "The engagement is off, Trey!" I storm out.

I pull up to my driveway. Trey's mother is waiting for me on the front porch. Her eyes are bulging red and glassy. I bet she was smoking marijuana in my house. She looks ready to cuss me out. Devorah

DeVaughn storms toward my car like a wild wildebeest, arms wailing, mouth flapping. I exhale, grip the wheel, and slam the gear into reverse. Thank God I didn't turn off the ignition. Trey's mama's got a spoon in her hand. The blueberry cobbler never had a chance.

"Hey! Trey told me what you did. You burned his face. What kind of woman throws a pot pie in her fiancé's face? I baked that at 400 degrees. Hey! Where you think you going?" his mother yells.

Good question. Where am I going? Lord, I didn't feel like hearing I told you so, so the only place for true peace and quiet is my bakery. I look at my phone. Still dead. I say a small prayer for little miracles.

I park in the back alley behind the dumpsters. Just in case, Mama DeVaughn or Trey drives by looking for me. I've seen enough of those two for quite some time. Maybe for the last time. I unlock the back door and step into the sanctuary of my kitchen. Calm immediate washes over me. I spared no expense remodeling my professional kitchen. Every appliance is top of the line. Four convection ovens, professional grade. Two stainless steel refrigerators. A huge island made of oak. And meticulously displayed measuring cups, rolling pins, cookie trays. Everything is in its place. Including me. This is my place. Whose knapsack is on the floor? Someone's in here. I pick up the rolling pin. Put it back down. Pick up a cast iron skillet. I creep into the front of the bakery. Empty. There's only one other hiding place. The pantry.

"Whoever's in there, come on out! I've called the police. I have a gun. I have two guns."

The pantry door slowly opens. Now what? I didn't think this through. I can't subdue whoever's hiding in the pantry.

"On second thought. Stay in there. I'm leaving. You can have the place."

The intruder steps out.

"Mustapha!"

Wearing a wife beater and jeans, holding his hands together, he apologizes for being in the bakery during closed hours. I notice his shoulders are very well defined. I also notice he can't look at me. He's too embarrassed.

"What are you doing here? Are you living in my pantry?"

"Only until I save enough for one of those single room occupancy hotels downtown. I was staying at bus shelters but I figured staying here was better. I could watch the place at night. You know there's been a few burglaries. But, I didn't touch nothing. I only ate my own food. I made sure to clean up before you got here in the morning. I'm real sorry, Ms. Trammell, I didn't mean no harm I just didn't have nowhere else to go."

The whole time he's talking he's gathering his things into his knapsack. He looks up to see me stuffing pieces of pie crust in my mouth. I'm not listening to him. I'm agitated and exhausted.

"What are you doing here? I mean, no disrespect. It's your business, I mean, it's your bakery and your business what you're doing here. You just never come on Mondays. Is something wrong?"

"Hmm? Yeah. Ummm… no. I don't know. I've been up all night. I need to sleep. I need to calm down. I'm tired. You know? I'm tired."

"Well, I kinda hooked up the pantry. There's a cot in there you can sleep on, I'll get out your hair."

"Wait. You don't have to go. You can't live here. But you don't have to go now. We'll figure out something for you. Have you had breakfast? I'm kinda hungry. What about you?"

"Yeah. I can always eat."

I turn on the stove. Reach for the frying pan. Mustapha takes the pan away from me.

"Why don't you lay down and I'll make breakfast. We have eggs, flour, sugar, I can make you pancakes. Blueberry pancakes. You like blueberries, right?"

"You're going to cook for me?"

"I can do more in the kitchen than lift fruit crates. Breakfast is my specialty. I burn, girl." Mustapha starts breakfast as I go into the walk-in pantry. There's an army cot nestled between the flour and sugar sacks. "How long have you been staying here?"

"Not long. A couple of weeks. But I'll find somewhere else to stay."

"Maybe it's a good thing you're here. Three businesses were broken into over the past month. You staying without telling me isn't right. But I understand needing a safe space to lay your head."

"Why don't you lay down and I'll wake you when breakfast is ready?"

I lie on the cot and pull out a book out from under the pillow. *A Life Inside,* a prisoner's notebook. So that's why he's so fit. He's been in prison. Been? Maybe he still is. Lord have mercy. Who is this man?

ELEVEN

MARIAH

Cliff has not been at work since the showdown on Rodeo Drive. I'm trying not to think about him while Teddy, our music editor, presents his version of our sizzle reel. We use the reel for new client pitches, and Teddy put together a fast-paced, hip-hop/sound design sequence for our presentation to Square Enix, the mobile app gaming company. Usually, Cliff weighs in on this sort of stuff but like I said, he's been MIA for a week.

My marriage is over. This time, not even cancer can put us back together again. What our marital failure means for Oyster Music is a mystery. My ego tells me this place can't go on without me. However, common sense tells me everyone is replaceable, even me, and I never drew up a contract adding my name as co-owner of the company. Legally, Oyster Music belongs to Cliff even though he doesn't do shit and even though the company didn't make real money 'til I came along. I'm the president but Cliff remains the CEO and founder. But the good news is we're married and I have contributed a whole hell of a lot to the success of Oyster, so I'm entitled to at least half. Half is good but not good enough. I want it all. Oyster Music is mine. It's the baby I never had and I'm not going to split it in half when I put my whole life into birthing it.

Two beefy security guards bust in, interrupting my internal tirade. They flick on the overhead lights and motion for Teddy to stop working. One of the guards stands next to the open door while the other stands next to me. I recognize the one standing by the door; I think his name is Henry or Henroc or something. We hired him to work the door at one of our parties. The other one looks like he's dead inside.

"Mr. Ash wants to see you, out in the hall," Henroc says.

"Tell Mr. Ash I'm busy."

"Out in the hall, ma'am," the other guard standing next to me says. He pulls my chair out.

"Wait a minute. Don't touch me. Cliff!" I wait for his answer.

"Please ma'am," Henroc says, a little nicer this time.

"Teddy, I'll be back in a minute, cue the reel from the beginning."

Teddy looks concerned but turns around and keeps his head down.

The guards lead me down the hall toward the receptionist, toward the common area where the lounge and kitchen are located, basically, where everyone can see me. Clifton waits for me, holding a clipboard. The guards position themselves on either side of me.

"If this is because of the other day, I don't care what you two-"

Clifton holds up the clipboard, and reads, "Mariah Stewart Ash, you are hereby fired from Oyster Records and will be escorted off the premises." The guards move closer to me. "Your personal belongings will be boxed and shipped to you." The guards gently grip my arm.

I try to shake loose. "Take your banana hands off me!" They don't. "I built this company. You can't fire me."

"I can, I have, and you are fired."

"My God, Cliff, what's happening to you?"

Clifton resumes reading. "If you trespass onto the premises, I have the legal authority to call the police and have you arrested. If you do not leave immediately, I will have you arrested."

"I was going to be civil. But as usual, you want to do things the stupid way."

"That's your problem. You never had any respeck for me."

"Spit the marbles out of your mouth. It's respecT with a T! You idioT!"

"Get her out of here," Cliff tells the goons.

"You're making a mistake, Cliff. When you come back to me, begging me for help, you'll be sorry."

"See, that's where you're wrong. I don't need your help to sell my company."

"You can't sell Oyster. We have employees. They depend on us. You wouldn't do that. You're lying."

"I don't need to lie."

"You don't have to sell our company. Sign it over to me. I'm running it anyway. You'll never have to work another day of your life."

Negotiating with him, right now is a long shot but you have to ask for what you want and I'm practically pleading with Cliff to take the high road. He strokes his chin, but I know he won't change his mind. He's mocking me. Drawing out the moment to give me hope before he dashes my dreams. He rests his hands on my shoulders. "The world is your oyster, Mariah, be the pearl." I slap him. Hard. So hard, he staggers back, shakes his head in shock. A red handprint spreads across his left cheek. We square off, finally seeing the deep-rooted resentment in each other.

He turns to the guards. "You want to get fired too? Get her out of here!"

I struggle as the guards pull me out the door. The bewildered employees watch. "You can't fire me! I run this bitch!" The employees stand transfixed, watching me make a spectacle of myself. "Get back to work!" Rose steps toward me, holding up her phone for a better angle to record everything.

"What are you looking at?" I shout at her.

"Ohhh, so sorry." She smiles at me, tapping her phone. ""Upload. Post. Score."

*****

So, that happened on Monday. I awaken on Wednesday, in my work clothes with all the windows open and the air fresh and crisp. I feel surprisingly rested. My head is clear. I'm not hot. Guess my body called a time out. Cliff won that round. He threw a fatal blow and knocked me on my ass. The best thing for me to do is lick my wounds until I have the strength to tear him apart. What's that noise? Something's pinging. Must be my phone. I have it set to ping for any mention of my name or Oyster Music. I know I should get up and at least check my phone but I'm not ready to put on my big girl panties. I don't feel like being strong today! Can a girl get a moment, take a knee, call the game on account of rain? You don't realize how fast you go until you hit a brick wall and I had a head-on collision. My body's in shock. For the first time in years, I'm in bed at three in the afternoon. And it feels good. Beyond good; it feels necessary. I should spend more time in bed. The $1400 mattress the salesman talked me into has a foam top that's guaranteed to whisk away body heat so I can sleep at the optimum temperature while it contours to my body's curves. He was right. Best investment ever. Cliff hated the mattress. It was one of the reasons he moved out of our bedroom to the other side of the house, or so he says. Not that where he slept mattered. We weren't having sex anymore. We weren't cuddling. All we were doing was sleeping on the opposite sides of the bed, ignoring each other.

I should get up. I should make coffee. I should make calls and plot my attack. At least plot my exit strategy from Oyster, from Cliff, maybe even from Los Angeles. I should be protecting my assets, calculating my projected losses, lawyering up. But I can't get up. Ping! Ping! Ping!

Down goes Mariah. Okay, get up and face what's left of your declining stock, Mariah.

I sit up, like a dejected hunchback. Thrown out of my own company. No one came to my defense. No one stood up for me. No one lifted a finger or batted an eye. They stood and watched. I'm going to assume they were in shock. But I do recall seeing a few phones pointed my way. Rose. I bet she recorded it. They're probably having a good laugh right now. 3:10 pm. Damn this bed feels good. This bed is my only friend. No one can hurt me as long as I'm in this bed. When was the last time I laid in bed past 7 am? Not never. I would never allow myself. I don't know why. Early bird gets the worm is bullshit if another bird can take the worm out of your mouth. Cliff certainly had no problem sleeping in. I spoiled him. I let him get to a place where he felt he could treat me like an employee. I blame myself. Did I just blame myself? Like a battered woman? If only I hadn't, maybe I should have; I know his moods, he's just acting out. And here I am. This is what happens when I lay in bed too long. This is why I don't. As long as I'm working, I'm not wallowing in self-pity.

I'm up! Cliffie. Clifton Ash. My husband. My mentor. My albatross around my neck. There are times when I second guessed myself for not having a baby but I can honestly say Cliff was the closest thing to a child. The attention he required wouldn't leave room for a baby. What kind of degenerate does this? An ingrate, that's who. He humiliated me.

In front of everyone. All my employees. And her! She was taping the whole thing! Hold up. What did she say, upload, post, score? Did that streetwalker post a video of me? Where's my phone?

I walk down the hall and make a mental note to take down ALL the photos carefully curated on the walls. Our success. My hard work. His accolades. His face has got to go. And my face, the pained grin, the college-try, go along to get along attitude I see behind every smile. They gotta go too. I won't even bother with an estate sale. I'll hire an assistant to throw them out. Speaking of assistance, I can't believe no one came to my defense.

There's my phone. Fifty messages. Three voicemails. Two of them from Vanessa and Toni. One from Human Resources. I already know what that's about. Exit papers to sign and handing over my key to the building. And a ton of google alerts. I click the link and see me being dragged out of my company while yelling, 'I run this bitch!' What the hell? Four thousand and eleven hits. YouTube's comment section ranges from she deserves it to that's a damn shame. I check the avatars and names. None I recognize from work. The clips are posted by @Flippingorgeous. Must be Rose. Yeah, we got it, you're Filipino with fake lashes and breast implants. You probably have tutorials on how to apply blush while banging your boss's husband. How to draw the perfect cat eye while doing nothing at your desk all day. You're an inspiration to a generation of entitled streetwalkers. I still can't believe that ingrate kicked me out of my own company. That's what I get for not making him make me an equal partner.

My only fear is public humiliation. Poppa Joe's rolling over in his grave. Mother, bless her, is on a golf course in Vegas, not giving a hot damn. Ever since Poppa Joe retired from the Air Force and died, mother relaxed her exacting standards. Good for her. Wish I could follow suit.

I call Human Resources. "Vincent Maldonado, HR."

"Vinnie, it's Mrs. Ash. What's Rose Abad's home address?"

"I'm sorry, Mrs. Ash, I'm not allowed to disclose confidential employee information to the public."

"Don't play games with me. I hired you. I bought all them damn Girl Scout cookies from your daughters. And you know I don't even like sweets. Now there's a video of me posted by Rose and there are even memes of me set to music… Oyster music! I want those employees' addresses too. I'm suing 'em all. And while I'm at it, I want to fire 'em. All of 'em. Today. You hear me?"

"Yes, ma'am, I hear you. And I'm actually glad you're calling. I have paperwork Mr. Ash instructed me to send to you. It's your severance package, ma'am."

Silence.

"Mr. Ash also instructed me to gather your personal items from your office, which I will do today. Shall I send them to your home address?"

"Don't touch anything in my office."

"Ma'am…"

"Stop calling me ma'am!"

"Yes, Mrs. Ash. Mr. Ash is renovating the top floor. He's removing your office. Whatever is there when the new furniture arrives will be discarded, ma… Mrs. Ash."

"You wouldn't have a place to work if it wasn't for me, Vinnie."

"So I'll send your things to your home address then."

"Are you enjoying this, Vincent?"

"You're a fair employer. Firm but fair. I have my doubts about the future of Oyster without you. And if I may add, I saw the clips of you on the Internet. Social media is a two-edged sword. You can either let it disembowel you or you can wield it to your benefit. Just so you'll know, Mr. Ash has instructed everyone not to take your calls and has ordered me to fire anyone who speaks to you. So if you call, we're obligated to hang up on you. I'm sorry, ma'am, please don't take this personally." He hangs up.

There's a knock at the door. I don't have to look out the window to know it's Vanessa and Toni.

*****

Sitting under the canopy next to the pool, Vanessa and Toni reassure me it'll blow over.

Toni giggles. "Mariah, you gotta admit. It is funny."

166

"Actually, it's not. Now when people see me, all they're going to see is me being thrown out of my company, screaming and carrying on."

"I run this bitch!" Toni and Vanessa yell in unison. They high five each other.

Ping! Ping! Ping! Damn it. "My employees probably have it as a screen saver." I reach for my phone and mute it.

"Or a ringtone! I run this bitch. Maybe even a t-shirt," Toni adds, waiting for me to agree.

"You're not making me feel better."

"I get it. You're ruined. You'll never love again. Cliff is a jerk. Which honestly speaking, I've never said this to you before but he's always been kinda weird. Is that okay to say now that we can agree he's an asshole? But what you've forgotten about yourself is that you're a military grade, industrial strength cockroach. And I mean that in the best possible way. Nothing can crush you. Nothing can kill you," Vanessa counsels.

"You're a survivor," Toni says. "Like the Beyoncé song." Toni hums it, jerking her shoulders to the beat inside her head.

"What's the point of surviving if I'm a loser? My brand is plummeting."

"Pivot, darling, pivot. Use your business acumen to bring him down. That's your company. He's your husband. Clean house, Mariah. Check his accounts, his purchases. That's how I found out Fred bought a house. I still don't know where he moved our money but I'm working on it. The Internet is information central."

"Trey isn't online. Me either," Toni says.

"You know what? Cliff wanted to humiliate me. He pushed me so I would act a fool. He did it in front of everybody to embarrass me. He probably told Rose to record me and had her put it on the Internet to ruin me." The ladies nod in agreement. "Cliff wants to go there. This is how he wants us to be then I'm going to be that. I'll show him what humiliation really feels like. I'm going to find that thing he's ashamed of and broadcast it to the world."

"And then what? What's the end result of mud on his face?" Toni asks. "I don't get it. An eye for an eye but then you're both blind."

"Anyway," Vanessa says. "We're here for you and if you want to blind him and broadcast it for the world to see, we got you."

Now I'm not so sure. Toni does make sense. She has these moments of clarity, kind of like an idiot savant. She's right. I need a bigger goal.

"The only problem is Cliff is milk toast. He doesn't have any skeletons. No financial misdeeds, I made sure of that. No affairs, not really. None that would matter anyway. Aside from acting like a spoiled brat, there's nothing out of the ordinary. He lacks imagination," I say, resigned.

"Maybe it's not him but her," Toni says.

"What if it's him and her?" Vanessa adds. "Call HR, pull Rose's records. Where does she live? Who is she? Where'd she come from?"

"Oh! Is she legal?" Toni asks.

We look at her, surprised.

"What?" Toni asks.

"I already called HR. There's a gag order. No one will speak to me at Oyster."

"Whoa. You're the boss," Toni says, shaking her head.

I ignore her. Sometimes her naivete is charming. This is not one of those times.

"I'll find another way. Her social media name is Flippingorgeous."

"Good name," Toni says. "What do you want, Mariah, besides making him a laughing stock?"

"I want my company, in my name. I want him out. Out of Oyster and out of my life."

Vanessa checks her phone. "Hey, you're officially viral. 10,000 views and climbing. Listen, all news is good news. It's when they stop talking about you that you have to worry." Vanessa snaps her fingers. "Hey! You bought him a Bentley! You bought it, right? It's yours, so call the dealership and activate the GPS. Then track him or track her, whatever, but let them lead you to the dirt." Vanessa bites a water cracker. "I used to do it to Fred all the time, until knowing hurt more than not knowing."

"You're a genius, V. A conniving, deviant genius," I say, stunned by her stealth.

TWELVE

VANESSA

Across town at a modeling agency, a receptionist applies her makeup while at the front desk. She looks up. A blank look of idiot confusion gives way to a smile slowly spreading across her face.

"Vanessa Noisette. Brett Adams is expecting me."

"Down the hall, corner office," the receptionist says, stifling a giggle.

Hater. They're all haters. I walk past a row of secretaries. Each one stops and stares at me. Aware that all eyes are on me, my walk turns into a runway strut. Wearing my Ms. Cali sash over a shimmering gold lamé mermaid pageant gown circa 2001, I pageant wave to each secretary, basking in their admiration. I still got it.

I stop at the entrance of Brett's office so he can take in all my shiny glory. He sees me. Coughs to clear his throat. "Vanessa!" He rises to greet me. He certainly changed from the hustler of the early 2000s when he was known for wearing rose-colored Gucci frames and bedding exotic bi-racial women. Now, he's twenty pounds lighter, wearing hemp clothing and a crystal around his neck to ward off evil spirits. Brett Adams is the Russell Simmons of the modeling world. Zen master, no stress, holistic approach to beauty and business, but don't let the namaste and hushed tone fool you. He'll get grimy if anyone messes with his money. He still has the Harlem accent though. Los Angeles didn't strip him of everything.

"Brett. It's been years."

"Yes. Many, many years. Please sit down."

I saunter toward the window where the light is better. Do a three-point turn and finish with a glance over my shoulder.

"Remember this gown?"

"I helped you pick it out for the pageant. Why are you wearing it, Vanessa?"

"I want you to book me. You can see for yourself, I look great. I'm still pageant size. A perfect size two."

"Please. Have a seat, Vanessa. I'm sorry to hear you and Fred are divorcing. You two made a great couple. I was always fond of Fred. And you know I have a soft spot for you."

I remain standing. I'm not going to discuss my marital situation. I'm not here for condolences.

"Life goes on, right, Brett? Do I look down? Do I look unhappy? I'm great! My priorities shifted and I want to get back in the game. All the magazines say forty is the new twenty!"

"Except when you're standing next to a twenty-year-old."

Brett pulls out a chair, forcing me to sit down.

"Magazines are in the business of selling a fantasy. So first of all, don't believe anything you read at the supermarket. Listen, you and I practically started out together so I'm gonna keep it one hundred with you. I can't help you."

"Brett. You're Brett Adams. You can do anything."

"I can't do that. If I could, I would. The reality is, you're too old but not old enough. You're in that middle limbo nether region. Five years ago, maybe. Under the Obama administration when clients were open to the Michelle Obama effect, you could have been relevant. But now." He shakes his head. "You're how old?"

"How old do you think I am?" I face the light, showing off my best feature, my profile.

Brett clears his throat and redirects my attention outside the window. "You see those two billboards dominating Sunset Blvd? That's me. Those are my models. Eastern European is the look. With this new administration, clients want Ivanka Trump. Maybe Melania for some of the risqué stuff. That's what's hot right now. I'm not saying it won't change, everything is cyclical but right now, that's what's hot."

"What about The Gap? Or Apple? They're inclusive. They advocate diversity."

"Vanessa, you're rounding forty, right? Okay, don't answer that. You're too old to appeal to new mothers and too young to reach the retirement demo. No one cares about a woman in her forties. Sorry. I know. I know it's harsh but I'd rather you hear it from a friend. I didn't make the rules." As Brett talks, he checks his emails.

A tall, leggy Eastern European model bounces into the office. "Oh, am I interrupting?" I look up to see youth standing in the door. Fresh faced. Tank top and barely-there shorts. No bra. She's twenty. Brett holds up his finger. The leggy Eastern European leans against the doorway, the light hits her face, highlighting her cheekbones.

"You must have a guardian angel. You want a job and I got one," Brett says to me.

"Yes! When?"

"Now. The girl walked off the set. So, you've got to get over there now."

"Yeah, sure. I'm ready."

Brett leads me to the door. "The receptionist will give you the address. We can talk about the fee after the shoot. You're not doing it for the money, right? You just want to get back in the game. Let everybody know Vanessa Noisette is back. Call me when you get there."

"What's the product? Cosmetics? Lingerie?"

"You don't care about that sort of stuff. It's a gig. You want to work, right?"

"That's why I'm here. But I want to know what I'm walking into." I'm starting to have doubts. It isn't like Brett not to be direct.

"You're the before model."

I blink. "Before what?"

"You're the woman the husband leaves for a new, younger wife. You can do this. Don't make it personal. Or make it personal if that helps you emote the right emotion." Brett looks me up and down. "They'll give you clothes when you get there."

"I'm nobody's *before*," I state.

"Then come back in five years, maybe I can get you an AARP ad. The truth is I'm not that kind of agency. I specialize in the new. Not the old."

I muster the last bit of my dignity and walk away from Brett and the perky model.

"Who's that?" the model asks.

"That's you if you don't listen to me," Brett replies.

I walk past the row of snickering secretaries. I pull off the Ms. Cali sash. It drops to the floor. I walk on. I continue past the receptionist and unzip my shimmering gold lamé dress. It drops to the floor. The receptionist looks up, mouth agape in astonishment. My head held high, I walk out of the building in lingerie and heels.

In a total daze, I walk into traffic on Sunset Blvd. Past bewildered drivers slowing down to snap photos to post to Snapchat, Instagram, Facebook. At least I'm not being ignored. I admit, even in a state of delirium, I waved at the flashing lights. Maybe I was having a flashback beauty queen moment. I can't tell you when the white camera flash became red and blue flashing lights from the approaching police car. I remember the officer ziplining my wrists with those barbaric cheap plastic straps and Brett running after me with my sash and gold lamé gown. A few moments later, Brett slipped something into the officer's hand; probably a couple of hundred dollars or his business card, I couldn't tell from inside the scratched police car windows but whatever he gave him, I ended up going home instead of to a holding cell on a 51-50.

The minute I get in the house, I demolish the monkey bread. I scarf it down. I don't even bother to pull it apart. I just grab it and shove it down my throat while uncorking my last bottle of expensive wine that I was saving for a special occasion. Since I didn't foresee anything special happening to me anytime soon, I skipped the glass and took the bottle with me into the bathtub for a good cry.

If daddy could see me now, he'd blame himself for not raising me to choose a better man. Before I married Fred, he told me it's not a commitment if you can change your mind. He said choosing a mate was the most critical decision a woman would ever make. Pay attention to how a man treats you, how mad he gets, how he acts when he's angry, what makes him angry, scared, jealous, insecure. What does he need to feel good about himself? And then ask yourself if you can handle him and still feel good about yourself as a woman. How do you feel around him? Not about him but around him? Are you happy, content, on edge? How do you feel when you leave his company? Empowered or depressed and confused? Daddy was smart. My parents stayed married through the civil rights era and through a life with no parole prison sentence. What marriage could sustain that? Momma visited him once a month, taking that long ass bus ride, always dragging me with her. Their vows were sorely tested and they survived it. They survived temptations, prison, dementia. Their vows meant something. Outwardly, they didn't seem to have much in common. Momma was conservative and daddy was a hellraising hustler. But fundamentally, they were cold water on a hot day. Just what the other needed.

Momma drilled into me to marry the man who would provide for me and protect me and who makes me feel good about who I am. He has to KNOW you're the one for him and do everything he can to convince you he's right. Otherwise, she warned, he'll use you and then abuse you. And once a man no longer respects his woman, she's doomed. Having a man work for your affection and time will teach him to cherish you. Momma didn't believe in equality. She believed men needed women more than women needed men, and when women forgot that simple fact, the relationship was sure to fail. Women were delicate flowers with wills of steel. And under no circumstance should a woman ever, never, never, never, ever act like a man by lifting anything heavy or paying for anything as long as her man was around. When a woman binds her future to a man it's his duty to help her rise and not drag her through the mud. It may sound archaic now but the balance works and has worked for thousands of years. So knowing all this, why am I sitting in my bathtub guzzling pinot noir? 'Cause of Fred's daddy.

Fred's daddy did a number on him. I won't say he hated me. I never took his slights personally. A misogynist is a misogynist with every woman. He had no respect for any women, not even his mother, I suspect, so I knew I wasn't special. But I was an inconvenience that wouldn't go away. His daddy, Farley, was one of those old Southern Black men who secretly hated themselves because they weren't white. Misery was his constant companion. Misery and fortitude. Fred's daddy thought women were either gold diggers or slut hounds. He did love one female, his hound dog, Luvvie. He treated her better than his wives. Luvvie outlasted four marriages. Farley had the audacity to stand up at our wedding and lecture me on the role of the woman. I'm glad daddy stood up to cut him off and talked about the role of the man. Farley sat back down then. Daddy is 6'5" with prison weight. He got a twelve hour prison furlough for good behavior. So yeah, Farley sat his doughy ass down.

I overheard Farley telling Fred, he didn't have to marry someone like me. At best I was side chick material. 'A beauty queen can't help your career. The only thing she brings to the table is a crown and a sash.' And I'll never forget Fred's response. He said, 'That's what my queen is supposed to bring'. Farley died ten years later. Although I didn't shed a tear, I did feel bad that he died alone and his body was found three days later with Luvvie crawled up next to him, also dead of a broken heart.

Unfortunately, Farley died in-between marriages. He had a heart attack while divorcing his fourth wife. She was a nurse, and if he had treated her better she would have been at home to call 9-1-1 and save his backwards ass. If he had treated any of his wives better, he'd be alive today since all his wives were nurses. He wanted Fred to marry a nurse. 'She'll keep you alive. Nurse you back to health. 'A beauty queen can't do nothing but prance around in a gown and play the violin.' Farley was secretly jealous of his son. However, he not so secretly made passes at me. Other than at the lawyer's office, I never said anything to Fred but I suspect he knew. He stopped leaving me alone with him and finally agreed to stopped having him at the house.

I think I have another bottle hidden in-between the linens. I step out of the tub filled with Epsom salts and coconut oil and pad over to the closet. Yep. An oldie and a cheapie bottle. Not that it matters, the second bottle will taste as good as the first. Standing naked, dripping wet, I fish around for a bottle opener and realized the house is silent. Gloriously silent. There is no Fred to scold me for drinking, even though, I tell him I'm having a pinot noir, the lightest of all the reds. I had to hide a couple of bottles throughout the house. A husband doesn't need to know all his wife's secrets. I can finally sip in peace. Fred would go on and on and on about two glasses of wine. Wine! Not scotch, bourbon or whiskey.

That I could understand. But wine? He was on steroids! At least wine is good for the heart. Well, I don't have to hide anything anymore. I need to chew on that thought. I don't have to hide anymore. What else am I hiding from my husband? What am I hiding from myself? I can cut my hair if I want. Fred likes long hair and forbid me to cut it. That's one less thing to debate. I've been thinking about cutting my hair short and going platinum to stop hiding these pesky grays. Hell. Now I can. I can do whatever the hell I want. I don't have to debate, negotiate, or any of the other concessions I've conceded over the years.

"I'm free," I say aloud, wiping the sweat from my face. "I can do what I want. However, I want. Whenever I want." And the only thing I want to do right now is what I'm doing right now. Sipping my wine and soaking my body. I'm out of tears. I'm out of fucks.

I turn on the wall mounted TV and flip through the channels, settling on E entertainment. I reach for my eye mask and press the remote, turning up the volume. "Senator Herschel Harris is seen boarding a plane with his new bride. A career politician representing the great state of California, Senator Harris was previously married to socialite Jocelyn Downes Harris. We were unable to contact the first Mrs. Harris for comment." Herschel helps his bride, still in her wedding gown board a private jet. They turn around and wave to the cameras.

Uh-oh. My wine spills into the tub as I grab the phone to call Jocelyn.

THIRTEEN

JOCELYN

Just when the caterpillar thought the world was over, she became a beautiful butterfly.

I awake to read this quote on a poster of a butterfly escaping from it's a cocoon hanging on the wall above the bedside table. This is Toni's way of encouraging me to stay positive. She used to have the same poster hanging over her desk in the dorm room we shared. There're also fresh cut pink and yellow roses, pink and yellow balloons and three cards. I know they're from the ladies. Pink and yellow are our sorority colors. It's very thoughtful. I hoped their visit would reunite our sisterhood. As soon as I'm on my feet, I'll invite them to the Vineyard. Maybe I'll invite Nurse Gwen too.

Nurse Gwen. There's more to her than a manufactured body and thick Jamaican by-way- of London accent. I got to know the woman behind the short nurse's uniform. Nurse Gwen can insert an intravenous drip while chatting on the phone to a sugar daddy, cooing and cajoling until she shows up with a new diamond necklace. Don't hate the player. I'm not in any position to turn on the only person who feeds me smoothies and empties my bladder bag. So I lie here and groan at the appropriate breaks in conversation when Nurse Gwen shows off pictures of the latest octogenarian white man who took her to dinner in

Palm Springs or on a shopping spree on Rodeo Drive or boating to Catalina Island.

Speaking of dating, who's the lucky man in my future? I won't date anyone seriously, of course, just a few high profile men to get Herschel to notice me. Someone on Capitol Hill. Or, someone in the press corps covering the White House. Whoever he is, it'll be someone who will cross paths with Herschel. I can see us running into him while we're on a date and he'll be surprised to see how well I'm doing without him. And then I imagine he'll call just to check in and inquire about the house at Martha's Vineyard, and then after a few calls and pleasantries when he sees I'm not at all bitter, I'll call him with a distressing matter that only he can solve. Men like that sort of thing. Hero worship. Play to their egos and they'll always return. Afterwards, I'll reveal my new body and our next chapter will begin. We'll laugh about the past. The separation. The divorce. The affairs. He'll admit that he was acting out. That he was subconsciously telling me not to take him for granted, to be kinder, appreciative, loving. I'll say that I learned my lesson. I'll let him know that I'm a changed woman. Literally, I'm changing as I lie here in my cocoon. Wrapped, bandaged, stitched. My body and soul are on the mend. I read the butterfly poster for the hundredth time. Yes. I am a beautiful butterfly. Just wait until Herschel sees me. We'll be like we used to be before I got old. All I have to do is wait and let my scars heal. My skin's itching again. It's about time for Nurse Gwen to turn me.

Per Dr. Kiss' breakthrough recovery procedure, all patients who've undergone multiple surgeries recuperate on a special suspension bed that's a cross between a hammock and a chicken rotisserie. Instead of you turning over, the bed turns to help with blood circulation and to prevent blood from pooling. When I start itching, it's time to turn me. Right now, my back is itching, so I need to rotate on my side. Luckily, I haven't had any complications except for a seroma under my breast. Nurse Gwen drains the pooling blood throughout the day. She assures me it's nothing to worry about. I press the emergency button and Nurse Gwen enters, looking distressed.

"You put yourself through so much and this had to happen." She walks in wiping her eyes. I knew it! There is something to worry about. A complication. I knew the itching was a bad sign. I want Dr. Kiss right now. I grunt to get her attention. She looks at me and turns on the TV, scrolling through channels until she stops on my husband, ex-husband, soon to be my husband again, Senator Harris. Nurse Gwen hits pause and rotates my suspension bed until I'm entirely upright with a clear view of the TV. She places a comforting hand on my shoulder. I'm wondering if Herschel's all right. I stare at his face, his graying temples, that smug smile that I fell in love with, and pray that he's okay. I grunt for Nurse Gwen to release pause.

"First, let me increase your morphine level. You'll definitely need a higher dose." Nurse Gwen adjusts my morphine drip. "There. That should make it easier. Let's wait a moment for it to take." She waits until the warmth rushes through me. Now my heart is racing. My heart monitor is beeping like crazy. Nurse Gwen glances at my skyrocketing blood pressure.

"He's dead?" I manage to choke out the words.

"Worse." Nurse Gwen hits play and Senator Harris waves to the camera. What's worse than death? It can't be that bad if he's alive. Thank God he's alive. And looking good. The man can wear a suit. And now that his hair is graying on the sides, he looks even more distinguished. Men have it so easy. They can age and look better. Women, we have to go to Dr. Kiss. I moan and blink rapidly, communicating with Nurse Gwen to turn up the volume. We've worked out a wordless system. Rapid blinks while staring at the TV means sound up. Closing my eyes means volume down. A left blink means to change the channel. But right now, I'm blinking like crazy. Not to turn up the volume which Nurse Gwen has on 100 but because I'm blinking back tears. My Herschel is emerging from a church next to a woman wearing a wedding dress, and it isn't me. I don't understand. Is he married? He married the maid. That bitch? This can't be true. This must be the fake news I keep hearing about. I look to Nurse Gwen for an explanation but she's checking her phone and stepping away. And then I see it. That woman in the wedding dress, the one holding onto my husband, shields her belly. I lean forward and unbelievable pain shoots through my midsection. I saw it. I can't pretend I didn't. Shielding a belly can only mean one thing. She's pregnant.

Nurse Gwen returns and changes the channel and lowers the volume. "We'll watch something relaxing. Helps the fluids drain and reduces swelling." She turns to House Hunters International where a couple is touring homes in Belize. He wants something close to the beach. She wants to be in the center of town. The agent is trying to help them compromise. I'm numb. My body is shutting down. I know it's shutting down because I don't want to live.

And then my heart stops I know it stopped because there are all kinds of beeps and alarms and I can see Nurse Gwen checking the monitors and pounding on my chest to start my heart. I see it all from up here. I see my bloated body wrapped in stained bandages. I do look like a rotisserie chicken. I look desperate. And sad. And alone. The paramedics arrive. They must be staying on the premises. They got to me so fast. They're trying to revive me. Yelling things like come back, don't give up. I wasted my life. Wasted my ambition. I didn't even leave a pretty corpse. I hope Dr. Kiss can fix me before my viewing.

Jocelyn Downes Harris
March 2, 1980 - May 15, 2018

Being dead is no excuse to miss your own funeral. The actual act of death is weird. My life doesn't flash before my eyes, that will happen later. There is a light and my mother and father greet me with forgiveness. I feel an overwhelming sense of love and calm and I have the option to go back. I decide there's no reason to return to the living. I know in an instant of all-knowing that I didn't live up to my potential and that I never would. Not in that lifetime.

In my haste to reinvent myself, I forgot I had God-given talents worth holding onto. I used to be smart. I mean, really smart, like an academic protégé. I was witty. That used to bother Herschel, so I toned down my quips and comments, all the way down until I even stopped thinking clever thoughts. And I used to be ambitious. I traded all the great parts of me for status. There I said it. Now that I'm dead, I can finally admit the truth about myself. I never thought I could actually be something. My brother was smart. A genius. And where did it get him? Two heart attacks and a stroke while juggling a $50,000 a year job and a sullen family. I couldn't chance being book smart and working poor. It was easier to champion someone else's dream, especially when he comes from a successful family. I never believed I could be a major Me that's why I became a Mrs. Him.

What they don't tell you about being dead is that when your life is flashing before your eyes, you're reliving how you made other's feel. You see yourself talking to others and you feel what they're feeling interacting with you. I hurt a lot of people's feelings. I wasn't kind. I wasn't generous. People didn't trust me. They thought I was always scheming. And they were right. I felt my mother's disappointment when I didn't invite her to my wedding. I felt my father's anger when I wouldn't answer his calls. They forgave me for shunning them. They had to. I'm in heaven, forgiveness is part of the deal.

I have no concept of time. I only know I want to come back for my funeral and here I am at the Hopper Funeral Home and Crematory. Not much of a crowd. Just my girls, wearing sunglasses to hide their sadness. Some of the tears are for me but mostly they cry for themselves. As they approach my casket, Toni giggles.

"I'm sorry, I laugh when I'm nervous."

"Maybe you should go outside," Vanessa says.

"What difference does it make? It's just us," Mariah says as she takes the lead and steps up to view my body. "Oh my God. Look at her." They stand over my body.

I gotta hand it to you Jo-Jo, if you're going to die, this is the way to do it. Beautifully, Vanessa thinks to herself as she views my immaculate body and perfect face.

"She looks ten years younger," Mariah comments.

"Dr. Kiss outdid himself. She's never looked better," Vanessa remarks, caressing her own neck.

"If you're going to meet the Lord and Savior, you ought to look your best," Toni claims, nodding for emphasis. Toni looks around. She finally notices that the room is packed with flowers instead of people. That's what happens when you value things over people. "So no one else is coming? Not even her staff?" Toni inquires, confused that no one else is there.

"We're here. We're someone, not no one," Mariah says. "Jo-Jo's here. We have flowers. Sympathy cards. It's not supposed to be a party." Mariah checks the sympathy cards attached to the elaborate arrangements. "Hotels and airlines, spas and salons, Neiman Marcus. This one is from The Beverly Center. A realtor from Martha's Vineyard and the pink and yellow flowers are from Alpha Delta Zeta. See? This is Jo-Jo's whole life and everything that was important to her, right here in this room. Like an Egyptian Queen entombed with all her favorite things. Sad." Mariah sniffles. The ladies look at her, shocked by her rare show of emotion. Mariah waves off their compassion. "I'm premenopausal."

"I believe death is a home going. It should be a celebration of the soul returning to Christ," Toni states.

"Not when you commit suicide. Is that still a sin?" Vanessa asks Mariah.

"Only if you're Catholic."

"I heard her heart stopped," Toni says. "But I think she died from a broken heart. She had to have seen Herschel's wedding on TV."

"Jo-Jo died long ago. Not to be dramatic but she's been slowly dying ever since she had her first abortion," Mariah adds. Dabbing tears from her eyes. "I never cry. I'm not sad. She's definitely in a better place. Jo-Jo wasn't a quitter. I can't believe she'd do this."

"She had an abortion?" Toni loud whispers.

Quickly looking around to see if anyone heard her, she forgets that no one else is there except them and me. I shouldn't be surprised, out of all the things Mariah said, this is the one she's concerned about. Yes, I had an abortion. Yes, I lived with the hard choice. Yes, I regret it.

"Three," Mariah says, choking back the swell of sadness.

Mariah's sad for herself. I'm not offended her tears aren't for me. She's alone too. All the ladies are wondering if I'm their fate. If they'll end up unloved and misunderstood. None of these things will happen to them but they don't know that yet and it's the unknowing that will help them push through the doubt.

"Mariah, here." Vanessa holds out a valium. "Do us all a favor and take it."

Mariah takes the valium. "I'm not sad."

"The valium will make you pleasantly numb."

Toni sits and fans herself, whispering a prayer for the aborted fetuses. The ladies step aside, letting Toni have her moment.

"Look. I bet it's from Herschel," Mariah says, referring to a small wreath. "She hates… hated carnations. She called them funeral flowers." Mariah checks the card. The carnation wreath is from Herschel. "Knew it. The bastard."

"Don't be so hard on him, Mariah. He didn't send the flowers, his secretary did," Vanessa says.

"If you're going to send flowers to a funeral, it's an appropriate choice, don't you think? What is he supposed to send, red roses?" Toni counters.

"Why are you sticking up for him?" Mariah asks.

"I'm not sticking up for anybody. This is a funeral. He sent funeral flowers." Toni states.

"It's her fault. I'm so sick of women thinking they can change men. She brought this on herself," Mariah says.

Toni gasps. "She's dead."

"Her own doing. She didn't have to get multiple cosmetic surgeries. You saw her suspended from the ceiling. Looking like a fly in a sadistic spider web. I'll say it again. She brought this on herself. She blames… blamed Herschel but he didn't break her heart. She broke her own heart."

"Wow, Mariah. Bitter, much?" Vanessa says.

"Not bitter, V. Realistic. Herschel has always been and will always be Herschel. He's selfish. She let him walk all over her. It takes two to ruin a marriage. She didn't have to… end up here. There was nothing wrong with her! There are other men in the world. Plenty of men just waiting to break her heart. She didn't have to let one man crush her. This is what happens when you can't see beyond your man."

"Maybe we shouldn't talk about this in front of her," Toni says.

Mariah ignores her.

"He was never going back to her. I know it. You know it. And Jo-Jo had to have known it. She knew…" Vanessa stops talking. Her face lights up.

"She knew what?" Toni asks.

"She knew her husband." Vanessa looks down at my smooth newly reconstructed youthful face. "Jocelyn, I swear I will not let you die in vain. I promise you I will learn from you and not let this happen to me."

"What is that supposed to mean?" Toni asks.

"It's supposed to mean it ain't over 'till it's over," Vanessa answers, smiling triumphantly at Toni.

Toni shrugs, more confused than ever. "Let's say our goodbyes," Toni says.

"I don't want to say goodbye. See you later is better," Mariah says.

Mariah doesn't like to say goodbye. It's a military thing.

"Okay, however, we want to wish our sister a safe passage home. There are no rules. Personally, I don't have any words," Vanessa adds.

My sorority sisters, the only sisters I've ever known, my closest friends who I spent too little time with, stare at me, lying in my casket. C'mon girls, say something. I hear you speaking to me with your hearts.

"She's wearing the eternity ring," Vanessa notices. The ladies lean in. They touch their own sorority rings.

"What was her quality?" Toni asks.

"The eternal bond of sisterhood," Mariah remembers. "Vanessa was grace. I was strength, and you were supposed to improve the lives of women everywhere. Or, something like that."

"She brought us back together. I'd say she fulfilled her purpose," Vanessa says.

Toni takes Mariah and Vanessa's hands. "Please Lord, watch over our sister. Make her an angel in your army of love. We ask that you, Sister Jocelyn, find peace in heaven and welcome us into the fold when it's our time to see our Heavenly Father. In Jesus name, we pray. Amen." Toni lifts her head. "Do you think she heard me?"

Yes, Toni. I hear you.

FOURTEEN

VANESSA

A white Phantom drives up to my house. Even though I've never seen the car before, I know who's driving it. Fred always wanted a Rolls Royce but I wouldn't let him get one. No car is worth half a million dollars. Not when you have a bad knee. Guess he's finally getting everything he wants, no matter the cost. I watch him roll down the windows. Please don't honk, I know you're here. The whole neighborhood knows you're here. They can hear the corny jazz you're listening to. Three quick honks get Breanna moving upstairs. I hear her pulling something down the stairs. I enlarge the image on the video monitor to get a better look at Fred's new car idling in the driveway. A new car! While I'm scraping money together to get my beauty business off the ground. And is that a woman in the passenger seat? I peer closer to the screen and watch Fred's girlfriend shake strands of red hair out the car window. "Mom! Dad's here!" Breanna calls out from the hall. I shut off the intercom. Must be nice to be a douchebag driving a new car with a skank by your side. Great example for our daughter. Nope. I'm not going to be angry. Be calm and carry on, Vanessa.

Shifting my attention to mixing shea butter and coconut oil in a bowl, I do my best to look unbothered for my daughter's sake. I take a restorative deep, deep inhale of lavender oil and I'm transported back to

193

my childhood bedroom where momma insisted on keeping lavender on the window sill. "It'll give you peaceful dreams," she said. "And when you're awake, you'll see a touch of beauty."

There were touches of beauty throughout the Noisette home. We didn't have much but we had touches of beauty, little surprises, like lavender plants in the bedroom and pitcher of water with lemon and lime slices. After pop was sent away, momma did everything to keep poverty from taking over our tiny apartment. Most of the time it worked, except when she was missing him. Those days and nights were long and dark and no amount of beauty could cover up momma's depression.

What people don't know about beauty queens is that we smile through the pain. Believe me, we know how painful the illusion of beauty can be. We'll smile through anything. A wild hair in our butts. A menstrual cramp. Our father in prison. Smile. Pivot. Wave. My mother losing her mind to dementia. Wave. Pivot. Smile. A half-witted answer that ends in 'world peace'. Beauty is all smoke and mirrors. Beauty queens are held together with Vaseline and hairspray. Not only is beauty painful, it's downright crippling. The only thing that matters, the only thing that's real is family.

My mother lost her mind to dementia but she never forgot my father. When she couldn't recognize me or remember my name, when she was convinced I was her dead sister, Sarah, she'd ask for her husband, Bert. When she was really in anguish she'd call out for

Bertram. Near the end, she asked for Bertram a lot. She'd get dressed and wait for her husband to come home from work. And when he didn't, she didn't understand why. She accused me, her sister, Sarah, of running him off. She'd spit at me, well her. It was heartbreaking. The love she had for him was true and dementia couldn't diminish it. Pop and I came up with a plan. I told her he was away fighting a war in the middle east and gave her a letter. I explained the number next to his name was his roster number to identify his platoon and unit. That calmed her down and she promptly wrote him every day. They became pen pals. She asked about the food, the weather, the people. He must have been very busy at the prison library because he always had detailed answers. She kept his letters in a gold box next to her bed so she could touch them every night. Theirs was a deep love. Not like the ADHD passing for commitment these days.

Breanna drops a bulging travel bag on the kitchen floor.

"Did you leave anything in your closet? You're coming home tomorrow morning."

"Oh, Dad didn't tell you?"

"Let's not play Dad didn't tell me. What didn't *you* tell me?"

"Dad's taking me to Las Vegas."

"No. You're not old enough to go to Las Vegas."

"But I want to go! And I'm going with Dad! You're the one who said we need to spend more time together."

"I never said anything about spending time in Las Vegas."

"What difference does it make where we go? I don't see the problem."

"You better watch how you speak to me, little girl. Just because we're the same height does not mean you're grown."

Breanna stands there searching for another tactic.

"We're going shopping for your Cotillion dress this weekend or does that not matter to you anymore?" I ask.

Breanna grabs my arms. "Please! I don't like shopping in LA. The sales people are rude. I don't look like you. I'm not a size six."

"I'm a size two."

"Mom. Stop. This is about me right now. Shopping in Los Angeles is torture. They treat me like I have two heads."

I angrily clear off the body butter ingredients from the counter. It's true. Salesgirls can be bitches. And there aren't a lot of stores for Breanna's unique square body and skinny legs. Plus she's got large breasts. At some point, Dr. Kiss will perform a breast reduction on her. Maybe for her eighteenth birthday. "They have the same malls in Las Vegas as they do in Los Angeles. I know you. You don't like shopping anywhere. There must be another reason you want to go."

"The Raiders have an exhibition game and ESPN wants Dad to be the lead announcer. It's a big deal and might make his career or something like that."

"Oh. Is he thinking about moving to Las Vegas?"

Breanna shrugs, dips her finger in the creamy shea butter mixture. "What's this?"

"Body butter."

"Wow, Mom. You're like the Martha Stewart of skin care DIY."

I load the dishwasher. The car honks again in short irritated blasts. The perfect sound for Fred's emotional disability. Short. Abrupt. Annoying. I can feel Breanna's anxiety rising. She'll just have to sweat it out and wait for my consent. Fred can wait too. Everybody can wait until I get good and ready. I whip the butter harder.

"It's better this way. I can watch the game and Dad can buy my dress that way you don't have to ask him for the money."

I stop mid-whip. What did this heifer say?

"You guys are still arguing about money, right? That's why you're making your own lotion because you don't have any money."

And she's still talking! If I had said something like that to my mother, I would've gotten slapped into next week.

"You're not going anywhere."

"What did I do?"

"I'm not one of your little friends. You speak to me like I'm your mother. You understand?"

"Yes, ma'am."

"What your father and I discuss are between us. Don't get in the middle."

We both take a moment to calm down. I did jump on her a little hard. All Breanna did was speak the truth. It's not like it's a secret that money's tight around here.

Breanna rubs the body butter on her hand. "I think it's great you're starting your own business. What's that saying about mothers being inventors because they have to."

"Necessity is the mother of invention."

'Yeah, that sounds like it." Breanna smells the lotion on her hands. "Smells like springtime. Like a meadow of lavender in the south of France."

"I'm still working on the consistency. It could be thicker," I say to ease the tension.

Breanna dips her finger in again. Rubs it into her arms. "It's luxurious, like liquid cashmere. Hey! That's what you should call it. Liquid cashmere. You could have your own beauty line like the Kardashians. "

"Okay, Breanna. You're laying it on pretty thick. And I don't mean the body butter."

Bree's phone rings. "Dad's getting mad. Can I go? I'm sorry I didn't ask. I forgot. But I promise to call you when we get there. I'll call while I'm shopping and I won't buy a dress until you approve it."

"Is it just the two of you going?"

"She's coming." Breanna deflates. She avoids looking at me. "How long is this going to go on? You're just letting him walk all over you."

I take another moment to not tell her to mind her own business. Instead I say, "Sometimes people grow apart. Sometimes people aren't as sensitive as you'd like them to be."

"Do you still love dad? I think he still loves you. When they're together it seems forced. Like he expects her to act like you. Are you waiting him out? Doing one of those 'if you love someone let them go and if they come back to you they're yours forever type thing'?" Bree looks up at me, expecting an answer that I don't have.

Discussing my relationship with my daughter is the last thing I want to do but here we are, doing it. "Since when do you watch Iyanla Vanzant?

"I read it on a poster. Seriously mom, do you still love dad?" Bree insists, bracing herself for the worse.

I hug her. "Love is many things. It changes. It grows. If you're lucky, it'll grow and mature and take your shoes without asking. Do you have my shoes in there?"

"You're changing the subject."

"So that's a yes. You can't even walk in them. I don't understand how a generation of women can't walk in heels."

"I've been practicing."

"In my shoes? Girl, give 'em here."

Breanna pulls the blush laser cut Yves Saint Laurent six-inch platform heels out of her bag.

"You don't even like high heels."

"Well, I can't wear sneakers. Isn't there some rule that I have to wear heels with a gown? Why do women subject themselves to torture? You can't even run in them."

"They're not for running. They're for gliding across the room. Show me what you got."

She slips them on her feet and wobbles toward me like a baby linebacker. My baby girl is not graceful. She's all meat and muscle with no booty or waist. I hold out my arms and Breanna grabs me before twisting her ankle. I try to hold her up but down goes Frazier. We both land on the floor, laughing.

"Are you going to be okay?" Breanna asks, giving me back the shoes and suddenly feeling guilty about leaving me alone for the weekend.

"Honey, don't worry about me. I have plenty to keep me occupied." I hug her again.

"So I can go?"

Now I'm stuck. If I say no, it's because I'm jealous of Fred's THOT, Heidi, making the skank more important than Bree's time with her father. I have to say yes to prove the skank is a non-factor. "No barely there body-con or halter dresses. Down to the knee or longer."

"As if. Thanks, mommy." Breanna hugs me.

"Now I'm mommy."

I help Breanna drag the luggage toward the front door. We stop on the porch, paralyzed by the sight of Heidi kissing Fred in the front seat. I put a reassuring hand on my daughter's sunken shoulder.

"Your father's going through something. Men do this. They get crazy ideas in their heads and forget who they are. But it doesn't mean he doesn't love you. You know none of this has anything to do with you. Or me for that matter. Dad is a little lost right now."

"I tried to hate him but I can't. It's Dad."

We decide to wait out the foreplay in the front seat by going over her weekend itinerary. Heidi is twenty-three. A natural red head. And on the come up. This is a whole new low for Fred. Kissing. In my driveway. The neighbors are probably watching. When we run out of small talk, Breanna looks at her dad making out with a white girl only a few years older than she is then glances back at me. Then back to watching them.

I finally step off the porch and walk toward Fred's car. Fred detangles himself from Heidi, wipes her lipstick off his mouth and gets out the car. Bree sidesteps his embrace. "Geez dad, get a room." He tries to help her with the bag, but Breanna refuses, so he stands there, helpless, by the car. Avoiding looking at me.

"Hi, Fred."

"Vanessa."

"So you're going to Las Vegas?"

"Yup."

"You could have told me."

"I don't need your permission. I can take my daughter anywhere I want. I come and go as I please with who I please."

"It just would have been nice to tell me you and Breanna are going away. That's all."

"That's between you and Bree."

"Nice car."

Fred doesn't say anything.

"You always wanted a Rolls Royce. Didn't think you'd chose white," I say as a not so subtle reference to the white girl in the passenger seat.

"White's easier to maintain," he says. I get his not so subtle meaning. Even if it isn't true.

"Jocelyn passed away. You remember her? Jocelyn Harris. We went to her wedding at Martha's Vineyard."

"The bougie couple? Yeah. I remember that. It was my first time eating on the beach at night. What's that called?"

"A crab boil."

"Yeah, that's it. Lobster, crab, shrimp. That was alright. She married old boy, the senator." Fred's face lights up, remembering the good times.

"They got divorced. And now she's dead. I just wanted you to know."

"You're not going to die, V. I heard you were picked up on a 51-50." Fred taps his temple. "Crazy runs in your family."

"You're despicable. There's no reason to bring up my mother. And she wasn't crazy. She had Alzheimer's. Don't go there."

"Hey, I just came to pick up my daughter. I'm glad you look stable. I'm doing you a favor by taking Bree for the weekend. It'll give you time to get yourself together." Fred smirks.

I just look at him. No expression. No malice. I just look at him and see him becoming his father. He leans closer to me and whispers, "I don't know what you're trying to pull, but you're not getting any money out of me. The prenup is ironclad."

"Honey, we have to go if we want to beat traffic," Heidi whines from the car. I bend down to speak to her but she's applying makeup with the visor down to avoid looking at me. She carefully swipes lip gloss over her pout, expertly plumped by Dr. Kiss not so long ago. I recognize his lip with the signature Cupid's bow.

Fred looks around for Breanna who's standing right next to him. "Let's get this show on the road."

Breanna hugs me. "Love you, Mom."

"Love you too, baby."

"Vanessa."

"Fred."

He awkwardly gets back in the car. I can tell his knee is bothering him again. Heidi leans over to kiss his cheek and rubs his leg, making sure I see her touching my husband. She doesn't say anything but her eyes say it all, 'the best bitch won'. What she's too simple to know is that queens don't compete with hoes.

*****

Senator Herschel Harris waves goodbye as he boards a private jet with his new young bride. Pausing the image on the screen, I turn to the ladies. "Jocelyn's body isn't cold and they're honeymooning in Fiji." I splash more champagne into Mariah and Toni's glasses.

"Vanessa, it's none of our business," Mariah says, pushing the champagne away. "Herschel moved on. He's married, living his life and frankly, we should all do the same."

"Hello! This is your life. Jo-Jo's problem is my problem, is your problem, and your problem," I state pointing at each of them.

"Did you eat today?" Toni asks, pushing the champagne away from her too.

I ignore her and continue. "In sickness and in health. For richer or poorer. What the hell is all that about if at the end of the day, you can leave? The whole purpose of the vows is so you can't leave. You're supposed to work out your differences. Vows are sacred. Love is sacred. But look at us. Three beautiful, university educated, loving women with husbands who don't give a damn. Except for you, Toni. You never made it to the altar. My husband is trying to ruin me financially. Yours never loved you, Mariah. And you, Toni, well… I'll just say it. He's never going to marry you. We're too old and have known each other too long to waste time."

"You don't know what he's going to do." Toni says, offended.

"Toni. You have to face reality. He isn't going to marry anybody as long as he's living with his momma. C'mon now. Do you really believe after ten years, he's going to one day say today's the day I get married? After ten years?"

Toni looks away and mumbles, "Seven years."

"The point is, instead of lawfully wedded husbands, we have *awfully* wedded husbands." I raise my champagne flute. "Ladies. In the spirit of Alpha Delta Zeta, I offer a toast to our misguided sister, Jocelyn Harris." They reluctantly clink my glass. "Revenge is a dish best served with champagne." I continue savoring the taste of the Veuve Clicquot. Mariah throws a questioning look at Toni, who shrugs.

"I give up. What are you talking about, V?" Mariah asks.

"Yeah. Revenge on who now?" Toni adds.

"Our men." Pointing the glass at Mariah, I say, "You were dragged out of your own company and kicked to the curb like an old eight-track."

"Well, I certainly drove a long way to get insulted."

"Jocelyn forgot one crucial detail. Something we've all forgotten," I continue.

"I'm losing my patience, V," Mariah warns.

"She forgot she knows her husband better than anyone else."

"I can't do this with you today." Mariah reaches for her purse, ready to go.

"He knows her too," Toni says.

"Exactly! And the fucker used it against her. He knew Jo-Jo would do anything to keep up appearances. That's why she didn't fight back. That's why she was laid on her back mutating into a new person." I push Mariah's glass toward her. "That's why she's dead." Mariah sits back down.

"What does any of that have to do with me?" Mariah asks.

"Your man played you. Our men played all of us. They're not smarter than us. They're just more ruthless."

"And selfish!" Toni shouts.

"I'm not going to lose my home and live on the street while Fred honeymoons in Fiji. Are you, Toni?" I ask.

"No!"

"Are you, Mariah? Are you going to let Simpleton Clifton take your company without a fight?"

"It's more complicated than that," Mariah says.

"Mariah, you called me, crying, telling me how the security guard's fat banana hands manhandled you, how your employees watched and said nothing, how some of them looked away 'cause they felt sorry for you. You were humiliated by your husband, who you propped up for years, who you made excuses for because the truth is he's a shitty narcissistic partner, no offense, but he's been using you for years. It's not as complicated as you want to believe. It's simple and sad. And frankly beneath you."

"And what about your marriage?" Mariah says, offended.

"Oh! I'm the biggest fool of all! Sisters. I call to order the first meeting of Oh Hell To The No!" I pull off my wedding ring and drop it in my champagne. "Hell No! I'm not begging for crumbs. Pleading for scraps of money. Grateful for tokens of affection. And I sure as Hell To The No ain't going out on a 51-50."

Mariah stands. "I don't know what you want me to say."

"I want you to say and more importantly, I want you to believe, Oh-Heeeeell-To-The-No! Will I ever hold up a man while he puts me down."

Mariah scrunches up her face and looks at me like I chose her cowardly husband. "Oh hell to the no, will I ever treat a mouse like a lion." She pulls off her wedding band, drops it into my glass.

Toni still can't bring herself to look at me. She scrimped and saved for two years to buy her ring. Two rings! She may not be ready.

"My relationship isn't an ideal relationship but Jesus took the wheel and I can't get out the car now."

Oh damn. She can't do it.

"But when I think of Pookie's rat face sitting in the car, licking his lips at me. Twisting his face in that ugly grin, I just get so mad! What's so funny? So I'm fat. So what? You know who else is fat? Madame CJ Walker! Oprah! And every woman in your whole family who ever loved your dumb ass!"

Mariah and I look at each other. Is Toni finally having a psychotic break?

Toni struggles to get out of the chair, twists the ring off her finger and dumps it into the flute with the other two rings. "Laugh at that!" She stands with her hands on her hips, claiming her body, owning her space. "Oh-Hell-To-My-Last-Nerve No! I'm DONE! I'm done with Trey! I'm done with Pookie and Trey's mama! I'm over being a second mama to a grown man."

"Ladies, we're playing by a new set of rules. We're going to beat them at their own game," I tell them. We clink glasses. "And Toni, you're first."

Toni gulps. "Why me?"

FIFTEEN

TONI

Lord, please help me not make a damn fool of myself. Trey isn't going to like this. He doesn't like surprises. The last time I surprised him, the surprise was on me and a chicken pot pie was on him. He deserved that. A hot pie in the face with extra gravy. Serves him right for laughing at me and calling me names. Him and that stupid no good Pookie. What kind of name is Pookie? Sounds like punani. He'll probably be there, smirking as usual. And his mama's gonna be there too. Too bad I don't have any pies to throw in their sour faces. All I have is this piece of paper and Vanessa egging me on. She's always meddling! Nosey Nessa, always up in somebody's business. Lord, this isn't going to turn out well. Nothing good comes from confrontation. Back people up in a corner and somebody's going to the hospital or the jail cell. That's what Trey would say. He oughta know. All the times he backed me up in a corner and all I could do was nod and say, 'Yes baby, no baby, I don't know baby, that's not true baby, I'll fix you something to eat baby.' I cave every time I'm cornered. I've been cornered my whole life. Imagine that, your whole life lived in a corner. Not breathing too big. Not moving too far. Just stuck.

But I made Trey notice me that day. I stood up to him and his boys. I just don't know if I can call up the anger to do it again. How do I stand up for myself when I'm not backed into a corner? Women like Mariah, Jocelyn, and Vanessa don't have a problem speaking their minds. They expect people to listen to them. They demand to be heard. I don't know how to do that.

"Toni!" Vanessa snaps at me. Apparently, I've been ignoring her. "I've been talking to you this whole time. Have you heard anything I said? You're not getting cold feet, are you?"

"Dang! Yes, I heard you. I'm sitting right here."

"Okay, what did I say?"

"Something bossy, I'm sure."

"Do you want to be free?"

"I'm not a slave!"

"You have been enslaved, Antoinette. He has enslaved your mind with his penis. He ejaculated in your brain and you can't think straight."

"Pull over! Right now. Pull this car over."

Vanessa keeps driving. "I heard about women who let men walk all over them because they have cum on the brain."

"You're nasty."

"How else do you explain it? What else does Trey do for you? He doesn't treat you nice. He won't marry you. He uses you. So you have to get something out of it. You're getting sex, right?"

Trey agreed to wait until we were married before consummating our relationship. But that's none of Vanessa's business. So I don't feel compelled to correct her. It's nobody's business but mine and God's. I'm pure and I don't need to flaunt my purity. No, I didn't stay for the sex, 'Nessa. So there.

"He's held you captive for how long? Ten years? Eight years of indentured servitude. He's never recognized your worth. You're his property and it's high time you repossessed yourself."

"Dang! You don't have to shame me! Okay, Sojourner Truth, I said I would, so I am. Left at La Cienega." I tell her left which is technically true but it's the long way to the promised land. Not that I want to prolong her crusade to free me from my master but I need a moment. I don't like confrontations. I'm not like Mariah. She can go twelve rounds with the heavyweight champion of confrontation and win by a knockout. I'm more like the person holding the spit bucket. It's not glamorous and I'm not in the spotlight but I'm in the ring and I'm doing what I can to help the fight. But there comes a time when you're tired of being spit at.

"Use that anger. Not at me. I'm your girl. Save that energy for him. He's the one who put you in this situation but you're the one who's going to turn things around."

Oh Lord please give me the strength to do the thing that is the last thing I want to do but the only thing left for me to do. Trey ain't going to like this. He don't like surprises.

"Ready?" Vanessa asks, rubbing her hands together, smiling like it's Christmas morning.

Vanessa parks in front of Trey's car dealership. I sit in the passenger seat, feeling ill. Twisting a piece of paper in my hand. Why'd I let her talk me into this? This is a bad idea. Ms. Oh hell to the no. This is so typical of Vanessa. Running everybody's life.

"I already broke off the engagement," I say.

"If you don't do this, you'll end up taking his down-low-ass back," Vanessa says.

"You mean low down."

Vanessa doesn't answer.

"Nessa! Take that back. He's not... Trey is really close to his mother."

"Yeah. His mother. Right." Vanessa waves her hand, dismissing the subject. "Toni."

I'm almost afraid to answer. Maybe if I keep looking out the window, whatever made her say my name like she just exposed the broken pieces of my life.

"Toni."

I look over at her to see her staring at me with her big eyes magnified even bigger with those fake lashes flapping at me. When did she have time to put on fake lashes? I barely have time to shower, rub lotion on myself and pull my hair into a bun. I've never worn fake lashes.

"I'm assuming you never had sex with Trey. Have you ever had sex with anyone?"

I knew it! I should have kept my head toward the window. Her and her stupid fake lashes blinking at me.

"That's none of your business. I don't ask about your sex life."

"Ask me! I'll tell you. What do you want to know?"

"Nothin'! I don't want to know nothing about anything to do with that."

"So you're a thirty-seven-year-old virgin?"

"That's between me and the Lord," I say, turning around so she won't see the embarrassment rush across my face. I don't want to talk about this.

"Toni."

"Stop saying my name."

"I respect your religious beliefs. As a friend, I'm asking, have you ever slept with anyone?"

If she thinks I'm going to dignify her curiosity with an answer, she's mistaken. My lips aren't moving. I am done entertaining her.

"Your silence speaks volumes. This is very delicate, and again, I'm your friend, we've known each other a long, long time and you know I am not trying to embarrass you. Have you ever looked at your vajajay?"

"What does that have to do with anything? You can take me home."

"You gotta love yourself before you can love anyone else. There's nothing wrong with being in touch with your body."

I don't know what she's talking about. Of course, I love me. "You're the one who sounds touched."

"Are you or are you not a virgin? Are you married to God or did you take a vow of chastity? I'm just trying to figure out what spell Trey has over you."

"In answer to one of your questions, I don't have to see it to know it's there. All you need to know is that it's clean and it works."

"Okay, right on."

"I'm not comfortable with this conversation."

We sit in silence, which I am eternally thankful for. I need to calm down. Am I virgin? Have I looked at my v-jay? I'm too old to think about these things. Every month I'm reminded that I'm a woman and anything more than that is between me and my husband. Would be husband. If I had a husband that would be our business. Trey never pressed me into a compromising position. We go to the same church for God's sakes. He knows there's no sex before marriage. We both pledged to keep ourselves pure. Although as the years went on, I think I'm the only one keeping that promise. I don't have proof but I have a feeling, Trey is sleeping around.

"Stay focused and stand up for yourself, Antoinette. He doesn't love you. Doesn't respect you and he's been clowning you. For years."

Thankfully, she changes her tone. "Just tell yourself, you can do this. That's what I used to say before walking on stage for every beauty contest. I can do this. You do this, Toni." She reaches over and pushes my door open. Vanessa makes a fist, thrusts it in the air. "Stand in your truth!"

Walking up to the car dealership, I'm having an out of body experience. I'm hot. Maybe Mariah gave me her menopause. Focus, Toni. I can do this. I can do this. I can do this. I can't breathe. I can do this. I'm hot. I can do this. Why'd Vanessa park so far? I can do this. Oh, there's Trey's car. Who's in his car? Damn. Why do I have to do this today? Just keep walking, maybe he won't notice you.

"Hey, hey, chickadee, where you going, girl?" Pookie says through yellow stained cigarette teeth. "Hey, you got a pie on you?"

Ignore him. Nobody likes a fool but another fool. Keep walking. Then the car doors slam. All of them clowns are out the car. Pookie and the rest of Trey's boy band are behind me.

"What you cooking up today, Ms. Toni?" Pookie says like a plantation Negro mocking me.

I can't turn around. I'd have to walk through them to get back to Vanessa. I have to keep going. I clutch my purse. Yes. Keep going. I can do this.

"Let me get that for you, Ms. Toni." Pookie does an elaborate doorman bow. He smells like cigarettes. The other nitwits lean close to me, breathing down my neck. I can do this.

I meekly enter the shop. Trey is busy pushing a couple to buy a new car outside of the price range. He doesn't notice me. Years of shrinking my existence and making myself smaller, I've perfected the act of disappearing in plain sight. I don't expect anyone to notice me. Pookie and the boys walk past me to the TV area across from Trey's desk. Pookie signals to Trey.

"Toni?" Trey looks over the head of a couple he's overcharging with an insane interest rate and unnecessary fees.

"Oh hey. You know, I just came by to... um... you're with a customer. I can come back later."

I turn to leave and catch a glimpse of Pookie shaking his head and smirking. Humiliated, I shuffle toward the door, wishing I could disappear. Through the wall of windows, I see Vanessa in the car watching, also shaking her head. I bet she thinks I can't do it. Meek little doormat Toni. Vanessa gets out the car. Pumps her fist in the air. Take a stand!

"Trey DeVaughn!" I turn around, hands-on my hips, gathering strength from my core. "You owe me $250,000!"

Trey's mother, Mrs. DeVaughn, comes out of an office, an older, bitter version of me if I'm not careful.

"Who's yelling out here?" Mrs. DeVaughn asks.

"Excuse me, Mrs. DeVaughn. Trey owes me $250,000."

"Don't pay her no mind, mama. She off her medication."

"I tallied up ten years of IOUs and you owe me, Trey."

"You crazy. Go home. Refill your 'scripts." Trey blows me off, making a circle around his ear, the universal sign for crazy, at his customer.

"You took $250,000 from me." He is not going to blow me off. "I kept all the IOU's." Standing over his desk, I hold my purse upside down and dump $250,000 worth of IOUs on his head. "Now tell me I'm crazy. Here's proof!"

The couple stands up. "We'll come back another time." The man is leading his wife toward the door. Trey shrugs, flicking the notes off his head.

"You have two weeks to repay your debt or I will liquidate your assets. You don't want to mess with me Trey DeVaughn."

"I told you not to get involved with her! I told you she wasn't good enough for my baby boy. Trey! I warned you about these thirsty women. You believe me now don't ya? Mama always knows best," his mother says, standing on the other side of the desk, staring me down. Assessing how crazy I am.

"Don't even worry about this drama, mama. She's trying to force me to marry her fat ass. Toni, an IOU don't mean shit. That's why I give 'em to you," he says, not daring to stand up and face me. He knows better than to test me this time. There's nothing funny about me this time. I got his attention. And my power.

"That's what I thought you'd say." I slam a loan document on his desk.

"What's this?" Trey asks.

His mother snatches it up first.

"The bank wouldn't approve his credit. He begged me to take out a loan on the dealership. All this belongs to me and the bank." Folding my arms. I won. Checkmate, mama.

"Is this true?" Trey's mother asks him.

Trey looks over at his boys standing by the wall.

"I had to make some moves to get things up and running."

"Pay me what you owe me or I'll repossess this building and every car on the lot." I point to the classic cars. "Including those."

He looks at his prized possessions. "Hey, listen here baby girl. I get it. You're upset about the other day. Look. Pookie is Pookie. That's my boy. He don't understand relationship stuff. I'll talk to him. You want to get married? Name the date. I'mma show up. Okay? I'll fucking show up. Mama. Change the bed sheets! I'm getting married."

I'm stunned. He finally took the step I've been waiting for. "I've been waiting seven years to hear you say that."

Trey smiles at me. Cocksure of himself. "See, I know what you want. I got it."

"What I want is for you to pay me my money. Or all this is mine. Technically it's mine now. Those cars are mine. This desk is mine." I take the pen out of his hand. "This pen is mine. And this!" I pull Trey's engagement ring off his finger. "You owe me, Trey DeVaughn. And as God is my witness, you're going to pay up."

Trey's mama balls up the loan papers. "Get out! Everybody! Out! Don't y'all have jobs? Trey! Get in the office! Now!!"

"Mama, it's not my fault!"

I walk out, spinning Trey's ring on my finger, head high, walking on sunshine. Triumphant, I get in Vanessa's car and slam Trey's ring on the dashboard.

"I did it. I. Did. It. I stood in my truth and did it. Ooooh, my hands are shaking. I have goosebumps."

"That's ten years of poison leaving your body." Vanessa drives off.

"OH HELL TO THE NO!!! I yell out the window at Pookie. He motions jerking himself off but I don't care. I stood up to all of them and it felt good.

SIXTEEN

MARIAH

Vanessa's Hell-To-The-No-Club is too little too late. My battles can't be solved with a catch phrase and good intentions. I need a plan. At the very least, I need a stop gap solution to stem the hemorrhaging of loss around me. I'm losing everything and everyone. My company. My husband. I already lost my friend. Jocelyn's death came at the worst possible time. If I lose another thing, I'm going down for the count. "This is why I don't do friendship," I say aloud to no one. I'm alone. Just like Jocelyn. Alone with nothing and no one. I reach into the nightstand and take out the sorority photo of the four of us holding up our pinkies pledging eternal sisterhood. Jocelyn, am I a monster because I don't feel sorry for you? You did not have to be a cautionary tale. No one told you to sink all your hopes and dreams into Herschel. It's not like you were Vanessa. You had looks and brains. You were the smartest of all of us and you gave up on yourself. There's no other way to put it. You put all your eggs in one man. You didn't diversify. You hitched a ride on his coat tail and he eventually shook you loose. The least you could have done was use his money to fund a charity, establish a school, adopt children. I can't feel sorry for you. I can't even weep for you. Maybe something's wrong with me.

221

Vanessa cried at your funeral. Sort of. Her eyes were watery. Of course, Toni boo hooed between giggle fits. That's what she does. Her heart bleeds vanilla extract. All I saw was a waste of potential. You could have been so many things. You could have been anything. You had everything to live for. You were always selfish and short-sighted, Jocelyn. Well, I'm not going out like that. You're not going to catch me pulling a Jocelyn and just give up. I have too much self-respect. I refuse to lose. Mariah Stewart Ash is a winner.

And with that, I start crying. Bawling. Blubbering. Blowing Viola Davis type snot bubbles. I release a tsunami of tears. My well of loneliness churns deep within the core of me and erupts like a volcano. I cry so hard, I make myself dizzy and drop to my knees. Head bowed, hands sprawled out like I'm grasping at straws. I weep for the wasted years with a man who resents me. I weep for my own hypocrisy. I wasn't running toward freedom. I was running from repression. I weep because I'm tired of being strong. Who's my pillar of strength? When the dry heaves come, I keep weeping. I finally rock myself into sedation.

Sprawled on the floor, my thoughts return to Jocelyn. The social status of being a senator's wife meant everything to her. It was her identity. Who am I without Oyster Music? *Scheisse.* I gave that company the best part of me. I worked until I slept on my feet. Until my brain broke apart trying to figure out how to stay relevant. I can lose my marriage but not my company, that's my baby. I'm nobody without it.

I get up off the floor and rinse my face with cold water. I feel better. Much, much better. Crying is cathartic. Who was it that used to make herself cry every day? I thought she was nuts but she said it helped her focus. All the nagging self-doubt stuff and random bad memories were washed away. Now I understand. I'm drained but in a good way. I wonder what Cliff is doing now? Cliff is an idiot but he's no fool. By now, he froze my access to our joint accounts. Thankfully, I have a separate nest egg he knows nothing about. I'm not like the other ladies, tying up my money in a man, trusting him to provide for me. Nope. When Poppa Joe played Billie Holiday's song in the garage, *God Bless the Child that's Got Her Own*, I paid attention to the message. I knew she was singing the truth and issuing a warning so as soon as I could, I kept something on the side for myself because there are no guarantees.

Once, during a heated argument, Cliff pointed to all the clothes in my closet and told me everything in there belonged to him. That was his closet. My shoes on the shelf were his shoes, his purses, his dresses and I better not forget it. The more he pointed and shouted the louder Billie Holiday's song rang in my head. And I was so glad I had an offshore account. He never knew and I never told him.

For years, I've been skimming, my own money, preparing for who knows what. The more Cliff relinquished the reins to me, the more money I added to my nest egg. As he spent more money on expensive wines and escorts, the more I aggressively sought out new streams of revenue. Laying music tracks for advertising agencies was at the heart of our business but there was plenty of room to expand. I saw the future and it wasn't with Cliff. Forrest Gump, my all-time favorite movie said it best but I added a twist; instead of life being like a box of chocolates, men are like a box of chocolates. Milk chocolate and mouth-watering on the outside but until you bite into one, you don't know what you're going to get. Say you love caramel, you read the box description and it says caramel but it's all just speculation until you take a bite and lo and behold you find nuts in your mouth. All you can do is hope you don't have a nut allergy.

I tried to tell Vanessa once, not long after she and Fred were married, take care of herself. Make sure you don't have to ask him for every dime. Keep something set aside for yourself. I tried to tell Jocelyn too. Both of them looked at me like I was meddling in married business. I have to hand it to Toni, God blessed this child with her own. Her bakery is her bread and butter.

I wrap myself in a plush terry robe and check my private offshore account. $1 million. Yep. It's there, right where I left it. Breathing a sigh of comfort and humming God bless the child that's got its own..."

Marriage is a 50-50 crapshoot. I would never go all in on love and marriage. Men aren't knights in shining armor looking for maidens to rescue. Ahem, Vanessa. They're human and flawed and sometimes the right guy can meet the right girl but that's not my fairytale. There's no right guy for me. I honestly believed Cliff was the closest I'd ever get to the right companion. I have to face facts. I'm not built for domesticity and submission and every guy, even Cliff, needs a bit of that in his woman. My first adult boyfriend said I made him feel like an imbecile. To which I replied, 'You can't feel like something you aren't. I meant it in a good way. He took it in a bad way. He body slammed me onto the patio deck. In addition to being an imbecile, he was also a neanderthal. For years, I was attracted to the strong, silent, dumb types. They were good for a laugh and a roll in hay. They were attentive and fun until they weren't.

My phone rings.

"Ma'am. Your GPS is activated on the Bentley. You can access the tracking on your phone. If you want to stay on the line, I can help you set it up. Are you ready?"

I so appreciate good customer service. "Let's do it."

*****

I follow the Bentley all day. I'm not surprised she's driving the car but her errands are very surprising. I decide Mimosa Nails near The Beverly Center is the perfect place to confront her. Rose is sitting in a chair soaking her feet and sipping Prosecco. I slip the owner two hundred dollars to cut in front of the women waiting for the chair next to Rose and sit down. Rose is busy staring into her phone like it holds the secret to eternal life.

"Rose."

Behind her Gucci sunglasses, I can see her eyes do a double take so fast she damn near drops her phone in the basin. She starts looking around for an escape but where's she going to go with wet toenails and no shoes? She changes her tactic and gets indignant. She looks around for the someone to help her. Who's coming, Rose? One of the Thai ladies or Vietnamese or combination thereof who paint nails for tips? You're on your own, honey. Just you and me. And you don't stand a chance against me.

"I'll call the police if you try to harass me," she warns.

"Oh, you will huh? And when I tell them you're driving my car, who do you think is getting arrested for grand theft auto? Let's not get ugly. I'm not here to cause a scene so I suggest you sip your drink while I talk."

"Cliffie gave me the Bentley. The title is in his name. I checked. You already know I got your husband in check. And speaking of checks, I check the money he gives me every week, I check it right in the bank. I'll call the police if you start trouble. Then I'll call Cliffie. And I'll record the cops taking you away, screaming and crying and I'll post it on the internet too. Just like I did the last time you lost your damn mind. The best bitch won so don't fuck with me, Mariah."

I hear the little Thai girl scrubbing Rose's foot chuckle. I got to admit. I was a little stunned. I didn't know she had it in her and in perfect

English. Thankfully, I took my hormone replacement pills this morning so my emotions are steady. Otherwise, I'd be drowning this chick in the foot sink. I take a second, let Rose feel herself. Let her think she got me thinking about backing down. And then she opens her phone and starts playing Candy Crush.

"I changed my mind. Give me the paraffin too," Rose tells the Thai girl who is scrubbing the callouses off her heel.

"Yes, ma'am," she replies. And leaves to get the wax and plastic bags.

"I knew there was something special about you when I hired you."

"You still here? I'll let Cliffie know you've stalking me when we have dinner tonight at Matsuhisa. I changed my mind. I don't want fish. I want French. Where's the place you and my Cliffie used to go? Well, he's not sentimental." She texts Cliff. "Hi baby. Dinner tonight at the French place?' Cliffie likes to keep me happy," she says, twirling her hair around her finger.

"I know about the widow. I know about the marine. And I know about Ferdinand."

Rose puts her phone down. It's ringing. Cliff is texting her but she doesn't respond. She puts the phone in her purse.

"You and I have something in common, besides my husband. It turns out, we both need hormone replacement therapy."

The Thai girl carefully dips Rose's feet in the paraffin. Listening.

"I didn't ruin your marriage. Cliff came to me."

"Women are so different from men. A man isn't sneaky. He'll just face something head on and fight for it. Men are confrontational. But a woman. A woman plans and plots and waits like a spider spinning a web for the next fly to come along."

"Do you want your husband back? Is that what you want?"

"You can't give me what's already mine. Now. I wondered why you would need hormone replace therapy. You're too young for menopause. So I told myself to think outside the box. And then bells started ringing. Wait a minute, who else would need hormones..."

"You stalker. Too much time on your hands. No job. No husband. I feel sorry for you."

"How much money does my husband give you?"

Rose sips her champagne. The Thai lady doing her nails glances up at her, waiting for a response.

"Two thousand a week."

"Look at you! Living the American dream."

Rose shifts in her seat. The Thai girl, whose nametag says Suzie, keeps working, slowly painting each toenail but her ears are burning. In fact, I notice the whole salon has stopped talking. It's so quiet you can hear fingernails being clipped. An Asian lady walks in and loudly calls out to the girls, who quickly yell at her to be quiet. I don't have to speak the language to know what they said, because she shuts her mouth and starts busying herself slowly choosing a polish, glancing over at us.

"You earn two thousand a week to fuck my husband?" I swear I felt the entire nail salon lean in.

"Cliffie love me. We make love."

I hear one of the women on the other side of the salon say something to her co-workers. Who says something back. And the woman sucks her teeth and says something that sounds like whore.

"You may be making love but Cliff isn't. He doesn't know about you."

"You know nothing. That's why you have no husband. No job. No life," Rose says.

"I know you've been married twice."

Rose sips Prosecco, but I see her eyebrow twitch.

"I know you married a woman," I continue.

Suzie stops mid-polish and looks up at Rose.

"I'm no lesbian. I'm not like you," Rose says.

"You weren't a woman when you married her, Ferdinand."

Suzie gasps. She leans back and stares at Rose's petite feet. She quickly says something to the other women who gasp and stare at Rose, who keeps sipping although she's turning red.

"She was a widow, thirty years your senior. Her money financed your partial sex change. Then you met a marine. You married him then took his money and ran. I doubt he knew you were a man. Whoever did your sex change is an artist."

Rose turns to me and laughs. I guess it's some weird involuntary reflex to being cornered.

"Uncanny how delicate you look. You were probably born petite. What do you think, Suzie?" I ask the pedicurist. She doesn't know what to do or where to look she so stunned by the revelation of Rose being a transwoman. Finally, she decides to continue doing her job, polishing Rose's toes in Love Me Tender red.

"Cliffie knows," Rose says in an octave lower than she usually talks.

"He doesn't know. Whatever you're doing to him, he's not doing it to you. Look, Madame Butterfly, we both know Cliff is gullible and has mommy issues. Fooling him is no big acting feat. But the retired Marine is another story. He put a warrant out for your arrest. He's looking for you, Ferdie. All it takes is one phone call to put the two of you in the same room. I don't think Dr. Kiss would be able to repair your pretty face and put the pieces back together again."

"What do you want?"

"Delete the videos you posted of me. You know the ones I'm talking about."

Rose takes out her phone, types in a few prompts and shows me the clips are deleted. "There. Done. You go now."

I motion to the manager. "She needs a refill."

Rose shifts in her chair, but she doesn't say anything, just sits there avoiding all the stares. I can tell she's preparing herself for me to go off. But I'm done letting my emotions speak for me. So instead of lashing out at her, like I want to. Instead of smooshing my hand into her perfectly made up pie face, I resist the urge to humiliate the woman who posted my worst humiliation on the Internet for my business colleagues to see. Instead of doing any of that, I calmly negotiate a deal because that's what businesswomen do.

"I want dirt on my husband."

"You already know I'm trans, what more do you want?"

"That's about you. I need something on him. Get creative, Fred. And, if you think about walking out of here and driving into the sunset in my Bentley, I'll contact the authorities and then I'll call the Marine and let him know what you look like and where your family lives in the Manila. He seems like the type who holds a grudge."

For the next half hour, I sip champagne and get a pedicure. While my feet are wrapped in paraffin, Rose keeps drinking and talking. She explains her money chase. She fell in love with the widow who convinced her to get the operation and live her true life. The Marine was an opportunity she couldn't pass up. She realized older men were lonely and had money and were willing to believe anything she told them. The bullshit job she had at Oyster was a stop-gap solution to tide her over

231

until she met the next old fart to finance the rest of her surgery. Enter my husband, Clifton Stupid-Ass Ash. By the time I get my toes painted, Rose converts to Team Mariah. She agrees to give me daily updates on Cliff's shenanigans. On her way out, she even pays for my pedicure. Well, ain't she a classy broad. Us women have to stick together.

SEVENTEEN

TONI

I went ahead and blocked Trey from my phone but I'd give anything to block him from my life. These days without him have been eye-opening. I can breathe. I can listen to my thoughts. Good Lord, I can hear myself. I didn't know how much space he took up in my head. His voice rattling around my brain all day, every day. I don't miss him. His mama was right. I'm not the woman for him. I don't even know if there is a woman for him. Thank the Lord we never had sex.

"Are you sure you're ready for this?" Mariah asks for the hundredth time. "You know this is the act of no return. Demanding he pay you back for a loan is one thing but this thing we're about to do, this is a whole other level. He's going to come after you."

"What did he leave on your doorstep?" Vanessa says, putting on lip-gloss. She's lost more weight and she didn't have none to lose from the get-go.

"He left a pie. Something he got from Albertsons," I say. The disgust creeps into my voice. "Who brings a baker a store-bought pie?"

"What did you do with it?" Mariah asks.

"I ate it," I confess. They don't say anything. "Someone baked it. I didn't want it to go to waste."

"You ate it out of professional courtesy?" Mariah asks, but not really asking.

"Stay up on the competition, Toni. Smart," Vanessa says. I think she's mocking me. "Can we stop at Starbucks? I need a latte."

Mariah pulls into the drive through on LaBrea. Vanessa orders her usual skinny, no fat, triple shot latte. And Mariah orders an espresso, and I get my S'mores Frappuccino with caramel and whipped cream. I can feel the judgment. Whatever. I was tempted to order mint tea but they'd see through that. Why be miserable when I can have what I want and enjoy it? I offer to pay but Mariah swipes her phone app.

"You should serve lattes at your bakery." Vanessa suggests.

"My customers don't want lattes. They want coffee. You're the only one who comes around asking for lattes."

"When they build the stadium in Inglewood, you'll have more customers like me and we want lattes."

"There's Starbucks for customers like you."

"Just a suggestion." Vanessa sips her precious latte.

"You're snippy this morning, Toni," Mariah says.

"I know! I'm sorry. Trey kept coming by the house last night."

"The next time he shows up, call the police," Mariah says. "You can stay with me. I have plenty of room."

"He was probably creeping for a booty call. Was it a booty call?" Vanessa asks.

"I don't. We don't do that." I say and immediately wish I hadn't.

"I knew it! You are saving it for God!" Vanessa exclaims like she solved a mystery.

"If you must know, I'm saving it for my husband."

"So he wasn't there for your booty. So what's up? What did Mr. Trey want? In my experience, when they bang on the door, they either want to fuck or fight. Which was it?"

Wow. Nessa will not leave it alone. She will not bait me. Not this morning.

"Did he hit you?" Mariah asks.

"NO! Nothing like that. He just throws stuff. A lot. So, he did that until he tired himself out."

"Any of the stuff he throws hit you?" Vanessa asks. This time she's sincere. "I'm assuming he's throwing your stuff. Breaking your shit. I bet he doesn't throw a fit in his momma's house."

"Where were his boys?" Mariah asks.

"I don't know. He was alone. Then he sat on my porch and started crying."

"Oh, God. He's so pathetic. I'm sorry. I know he's your... he was your man but really? He's such a baby. Please tell me you didn't let him in." Vanessa stares at me. Waiting for me to give her the right answer. So I lie. I did let him in. The neighbors were looking. I had no choice. He talked my ear off for the better part of the night.

But I told Vanessa the only thing I could tell her. "I called his mother. She came and got him."

Mariah pulls into the parking lot of the car dealership. "They'll be here any minute. Let's get going." She pops the trunk.

Vanessa stick OUT OF BUSINESS labels on the windows and doors of the dealership while I padlock the front doors. Mariah's on the phone. Right on schedule, the moving trucks arrive to pick up the two dozen cars on the lot. Most of the cars will be sold at auction. The other cars are vintage. Old hip hop classics that Trey loved having around as part of his showcase. The '64 Chevy Impalas. El Caminos and Monte Carlos. And a couple of high-end luxury vehicles. I don't know where he got them but the titles say they belong to the dealership so they're mine now and Mariah agreed to keep them in her six-car garage. I think she's hatching some plan. Mariah's good at the long picture. Me, I prefer immediate gratification, like the cookies I'm going to eat with my homemade vanilla and lavender ice cream as soon as I get back to the bakery.

"Uh-oh. Here comes your boy," Mariah warns. Before I can say anything, Vanessa shoves me in the car.

"We're done. Let's go."

"What about the stickers and stuff?"

"Leave it."

From the backseat, I see Trey try to wave down the movers. They blow their horns for him to get out the way and continue driving off the lot.

"Mariah, let's go," Vanessa says. "I don't want to get into it with this guy."

"He doesn't see us. We're fine. I just want to make sure all the trucks pull off the lot."

Trey pulls on the padlocked doors to his dealership. "That bitch!" He tears off the repossessed stickers. Kicks the doors in frustration. Pookie and the rest of the boys gather round, peering through the window. Not much to see, just the office desks are left.

Trey's mother gets out of her car.

"I don't think you look anything like her," Vanessa says. "What do you think, Mariah?"

"Hmmm. It's not her look so much as it is her manner. I think you guys walk the same way. Kinda lumbering like."

"I want to go," I finally say. The last truck drives off the lot, not paying any attention to Trey's histrionics.

As we drive past, his mama locks eyes with me. She looks at me then back at the closed dealership.

"There she go! That's her. Right there. She's getting away!"

"Where you want to go? The police?" Mariah asks, driving like a mad woman down LaBrea.

"No!" Vanessa says. "Don't you watch the news?"

"The bakery. Take me to the bakery. He kept the neighbors up all last night."

"You said his mother came and got him." Mariah says.

"Mariah. Just go on and go to the bakery, please."

"That's the first place he'll go. That doesn't make sense," Vanessa says, looking through the rear window to see how close they are.

"Then let's go to your house, Vanessa." I say.

"Well, if she wants to go to the bakery, she knows what she's doing," Vanessa says. Yeah, I thought so.

Mustapha is pulling cookies out of the oven. For a moment, I forget about World War Three about to go down and inhale the scent of freshly baked chocolate chip cookies. Vanessa nudges Mariah and whispers, "And he bakes."

Mariah nods. "He looks like he bakes, well."

They giggle. Once again I'm wondering why they're in my life.

"You okay, Ms. Toni?" Mustapha asks, his apron covered in flour and sugar. I make a mental note to take a mental picture of him. Before I can answer his question, Mariah butts in.

"Trey is on the warpath and he's probably on his way here right now. Whatever you do don't escalate anything. I just want him out of here. Vanessa, lock the front door and flip the sign around. We're closed today," Mariah says.

Vanessa leaves the kitchen. Thankfully we're not open yet so there aren't any customers inside. "I don't like y'all taking over my business."

"Hey, you took a big step today. You took back your life and I'm not going to let him pull you back into a hole," Mariah says to me. She's good. She knows just what to say.

Vanessa returns. "He's pulling up and he's not alone. Tell me he doesn't have a key."

I shake my head. "He used to but I took it back."

Mustapha doesn't say anything. He just listens. Assessing the situation. He goes into the pantry and makes a phone call. I'm half listening and hear him mention the bakery and he gives someone my address. After a few minutes, he comes out.

"Maybe I should go outside and talk to him. I knew I shouldn't have moved so fast. What was I thinking, repossessing his business."

"It's your business, Toni. You took out the loan. You paid for everything. He worked for you," Mariah says.

"I knew Trey was going to get upset."

Mustapha shrugs. "His feelings mean nothing. If you're afraid of him, I can come over and sleep in the living room to protect you."

Protect me. I never had a man protect me before. I don't say anything 'cause he didn't ask me a question, he just stated it like he was my man or something. I haven't told the girls about Mustapha. There's nothing to say. He's my employee. He's just being nice. That's all this is for him, job security. Or he feels sorry for me. I need a cookie. Or a scoop of peach cobbler. I need to make peach cobbler. Everybody likes peach cobbler. Mustapha doesn't eat sweets though. Must be a religious thing.

"Trey gets so upset." I laugh it off. "Nothing I can't handle but … I hate confrontations. Ever since you ladies came back into my life, it's been one thing after the other."

"I know you are not blaming me for your dilemma," Vanessa says, all wide-eyed like the innocence she ain't. "We're here to help you."

Someone's pounding on the back door. "Open up! I want a piece of pie!" I nearly jump out of my skin. Pookie laughs at me. "Nowhere to run to, baby. Nowhere to hide."

I can hear Trey honking his car horn. "Toni! Get your ass out here."

I look at my friends and Mustapha. I'm trapped. I don't know where to go. Before I can say anything, Mustapha says, "Don't worry. I got this." He leaves the kitchen. Mustapha steps outside and stands in front of the bakery like a sugar coated, chocolate gingerbread man. He's still wearing the floured apron and his arms are folded making his shoulder and chest muscles bulge. He looks delicious. I shake the thought of yummy Mustapha out of my head. Toni, do something. I run into the kitchen and grab a knife. No. Not the knife. I don't want to get cut. I grab the rolling pin. Swing it around. Jab the air with it. "This'll do." I go back to the front and watch from the window.

Trey pops the trunk open. Oh Lord, don't let it be a gun. Slamming the lid down, he shakes a baseball bat at Mustapha. Whew. Trey paces the sidewalk swinging the bat. He gets his nerve up to rush the store but Mustapha doesn't budge. He doesn't even flinch. I have half a mind to call the police but nothing good'll come from that. Black men and the police. No.

"Get out my way, Mustang," Trey orders.

"I don't want to hurt you," Mustapha says.

"Toni!" Trey grips the bat. Points it at Mustapha. "You wanna get hurt? Step off. Toni! I'm not playing with you! Get out here and give me the key! You know what I'm talking about."

Just when I'm thinking, I should go outside, a dozen or so men from The Nation of Islam walk up to the shop. I don't know where they came from. They just came from all over, across the street, up the street, down the street, and they meet at my bakery. They fall in line four by four in front of my door, each dressed impeccably in a suit and tie.

"Oh y'all selling bean pies? Am I s'pose to be scared?" Trey yells in a shaky voice.

"Go in peace, my brother," Mustapha says.

"What's the matter? Can't fight your own battles?"

Mustapha gestures for the Nation to step back. "Women don't fight men. Men don't fight women." Mustapha unties his apron. Pulls off his shirt, revealing a rock hard body. "Only a weak man raises a hand against a woman."

Vanessa watches from a corner table, munching on one of Mustapha's cookies. I can almost spot glee in her eyes like this is reality TV and not a terrible day in my life.

"Who's that with the do-rag on his head. The skinny one that looks like an alley cat?" Vanessa asks.

"Pookie."

"Dookie?

"Pookie," I say slowly so she'll understand.

"Oh, he looks more like a Poop Butt if you ask me." She laughs, chomping on the cookies like it's popcorn.

"There's nothing funny about what's going on out there? What if someone gets hurt?"

"Even better! Girl, you got men fighting over you. I suggest you savor the moment. What's going on with you and Mustapha? Is he sleeping here?" she asks.

"You know that's a code violation," Mariah says, sitting next to me, doing something on her phone. She offers me a cookie. "He bakes a mean cookie and I don't even like sweets."

"You need an espresso machine. Girl, you better put some coffee on after the dust settles you gotta offer them something." Vanessa shoots me a double meaning look.

I turn away from her and back to the squabble outside. All this over me. Me? I can't help the little smile on my face. All this for me.

"I see you over there grinning," Vanessa calls out. "You got any sweet tea? They're going to be thirsty."

Trey's mama calls from her car, "Trey! C'mon baby. We gone handle this another way. This ain't over Toni!"

Trey lowers the bat. Backs away. He stumbles off the sidewalk, never turning his back on Mustapha. "Y'all gonna have to leave sometime. Ya hear that, Toni!"

I catch his glare and my smile dries up. Here I am, a grown woman, hiding behind the blinds. No, Vanessa's right. I'm good right where I am. Let the men handle it.

"If anything happens to Ms. Trammell, the same will happen to you. To each of you!"

I can't see who said it but it sounds like Mustapha's raising his voice in defense of me. I peek through the blinds again to see Trey throw his bat in the car.

"This is bullshit. C'mon man," Pookie says as Trey jumps into the driver's seat.

Mariah squeezes my shoulder. "It'll be okay. He won't come around anymore." Mariah's phone goes off. "Shit." Mariah grabs her purse.

"Where are you going? What's more important than what's happening right here?" Vanessa asks, standing in the middle of the bakery.

"Cliff is at my house." Mariah shows them the tracker is beeping red at her home.

"What?" we both say in unison. "What's he doing there?"

"I don't know. Rose sent me a text."

"His mistress? What you got going on, Mariah?"

"I have to go." Mariah rushes out as Mustapha enters the shop, followed by the men of the Nation.

Mustapha smiles at me. I am seeing him for the first time with his shirt off. I don't know where to look, so I settle on looking at the floor. Vanessa steps up and instructs the men to have a seat. Thankfully her hostess skills are on point. She asks the men if they'd like coffee or sweet tea. Most of the men choose sweet tea. Vanessa shoots Toni a triumphant look and rolls her hips into the kitchen.

"You don't have to worry anymore. He won't be back," Mustapha says.

"Yes, he will. Usually when I least suspect it."

"That one's a coward. He preys on the weakness of women because he lacks the courage of a man." Mustapha squeezes my hand. Flustered, I put on an apron and smile gratefully at the men who protected me.

"Y'all need sweet potato pie to go with that sweet tea and coffee."

Joining Vanessa behind the counter, I pull out every pie in the display case. "This is the most people I've had in the bakery since Bingo night let out at the fellowship church down the block.

"Girl, you better open your eyes and jump on that man. He likes you. It's not every man who will stand up for a woman."

"He's just being nice."

"Nice is holding the door open when you're carrying a bag of groceries. He protected you. Remember what Steve Harvey said what a man will do when he loves a woman. He'll protect, which he just did. And he brought his crew over to protect you too. He'll profess his love. I bet that's coming. And he'll provide for you. Look at all these cookies. He didn't bake 'em for himself."

"You're gonna have me believin'..."

Mustapha walks behind me and interrupts my train of thought. He smiles at me with that big grin that shows all his white teeth. I believe his eyes twinkled. He takes the tray of plastic glasses out to his friends.

"And he don't mind serving. Girl, you better open your eyes." Vanessa takes the pitcher of sweet tea and follows Mustapha around filling each glass. Mustapha looks up at me with the most pleasant look on his face. I'm so used to someone looking at me wanting something. Wanting a slice of this, a piece of that. It takes me a minute to see that there was nothing behind his smile, nothing behind his eyes. He doesn't want anything. Good Lord when I realize he just wants me to be safe, a sweat breaks out all over my body and pain eases out from the core of my soul and I have to steady myself against the counter. I'm whoozy. I feel Mustapha wrap his arms around me. He helps me into the kitchen, away from everyone. I grip the edge of the sink as he runs cold water and squeezes a towel out and gently places it on the back of my neck.

"You need to rest."

I nod. I don't trust myself to speak. If I open my mouth a howl from years of neglect will escape. Instead, I do what I always do, I bury it deeper, clamp it shut and get up to go back to work. When I stand, Mustapha holds me in his arms. A sniffle escapes. Mustapha lifts my head and looks at my eyes tearing up.

"Everything okay. You don't have to worry anymore."

I shake off my silly emotions and bravely look up at him. "I don't have time to be feeling sorry for myself when there's a room full of hungry men."

"Wait a minute. Sit down."

I plop down. All my weight plus the weight of the world on my shoulders collapsed on my poor stool. I look at him, haunched on his knees, patiently waiting for me to speak. And it all comes rushing out.

"I'm so stupid! I gave my heart to him. Even when I knew he wasn't worth it. I knew he didn't love me and I still wasted years on that man. That boy. I've been a fool. I let him take advantage of me because… 'cause I didn't want to be alone. I bought this stupid ring.... 'cause I didn't want people to say she's fat and alone." I say this through globs of snot stuck in my nose. My chest is heaving to hold back the wailing rising up through me. And Mustapha, bless his soul, doesn't tell me to stop acting silly or to pull myself together. He doesn't say anything. He just rocks me back and forth until the pressure eases from my chest and I can breathe again.

EIGHTEEN

MARIAH

What the hell is Cliff doing at my house? I better not get a ticket speeding through these streets. While I'm wasting time with Toni and her baby boy, Rose is with my husband in my house looking for dirt on me! She probably told him I spoke to her. She can't be stupid enough to ruin her gravy train and risk a pissed off marine finding her. Unless she thought I was bluffing. If she's setting me up, why send me a text telling me they're in my home? This doesn't make sense.

I press the gate FOB and wait for my gate to open. It doesn't. What the hell? I turn the batteries and try again. Still doesn't work. I buzz the house. My maid, Chatty Natty, answers. She's a great cook and housekeeper but the only way to get her to stop talking is a glass of wine.

"Mrs. Ash, the Mister is here with that woman and a man. They're are looking at everything. They're in your office. They are looking and writing things down."

"Buzz me in, Natty.

The gate opens. Cliff must have reset the gate code. I knew I forgot to get the FOB from him. It was on my list and I forgot. The devil's in the details, Mariah. There it is. The Bentley with OYSTER plates. The world is your oyster, BS. Be the pearl. How many nauseating times have I endured him saying that?

"Cliff!" I yell, dropping my bag on the foyer table. Chatty Natty points to my office.

"There in there, Mrs."

In my office, I see them unplug my computer while a man I don't know rifles through my filing cabinet.

"What the hell do you think you're doing?"

"Oh, Mariah. I didn't think you'd have the balls to show your face," Cliff says, leaning back in my chair. "Now that I see you, I'm thinking I should call the police."

"I'm thinking the same thing, Cliff."

"You think I'm going to sit back and let you steal from me? You should know me better than that." Cliff says, leaning over my desk, trying to intimidate me.

I look over at Rose. She stands behind him, ever so slightly shaking her head. Cliff looks back at her. She gets indignant. "I know baby. I told you, you couldn't trust her." Cliff turns back to me and Rose gives a slight helpless shrug.

"You can't prove anything, Cliff. And who is this?"

"He's a forensic accountant. He's gathering evidence. We know, Mariah. We know everything." Rose says from behind Cliff. I notice she's wearing a new pearl necklace. Be the pearl.

"Mrs. Ash. Salas Samonte, here. Hi. Mr. Ash called me and asked me to look into Oyster's books. My team found some inconsistencies and really I must say, disturbing …"

"You embezzled money, Mariah. You stole from the company, Mariah. You're a thief, Mariah," Cliff taunts. "And if you don't give me back all the money you stole from me, I'll send you to prison, Mariah."

"A husband can't testify against his wife, Cliff," I remind him.

"That's why Rose is here. She's a witness and so is he."

"We know about the money, Mrs. Ash," Mr. Samonte says.

"I'll tell you what, don't give me the money. I want to see your ass in prison. You ain't going to the nice prison for white collar criminals where you play tennis and swim laps. You're going to lockdown. I'm sure a lesbo like you can adapt. Did you know my wife was a lesbian?" he says to Rose.

"Only a lesbian would not have sex with my Cliffie."

Cliff takes the laptop and gives it to Mr. Samonte.

"You don't have the right to take my things…"

"All of this is mine! This house is mine! You think you could afford to live here? Oyster is my company. See, this is where you got confused. I'm the boss. Respeck that. Right, baby?"

"Big boss," Rose agrees. Kissing Cliff.

"That's right," Cliff says, kissing her back.

"Mrs. Ash, if I may step in. You have hidden away a significant amount of money that belongs to the company and therefore money that belongs to Mr. Ash."

"You got forty-eight hours, thief." Cliff cuts in.

"After you return the money and the books are balanced, then my work will be done. You and Mr. Ash can split your assets and go your separate but equitable ways. Unfortunately, if you do not return the money…"

"I'll drag your ass to court." Cliff cuts in again. "I'll ruin you."

"That's the worst case scenario. The way we're all hoping this will go is, I'll take these items. Go through them just to see what else you're hiding or not hiding and in the interim, you return the money to Mr. Ash."

"You can't have my computer."

Cliff chuckles. "Your computer? You don't have a pot to piss in. You don't even have a home to sit in, Mariah. You think I'm going to let you live here after stealing my money?"

"Hiding," Mr. Samonte corrects him.

"You gone. You out. In fact, you can get to stepping right now. Go on! Get!" Cliff steps toward me. Rose pulls him back.

"Don't upset yourself baby," Rose says. "We got her."

"And don't collect your clothes. Correction! My clothes that I let you wear! Get out of my house!"

I turn and walk out. Chatty Natty is listening right outside the door. She scurries away as soon as I open the door. By the time I reach my car, I get a text from Rose: *I had nothing to do with this! Team Mariah!*

Outside, Chatty Natty meets me with my emergency weekender bag filled with two days of clothing, my passport, and the money I keep stashed in my closet.

"I know you, Mrs. You have nine lives. You'll land on your feet."

I take the bag and drive off. I always knew this bag would be necessary. Poppa Joe would say, you have to keep your passport somewhere so keep it in a bag with some money and some clothes. You never know when an emergency will force you to leave in the middle of the night. You can't waste time packing. Grab your bag and go. Speaking of which, I don't know where I'm going. I'm just driving. And thinking. All I'm wondering is why I didn't see this coming. I thought I had her. And this Samonte character, a forensic accountant. I never heard of that. Regardless, I don't have any trails leading to Cliff or to Oyster. I replayed my encounter in the nail shop with Rose. Nothing springs to mind. I didn't say anything alluding to my money. The only person I told … was Vanessa. 'Are you squirreling away money?' Why would she ask me that? Did Vanessa set me up? I know she needs money but she wouldn't go against me and side with Cliff.

Before I confront Vanessa's, I pull into the Starbucks at La Tijera and Centinela. I park the car but can't unclench my fingers from the steering wheel. I see myself clutching the bars of my cell. Shuffling to the mess hall. Wearing an orange jumpsuit with my hair in cornrows, trying to fit in as the smart one who can help them appeal their cases. Sleeping on the bottom bunk. Sharing a cell with Cleo. I'm too old to go to prison! I've worked too hard for bed bugs and open toilets. I can smell the funk now. Damn it I'm sweating through my silk blouse. Calm down, Mariah. Keep calm, girl. Let go of the wheel. Where are my pills? How could Vanessa do this to me? Which countries have universal healthcare? I'm not going out like this. If I'm going to prison, we all going to prison.

*****

I return to Toni's Bakery to find the men gone, including Mustapha. Toni's creating gift baskets and Vanessa's sipping on iced tea. I look at them, my newfound old friends. Is Toni in on it too? I clear my throat.

"Hey! Look who's back." Vanessa dances over to me and pulls me to the counter where there are multiple pies with gift-wrapped jars and bottles. I silently accept the iced tea. Vanessa's not acting guilty. Then again she's a beauty queen, she knows how to fake emotions.

"What are you celebrating?" I ask.

"Life! Today is praise day. And if anyone needs a celebration it's us. So I'm praising my friends with goodies," Toni says, pushing a basket of homemade stuff I'm never going to eat toward me.

"I know I have a long way to go but I've come so far and I have my sisters to thank. Today was amazing." Toni pushes the giant gift basket closer to me. "Mariah, I made you blackberry preserves and strawberry jam. And I made a special streusel cake and apple strudel 'cause you like German stuff. All the ingredients are organic so Vanessa, can actually eat her basket of goodies. I made her nutter butters! 'Cause she used to love nutter butters, remember that, Mariah, she only wanted Nutter Butters and I made her beignets and croissants 'cause her maiden name is Noisette and that sounds French. Isn't your mother from New Orleans?"

"Guilty. So what happened at the house?" Vanessa asks me.

You can always count on nosey Vanessa to stick her nose in other people's business. I continue sipping my tea to keep from rolling my eyes.

"I just woke up feeling blessed this morning. I knew today was going to be special. And to have my two best friends with me, well I just want to thank you both." Toni cuts into an exquisite pie, the meringue is at least a foot tall. "I baked the lemon meringue pie because it's the happiest pie. Who doesn't like lemon meringue, right? Ladies. I just made a decision to renovate my bakery. Isn't this exciting. I just decided, just now. And I'm expanding my menu to include tarts."

Vanessa and Toni high five each other, they turn, hand raised to me. I stare at my German basket... "What am I supposed to do with these?"

"Eat them. Enjoy them," Toni says.

I loudly slurp the last of my iced tea. The ladies finally notice my dark mood.

"What's wrong?" Toni asks.

Shaking my head in disgust. "I should have paid more attention to my own life instead of helping you with yours."

"Mariah, just tell us what happened," Vanessa says.

"Why don't you tell me, Vanessa?" I say, confronting her.

"I don't have anything... what's going on?" Vanessa asks.

"You sold me out to Cliff. You set me up."

"I did no such thing!"

"How did he find out about my money? I never told anyone except for you."

"I'm confused. What money? Okay, more importantly, I never spoke to your husband. I have no reason to speak to him. Our paths don't cross and if they did, I would tell you. I'm not a sellout, Mariah. Slow down and tell us what the hell happened."

I can't bring myself to tell them. I don't trust them. "Just because we were friends once doesn't mean nothing now."

Toni gasps. She grabs my hand. "Whatever happened, we'll help you. Just like you helped me. We're sisters."

"You don't have enough money to help me."

"I can get a bank loan for $200,000!"

"That's not enough."

"Maybe it'll help you buy time or something."

"Toni, don't you ever stop being a doormat?"

"I'm not a doormat," Toni says softly, moving away from me.

"That isn't very nice," Vanessa says.

"Well, I guess I'm not a nice person. We can't all be Ms. Etiquette and Ms. Apple Pie. You can't possibly understand what I'm going through. It's not like you've done anything with your lives."

"Mariah!" Vanessa warns.

"I own my own business," Toni says.

"And you clear what? $5 a year."

"I don't do it for the money."

"Of course you didn't, Toni. You did it to keep Trey under your apron so you won't be alone."

Toni breaks off a piece of beignet, mumbling, "So."

"I was going to say something smart, Toni, but those big dumb eyes of yours remind me of Old Yella before his master shot him. So please, just stay out of it."

"Attacking Toni won't solve anything. We will help you with Cliff."

"What are you going to do, V? Make him a lip balm." I push the gift basket away from me and stand. "You want to know the real reason

Fred left you? He's as shallow as you are, the only difference is, you got old and he got rich."

Vanessa's mouth drops open.

"That's enough, Mariah," Toni warns.

"Newsflash, Ms. Baked Goods, the way to a man's heart is not through diabetes."

Toni reaches for a cookie. I snatch it out of her hand. "Just because you cook like Trey's mother, doesn't mean you have to look like her."

Toni's bottom lip quivers.

"You told Cliff about the money," I finally spit out.

"What money?" Vanessa asks.

"Don't play stupid, Vanessa. I know it's your signature move but not now. Not with me."

"What are you talking about?"

"He knows I've been skimming and 'squirreling' as you say."

Vanessa looks at me with a blank stare. Toni gasps.

"Mariah! You stole? That's a sin. You know that," Toni says.

"For once in your life, climb down off the cross and be a normal person. You don't get extra points for being a victim."

"That's not nice, Mariah. You're being mean. Meanie Mariah," Toni says.

"I really can't do this with you, Toni. I didn't steal my own money that I worked my ass off to earn."

"But Cliff didn't know. You kept it from him," Vanessa says.

"That's stealing. Embezzlement. I know because Trey's been stealing from my cash register for years. How could you?"

I throw up my hand to Toni. "I told you once to shut it."

"Thanks for proving why Cliff never loved you," Vanessa says. "You need to go."

"It was a waste of time coming over anyway. I just had to see the look on your face to know the truth." I pick up my purse.

"Where do you think you're going?" Toni blocks my path. "Sit the hell down, Mariah," Toni commands.

My instincts tell me I better sit the hell down or get tackled. Vanessa must have felt the same way, she sits too.

"The doormat has the floor and you will sit there and listen to what the doormat has to say. Everybody gets one pass to act a fool. Not that you deserve a pass after the awful things you said." She clears her throat. "Which may or may not have been true."

Vanessa raises her hand to testify and beams with pride at Toni. "Mariah, you're a pain in the butt. But you're our pain and we love you. Now we are going to help you. Whether you like it or not. You got that?"

"Doesn't sound like I have a choice."

"No, you don't so go on and tell us what he did." Toni sits across from me, waiting to hear the story. I really do love these girls.

"He knows. He had that Rose woman with him in my house in my office going through my files with a forensic accountant. I never told anybody about the money, never even hinted at it, never made a joke about it, nothing. You're the only person I told." I look at Vanessa.

"I didn't say anything."

"Yeah Mariah, you know Vanessa would never do that."

"Then how do you explain it?"

"I don't know. But we're all going to calm down and figure it out." Vanessa says.

"He threatened me with prison. If I'm going to prison, both you bitches are going with me."

"I'm God's daughter, don't curse at me," Toni says while cutting a slice of streusel cake. "Eat."

Vanessa remains calm, ignoring me. "A forensic accountant, huh?"

"I have two days to give him the money. And for the cherry on top, I'm kicked out of my house."

"Well, how much did you take?" Toni asks.

I don't say anything. I pinch off a bit of streusel cake. It's good.

"Okay, how much did they say you took?" Toni asks, getting exasperated.

I think back. Did they say a dollar amount? I shake my head, "I don't think he said how much."

"Mariah. Did the fancy accountant show you his credentials? Like a badge or a card or anything?" Vanessa says, sipping iced tea.

"I think he did. It happened so fast. They were going through my files, unplugging my computer. I think he showed me his card. Now I'm not sure."

"The truth is, you don't know who this guy is," Vanessa continues. "This is LA, everybody's always saying they're somebody."

"Well, clearly you did something because you're acting hella guilty." Toni adds.

"Remember what I said about Jocelyn's husband knowing how to hurt her. Cliff knows how to hurt you," Vanessa says. "He could have paid this guy a hundred dollars to pretend to be a futuristic accountant."

"Forensic."

"Whatever, girl."

"You think so?"

"Uh... yeah." Vanessa says, her eyes big, looking at me like I'm Boo Boo the fool.

"Cliff was always threatening to kick me out the house, telling me to go back to where I came from. I had to put money aside. I had to look after myself. I couldn't trust him to do it."

"He got you! See what they do? They use our weaknesses against us. The big question is, what did you say when they accused you of stealing?" Vanessa asks, offering me a beignet, ever the hostess.

"I didn't say anything. I turned around and walked out."

"Nothing? You didn't agree to give them the money, which would imply you were indeed guilty?" Toni asks. "I watch a lot of crime shows. Snapped is my favorite. Followed by Law and Order."

"No, I just walked out."

"He played you, girl. He pressed a button, launched a missile and blew your mind. The good thing is, you didn't play into his hand and admit anything. He suspects you took the money 'cause he knows that's the sort of thing you'd do to protect yourself. He's pretty sure you did but you never said you did." Vanessa waits for me to grasp that I walked in on a one act play, directed by Cliff starring Salas Samonte.

"Yep. He played you, girl," Toni adds, agreeing with V.

My mind starts to clear. Cliff was baiting me, trying to get me to incriminate myself but I didn't take the bait. "That fuck face! I'm going to get him. I'm going to get him good."

NINETEEN

VANESSA

Breanna clasps her father's hand as they wait in line with the other young debutantes. The ballroom is packed with parents and friends gathered to witness the Alpha Delta Zeta 75th Annual Cotillion. Twelve cadets from The Army and Navy Academy raise their swords as the debutante and her father walk underneath the arch. The Palisades High School orchestra plays a waltz from Sleeping Beauty as Marc Brown, anchor for KABC-TV announced the debutantes.

The only reason I recognized the music is because Breanna went through a Sleeping Beauty phase at four years old. I know everything there is to know about Aurora, the sleeping beauty. For a time, Breanna insisted we call her Aurora. When I asked her what made Aurora different from Belle or Snow White, she said Aurora and the Prince reminded her of Fred and me. I was a teen beauty queen and Fred was the prince who kissed me and awakened me to a dream life. When she said that, I stopped with that princess nonsense. I didn't want my daughter thinking a man was the magical key to happiness. Disney never got another dime out of me. I gave into Fred's wishes and enrolled Bree in girls' touch football, then girls' softball, then wrestling. She was terrible at every sport but she was great as a sideline strategist.

While she was on the field or on the mat, I start learned about African queens, like Queen Amina, Queen Makeda and Queen Candace and as I learned about these mighty women warriors, I taught my baby. Along with getting her into sports and teaching her about our ancestors, I stopped telling her she was pretty. Fred continued to lavish the pretty princess compliments on her but I stopped. It's not that I didn't believe she was beautiful, she's my baby, of course, she's pretty, but I didn't want her to believe being pretty was female currency.

Fred thought I was over thinking it and damaging her self-esteem. Whatever. Fred is Fred. Instead of telling her she was pretty, I told Breanna she was smart and athletic, witty and thoughtful and I told her that her mind would get her much farther than my beauty ever got me. As she grew up, I watched her develop into a young woman who would invite the new girl at school to the sleepover, who judged her classmates on their character instead of their latest phone. Fred and I instilled a healthy balance in her self-esteem.

A week ago, I dug out the Sleeping Beauty book and showed it to Bree. That heifer told me I still remind her of Sleeping Beauty, only this time instead of a prince waking me up to a dream life, I needed to wake myself up and get my own life.

'That's the problem with women. They've bought into the psychology of being rescued,' she told me. I did too a good job teaching her self-reliance. Maybe Fred was my prince who gave me a dream life but the dream is over and I'm hashtag woke.

From my table, I can see Breanna twitching with excitement in her Swarovski crystal studded combat shoes. Thankfully her gown covers them. Oh, yeah. Contrary to her promise, she did not show me the gown before buying it in Vegas. Maybe she was influenced by all the glitz and showgirl glamour because she chose a dress with all the bells and whistles. Ostrich feathers. Sequins. Crystals. And good grief it's tight. The only thing brighter than her gown is her smile. I told her she would stand out from everyone else and there she is, glittering like a Christmas icicle. I'm so proud of her.

"Do you tell her she's beautiful, or are you still not doing that?" Mariah asks as she hands me a drink from the bar. "Because she's gorgeous. I love the dress."

"I'm starting to, she needs to hear it now. She told me the other day that her friends are surprised I'm her mom because we don't look alike. She told me she asked Fred why I never tell her she's pretty and he said because I'm jealous of her. Can you believe that?"

"Breanna knows it isn't true. Cliff told me I would be jealous if we ever had a little girl. He reached deep for that one."

"Wasn't that a saying? Daughters steal their mother's beauty," Toni recalls. "Oh! Remember what's her name, who pledged after us. She was so pretty, she was homecoming queen and married what's his name, the Kappa. They had a little girl and what's her name broke out in adult acne and never got rid of it."

"She's right over there." A thin woman wearing a ton of foundation smiles at us. We wave back and mouth, 'hey, girl'.

"Laser resurfacing is real," I add. "We don't have to keep the face we're born with."

We turn to the stage. Marc Brown stands at the podium announcing the next debutante and her educational goals. "Mr. Arthur Riggs presents his daughter, Willomena Victoria Riggs who has been accepted to Spellman University."

I scan the room and see Heidi. "He brought her," I say, shaking my head at Fred's lapse in judgment and courtesy.

"Who are we looking at?" Toni asks.

"Fred's skank. Sorry, no other word comes to mind to describe her. Actually, not sorry."

"Which one?" Toni asks.

"Really, Toni, which one?" I counter.

"I mean, which one is Fred's skank, not which one of Fred's skanks is here," Toni says.

"That sounded like shade to me," I say.

"The newest skank is over there at that table." Mariah gestures to the table with the interracial couples.

"In the red dress," I point out.

Heidi is dressed in a skin-tight, short red bondage dress.

"I have to say, you see one skank, you've seen 'em all. Just once, I'd like the skank to be a size sixteen with an afro and ebony skin." Mariah snorts.

"I guess it's her debut too," Toni says.

"I'm surprised you're so calm, V," Mariah says to me.

Yes, I am calm. On the outside. I'm going to sit here. Sip my Chardonnay. Eat my dry chicken breast and celebrate my daughter. They don't have to know I took half a Valium.

"This is Breanna's night. Oh! There she is!"

I grab Toni and Mariah's hands.

"Mr. Fred, the Freezer, Jones presents his lovely daughter, Breanna Alexis Jones. Ms. Jones is a freshman at the prestigious Harvard-Westlake High School," the emcee announces.

The cadets raise their swords. Breanna and her father walk underneath them. A loud, shrill whistle cuts through the polite clapping. Heidi stands. Sticks her fingers in her mouth and whistles. Loud.

"She is getting on my last nerve," I warn.

"No couth," Mariah adds.

"Couth-less," Toni joins in, giggling.

"No couth or scruples. Who wears a red dress to a cotillion and her jewelry... ummm, uh oh," Mariah says.

"Jewelry?" Did she say jewelry? I turn around to see what she's flaunting. Mariah pulls me back toward the table.

"Don't pay that child no attention," Mariah says, holding my arm in a death grip.

I peel back Mariah's fingers and turn around to see a giant diamond engagement ring on Heidi's greedy finger. She catches my eye. Waves her ring hand. She even blows me a kiss. "I'mma kill that skank!" Before I can push the chair back Toni slams her hand on my shoulder, pushing me back down.

"Remember Breanna. Keep your eyes on Breanna. Don't turn away from Breanna," Toni counsels.

"Remember all those years of denial? Use it now," Mariah whispers.

I keep my eyes on the prize, focusing my attention on my baby girl. I clap as the last debutante is announced. Tears of anger stream down my face. The orchestra changes to an up-tempo. The cadets tap each father for their daughter's hand. The fathers bow and the debutantes curtsy in an elaborate display of handing over their daughters to these young, disciplined men.

"It's time for the parents' dance. Parents. Please join your daughters and their escorts on the dance floor," the emcee announces.

"Dance? I'd like to see him try. He can't dance with that knee." Dancing with Fred is the last thing I want to do. I can't trust myself not to throat punch him.

"You gotta do it," Toni says. "I can request the electric slide if that'll help."

"Mom!" Breanna calls out from the dance floor.

"If you don't, the skank will. Is that what you want?" Mariah asks.

Breanna continues to wave for me to join them on the dance floor. Fred, looking rather debonair in his tuxedo, extends his hand to me. I reluctantly get up and take his hand. We sway in perfect rhythm that seventeen years of marriage brings. Breanna, dancing with her escort, beams at us.

"We did it," Fred says.

"We? Oh, you speak French now?" I know it's a corny saying but I can't resist the shade. He can't resist chuckling.

"We raised a beautiful young woman."

"So why are you trying to raise another one?"

Fred smiles at Heidi. She waves her engagement hand at him.

"I'm feeling too good, V. You can't upset me tonight. We did everything right with Bree."

"Don't flatter yourself, Fred. While you were out whoring, I was home raising our daughter."

"You're so bitter. You can't stand that I'm finally happy."

"I'm not bitter, you moron. I'm disappointed. Learn the difference."

"Oh! I get it. You saw the ring. I asked her to marry me and now you're jealous. Sounds like a personal problem."

"Personal! I'll tell you what's personal."

A few of the parents dance away from us. Fred notices. He hates public disagreements.

"Lower your voice," he whispers.

"Not being able to buy groceries is personal. Having my credit cards declined after I've eaten dinner with friends is personal!"

"Mom," Breanna hisses, still swaying with her escort.

"Seeing a giant diamond ring on your skank's finger while I buy a rotisserie chicken from Costco and ration it over three days is very, very personal!"

Fred lets me go. He turns to Breanna. Shrugs. "I tried to be nice."

I kick Fred's leg from under him. "Try harder!" He falls to the floor, holding his dislocated knee. Now no one is ignoring us. The orchestra stops playing. Everyone's staring. Instead of being embarrassed, I turn to the young debutantes.

"Girls! Let this be a lesson to you. Never. Ever. Ever. Sign a prenup!"

"Mom!" Breanna shouts. On the verge of tears of shame, she stands there immobile.

"You told me to wake up. Consider me woke!" I yell back at her.

I catch Leona Ellis' eye as I storm out, followed by Mariah and Toni. Leona's the Supreme Grand Dame of Alpha Delta Zeta. That's her official title and I'm going to need every bit of her influence to get out of this mess.

*****

Later that night in my kitchen, Mariah shakes up my favorite college cocktail, Vodka Gimlets, three-fourths Stoli, one-fourth Rose's lime juice. Refreshingly spry back in the day when I young and carefree. Now, it tastes like a numbing alcohol bomb. I tell Mariah to go ahead and pour me two. Toni finds a pint of what she thinks is ice cream in the freezer.

"Why didn't you tell us you couldn't buy groceries?" Mariah asks.

"Because it's private," I say, taking the second drink from her.

"Not anymore," Toni says, digging out a spoonful of creamy goodness and relishing the taste. "What kind of ice cream is this? It's delicious."

"Body Butter." I watch Toni lick the homemade lotion off the spoon.

"How does it taste?"

"Tastes like lavender. I make an ice cream that tastes like this." Toni says, contemplating another spoonful.

"How much do you need?" Mariah asks.

"I don't want your money. I want my money. Did you see her engagement ring? At least, ten grand."

The front door slams.

"Bree! Honey, I'm in the kitchen."

Silence. I lean forward, straining to hear Breanna's motions when she appears at the door. She stands there looking at me. No outbursts. No tantrum. She just stands there, staring at me like a bird of prey trying to decide which limb to rip off first.

"I realize you and dad are going through a divorce. I get that you're in a bad place. I've seen you do a lot of desperate things to keep him but I never thought you'd publicly humiliate me."

"No, honey, that's not…"

She lifts her hand to silence me. It works. "The sorority cotillion was your idea. You wanted me to parade around like an ostrich. You wanted to present me to society. I hope you're proud of yourself. I'm the talk of the town thanks to you. I have to go to Harvard-Westlake with some of those girls. I'm D.O.A. Persona non-grata."

"Honey, I didn't…."

She lifts her other hand. "I'm the teenager. I'm supposed to be immature and rebellious. You all take it to a whole other level. You're petty, self-centered, bitter biddies."

Mariah clears her throat.

"That's enough, Bree. You can be mad at me but don't be disrespectful," I warn.

"Save it. This is not the time to give me a lecture on respect." Breanna takes a breath to calm down. "Dad and… her are waiting for me. Do not go outside and confront them. I only came in to tell you I'm staying with them, indefinitely. Do what you have to do to get yourself together, and mom, do it quickly." Breanna walks out.

I am stunned by her directness. So are the ladies.

"That was mature," Toni says, digging into the pint of lotion. Forgetting it isn't ice cream although it is delicious. "She has a great speaking voice."

"Stop eating the body butter, Toni." I pour myself an extra tall drink, listening for Breanna to finish packing and leave. On her way out, she slams the door, extra hard. She knows I hate the sound of doors slamming. It reminds me of visiting my father in prison. I don't blame her for leaving. A part of me wants to run away too. Instead, I sip on my third gimlet and turn to my girls.

"Maybe this is best. Breanna's safe. You can have some breathing room," Mariah offers.

"Mariah, I need you to find out where Fred's hiding my money."

"Ooooh! Ooooh! What's her name? The skank," Toni says, polishing off the pint.

I shake my head. "No way. Not possible. He wouldn't do that. Fred's not that stupid," I reason.

Mariah and Toni look at me like 'yeah, he is.'

*****

I'm at Goodwill on La Tijera, waiting for Mariah. Since Cliff kicked her out of the house, I don't know where she's staying but knowing Mariah she bought a safe house years ago. Probably a condo with a view of the ocean. Oh, there she is, standing at the entrance of the store searching for me. I wave at her from the wall of dresses I'm shifting through.

"This isn't what I had in mind when you said retail therapy. If I had known you were going Goodwill Hunting, I would have worn something more appropriate, like a track suit." Mariah flicks non-existent lint off her new cap sleeve cashmere sweater.

"If I would have told you, you wouldn't have come. It's good to see you! You've been M.I.A. since last week."

Mariah scratches her arm. "These clothes are making me itchy."

"They clean everything before putting them out. So... ummm... where are you staying?"

"I have a little place I go to clear my head."

"Mariah, you're like the CIA. You got safe houses and secret accounts. I wouldn't be surprised if Mariah isn't your real name."

"I'm just trying to stay ahead of the curve." She scratches her arm. "Let me loan you some money," she whispers.

"I don't need a loan. I don't need your money. I need my money. And for your information, I'm here because I like coming here. I like the hunt. I found the dress I'm wearing right here. Vintage Dior. I got it for ten dollars."

"Seriously, when you're done, come by the house. Cliff's at Martha's Vineyard for 4th of July. He's gone for the week so I have access to the house."

*****

Mariah's house is ten minutes away from mine but it feels like it's a world away.

She answers the door wearing a Moroccan kaftan. One of those flowy, colorful, silky numbers. It takes me a moment to realize it's her. I'm used to seeing her in pants.

"You look relaxed. Love the kaftan," I say, kissing her cheek.

"Hey girl," she says, stepping aside.

Mariah walks through her paisley living room. This must be Cliff's taste. Mariah is not ornate or ostentatious. She's the most minimalist person I know. "You need to hire me to redecorate your home. Something blue and coastal. Your house should be light and airy. It needs to breathe."

"As soon as my situation with Cliff is over, I'm selling the house." She says this as she quickly walks to her home office and media room overlooking the pool. Now this room is Mariah. Modern furniture. All clean lines and right angles, no overstuffed furniture here. No distracting prints. Sparse. Like a well-designed monastery.

I sit across from her desk and admire the trophies and awards she and Cliff accumulated over the years. I can hear the waterfall tumbling into the Olympic size Infiniti pool beyond the french doors. "Do you use the pool?"

Mariah stops typing on her new laptop and nods her head. "Did ten laps this morning. So I found out some things about Fred's finances. I have good news and bad news," Mariah informs me. Okay, let's get into it. No chit chat. I point to a pitcher of tea on the coffee table.

"Is that sun tea or Long Island Iced Tea?"

"At ten in the morning, it's sun tea." She pauses. "You want something stronger?"

"Depends on the bad news. Am I gonna need a drink or a Xanax?"

Mariah pours a glass of sun tea for me. Something tells me I'm going to need vodka. "According to you, Fred has $15 million in assets, real estate, cars, stocks, retirement and savings."

"Of course according to me. Who else would it be according to?"

"Easy. Drink the tea."

I watch Mariah's diamond panther ring sparkle as she types on the keyboard. "You bought the Cartier ring." I say, amazed by its beauty and by its hefty price tag.

Mariah spreads out her fingers, admiring the eighteen carat gold Panther head, encrusted with 136 brilliant cut diamonds and two emerald gemstones for its eyes. This is a major upgrade from her wedding ring, which was a respectable piece of jewelry but not drop dead gorgeous like the $15,000 sparkler lighting up her hand.

"I missed having something on my finger," she says, almost apologizing.

I don't blame her. If I had the money I would have bought a replacement ring too. I would have told people I divorced Fred and married myself and vowed to love me unconditionally through thick and thin. Amen. I feel a headache coming on. I skipped my customary mimosa this morning and went on a run as part of my renewed commitment to me. I won't do that again. I'm sore all over, my hip hurts, and I sweated my hair out.

"How's Cliff? How's the unholy alliance between you and the he-she? I ask. Mariah doesn't answer at first. I can tell she's counting to ten or saying whatever mantra so she doesn't rip me a new one. Mariah has a strong alliance to the LGBT and sometimes Y community.

"Do you want to do this now or not? Either way is fine with me."

"Before you get upset with me, just know that I'm overwhelmed and I'm underwhelmed. I'm everything and nothing. Just be my friend today and forgive me in advance." I watch Mariah exhale. Loudly. "Yes, let it out girl. Release the toxins. It's not your fault my husband's a louse." I say whatever I need to, to take the tension down a notch.

"He's a broke louse," Mariah says.

"Trust me. Fred has money. I made sure we wouldn't go broke. He has $15 million that I'm aware of. I know he didn't spend $15 million in nine months."

"You said he started a business earlier this year," Mariah says.

"That stupid bobble-head business did not cost $15 million!"

"I'm right here. No need to yell."

"Would you rather I cry? 'Cause I gotta do one or the other."

Mariah's my friend and she'll walk through the high end of hell with me but the minute she sees tears, I'm on my own.

"Clearly he's hiding assets. The question is where? Family? Friends, maybe? An off-shore account? Maybe one of his girlfriends scammed him," Mariah pushes.

"He wouldn't give it to any of the women he dates. But, did you follow up on Toni's idea and check the skank?"

"I need her social security number to dig deep but I did a surface probe and she doesn't seem to have any assets. But let's say he did transfer his money to her or to somewhere since it's not where it used to be…"

"Well then, I'm back where I started. I still don't know where our money is."

"But you know where it isn't. Money doesn't just disappear. There's a paper trail. Maybe he has a new bank account. Bree lives with them, maybe she can snoop around?"

Mariah reads the look on my face and knows it's a dead end idea.

"She's not speaking to me. I came here for answers. What's the good news?"

"We're going to figure this out."

I need some air. I get up and walk outside onto the balcony overlooking the infinity pool, I take a few deep breaths. Mariah joins me.

"Everybody said set aside money for yourself 'cause you just don't know when it's going to turn left." I grip the sun tea, wishing it was Long Island. Mariah doesn't say anything. "I know it's killing you not to say I told you so."

"You told me to mind my own business," Mariah recalls. "No, let me quote you right. You said, stay out my business."

"You're doing this now? It's not pretty to be petty."

"I was looking out for your best interest. There are no guarantees. I always say that."

"Mariah, tell me the truth. How big is that nest egg you buried?"

"I don't know what you're talking about. But I will say this. Cliff doesn't know how much money we make in a year, what our debt to income ratio is, our loan amounts, our interest rates, and that's his willful, lazy ignorance."

"Maybe he never needed to know because he trusted you."

"Yeah, well. I trusted him too and look at us now. The point is, think about Fred, think about how he spends his money, how he saves his money, and then you'll know where he keeps his money."

"If I can get into his house…"

"Snooping around his house? No, V."

"You owe me, Mariah. I don't understand why with all your degrees and all your success, friendship is a concept you still struggle with." I take a moment to calm down. "Mariah, sometimes I look at you and all I see is a business woman."

"You say that like it's a bad thing."

"In your case it's a limiting thing. Hands down you are the best at what you do. You wheel and deal circles around men. There is no glass ceiling that you can't smash and I'm proud of what you've accomplished. But we both know you suck at love. Any kind of love. Relationships. Friendships. Anything that requires you to put your own needs aside, you make excuses not to do it. You moan and groan. And I've never said this to you before, we've never talked about it because that would mean you'd have to be vulnerable but that's the real reason you never had children."

"Wow. Maybe you need to take a couple of laps in the pool. How did we go from me helping you to you insulting me?"

"The reason you don't have children is because you knew you'd resent then. You made the right decision! I get it. I'm a great mom and sometimes I resent my daughter. At least you were honest with yourself to know your limitations. You're selfish Mariah. I've always known this about you. And I've overlooked it because I had my own family and I really didn't need you for emotional support. But now it's different. I need you. My family is broken. My heart is broken. My life is broken. And I need you to not be your usual compartmentalized-what's the bottom line, 'I can only do this much for you because I've calculated the risk and I need more of a return on my investment Mariah. I'm begging you to be a better friend to me. I know people are an inconvenience for you but you're no walk in the park either, my dear."

Mariah plops a mint in her mouth. "Are you done?"

I know what's coming. I simply reach for my purse. "Fine, Mariah. Do you, and to hell with everyone else."

"Yes, I'm selfish. So what? You're vain. Toni's... Toni. What's that stupid poster Toni had on her dorm wall? Friends know each other..."

"... And love them anyway," I finish, walking to the door.

"Vanessa, I love you but I can't do the soap opera thing. Please stop acting like you're a candidate for Section 8 housing."

"Then help me find my money, Mariah."

Mariah grabs a box of surveillance cameras. "C'mon."

*****

When we get to Fred's house, his doctor's Mercedes is in the driveway. Luckily the security gate is open.

"Someone's home. Oh well. Let's have lunch," Mariah says, ready to drive off.

"Wait a minute. That's Dr. Palmer's car. I must have really popped Fred's knee."

I get out the car and sneak around to the back of the house.

"Vanessa. Are you crazy?" Mariah says, following me. "He's home."

Fred doesn't lock doors. I used to go through the house every night and make sure the doors were locked and the windows were shut. Just like I suspected, the back door is unlocked. Maybe I am crazy. We should have driven past the house after seeing Dr. Palmer's car in the driveway but I won't have the nerve to do this later. Sneaking through the kitchen, we pass an intercom. I tug on Mariah's kaftan and point to the monitors. I press listen and turn the volume up. I can hear Heidi's voice. "There you go, baby," she says.

Mariah nudges me out the way. She turns on the video surveillance and switches through the monitors until we see Heidi and Dr. Palmer propping Fred up in bed. I grit my teeth to keep from cursing him out. It's a natural reaction to seeing him.

"Freeze, we've been through this before. Couple days of bed rest. Keep your leg elevated to reduce the swelling," Dr. Palmer advises.

"Babe, get the massage oil. I need you to rub my feet," Fred says. Heidi cheerfully bounces out the room. As soon as she's in the hall, I watch her roll her eyes. I know the routine. Another night of rubbing his gargantuan smelly, sweaty feet. First the feet, then the calf, then the thigh and his whole old body until he snores himself to sleep. And then, she'll get the joy of listening to his farts. Careful what you wish for!

The doctor walks past Heidi, who is pouring herself a stiff drink.

"Don't worry. He'll be chasing you around the house soon enough," Dr. Palmer says.

"Yippee. Hey Doc, did you leave him any pain pills?"

"Remind him to *only* take one every six hours. As needed." He continues walking down the stairs toward the front door.

"Babe! I'm thirsty!" Fred bellows from the bedroom.

I'm touching buttons, trying to figure out how to switch screens to follow Heidi. Mariah slaps my hand. A little too hard. She points to the other screen. Heidi's in the game room.

"Coming babe!" Heidi cheerfully replies. She slams her drink on the counter. Fills a glass with tap water.

Fred is watching ESPN when Heidi returns.

"Baby, rub my feet."

Heidi plasters the smile on her face but those eyes don't lie. She's hating every minute of this. "Which one baby?"

"Both. And get in the arch. Yeah, that's it. Really dig in." Fred stares up at the ceiling. "She's never gotten that mad before."

"I told you she was bitter."

"She's eating leftovers. She hates leftovers."

"How does that feel, baby? Does that feel good?" Heidi asks, trying to redirect the conversation.

"Harder. Yeah, that's it. Move up to the calf."

Heidi smiles up at him. Blows him a kiss. He keeps staring at the ceiling.

"She fainted at the attorney's office. I told you about that?"

"It's an act, baby. You get a look at her hips. She's not missing any meals."

"Still. I should give her a couple of thousand a month."

Mariah hits me. Looks at me as if to say, 'See? Everything is going to be okay.' I have an uneasy feeling. We watch Heidi climb over his legs and straddle him. She speaks slowly, in a pouting, baby voice. "What about us?"

"Hmmm?"

"We have expenses," Heidi pouts.

"We have everything we need."

"We don't have a nursery."

I catch my breath.

"We don't need a ..." Fred looks at her.

"Freddie Weddie. You're going to be a daddy!" Heidi throws her arms around him. His eyes widen in shock.

Mariah and I both gasp. Only I can't stop gasping. Mariah clamps her hand over my mouth and tries to pull me out the kitchen. My hand catches on the table cloth and dishes crash onto the floor.

We hear Fred's voice again but it's not coming from the monitor. "I got a gun and I ain't afraid to stand my ground!"

"C'mon!" Mariah whisper-yells but I can't move. I'm frozen. Still in shock from the bimbo's baby revelation. Mariah slaps me. I focus on her face. Her eyes look a little too happy to have slapped me. She mouths, "Let's go."

I don't know how we made it to Mariah's car and down the block but we did. Mariah keeps checking the rear view mirror. My head is between my knees. I feel faint. "I don't think they saw us. You okay?"

I pull myself up and lean against the passenger head rest. "She's going to take Fred for everything we have."

TWENTY

TONI

Lord, before I get out this car let me take a minute to say thank you for all my blessings. I know I failed and didn't confront the devil but I promise if you see fit to bring him back in my presence, I will meet the call. You know I vowed never again to pray for a man, but Mustapha is The Righteous One, Lord. I recognize the soldier you sent to handle Trey and his band of hoodlums. I only hope Trey can move on and leave me alone. And Lord, bless Mariah and her nefarious situation. I know she did wrong by stealing but she did right by looking after herself too. And it's not like she took something that wasn't hers. I just hope that she can see her way through this dark time and into the light. And bless Vanessa, please let our Oh-Hell-To-The-No plan work out for her 'cause her husband don't care nothing for her and she's suffered enough humiliations. And Lord, if you happen to see Jocelyn floating around tell her we miss her and love her. Now I'm going to get on in this house and drop dead 'cause I'm beat.

The minute I walk in my house, I know he's there. I can smell the cologne I bought him last Christmas. He insisted on the Gucci cologne which cost me $80 with the bath soap and lotion and he gave me Chinese house slippers from the Swap Meet that cost $2.99. So I'm not surprised when I turn on the light and see Trey sitting on my sofa in his only church suit. He stands up, holding flowers, my favorite flowers, tulips, and a box of chocolates.

"Hi baby, I've been waiting for you to get home. I got a hot bath for you. I even put rose petals in the water. And I picked up oxtails and rice and peas from the Jamaican place. These are for you," he says, holding up the gifts. "I want you to know I'm not even mad at you. I get it. You right." He's still holding out the flowers and chocolates. I haven't made a move from the front door. "Don't you want 'em?"

Okay, let's get this over with. I close the front door. Take the flowers and chocolates. And sneeze. I never liked the Gucci cologne. Something about it tickles my nose. "How'd you get in? You don't have a key."

"Nothing can stop a man from getting to the woman he loves." He sits back down and pats the sofa for me to sit next to him.

"You broke into my house. I didn't call the police when you were following me earlier but you're not going to be coming to the house, breaking into my home."

"What's wrong with you? You've been acting different."

"I'm tired and I don't feel like any foolishness."

I don't want to sit down. I want to keep standing there so he'll know none of this is working but I'm too tired so I sit across from him in my recliner.

He pulls up his pant legs, drops his shoe on the coffee table. "Remember these socks. Every year, you get me socks, just like my mama. Matter fact, I told mama, you had the sock department on lock. Underwear too." Trey grabs his crotch. Smirks at me like an oily eel.

I can't take it. I stand up.

"Sit on down, over here next to me and relax. We go back like car seats, Toni. You and me. Toni and Trey. TNT. We're dyn-o-mite!" In a lame attempt to get me to laugh, Trey gyrates like Jimmy Walker in *Good Times*. I'm not amused but I get the giggling fits. And when I start laughing, I can't seem to stop. I see him for what he is. A clown. Guess I'm laughing too long and too hard 'cause Trey stops smiling and gets pissed.

"It wasn't that funny. You think it's easy for me to come here after you made me look like a fool?"

"What do you want, Terrence?"

"Terrence, since when do you call me Terrence? I'm Trey. Ace. Deuce, Trey."

"Uh huh." I yawn. Not to be rude, but it's been a long, long day.

"Damn baby. Give a brother a chance to get to know ya, so I can show ya. Right, right. I know what you need, baby. Like I said, the bath is hot. The food is hot. And here I am, sizzlin'. Ready to serve you in every way I can."

I don't budge. I don't sit. I just look at him. And I feel a little sorry for him.

"I said I get it. You want to marry me, c'mon let's get it over with and get married. Girl, you play for keeps, huh? I mean you played hardball out there. I didn't know you had it in you. Closing down my business."

"My business. I took out the loan. I made the payments."

"Our business then. You got my attention. You win. When you want to do this? I told you, tell me when and where and I'll show up."

"I don't want anything from you, Terrence."

"Stop calling me Terrence! I don't like the way you say it. You call me baby. I'm your baby." Trey pulls out an engagement ring. "Stop all this. Let's get married, tonight. Right now."

"Terrence…"

"It was my mama's. She said you could have it. She said we could move in. She changed the bathroom towels and everything. I told Pookie he can't ride in the front seat no more. That's your spot." Trey gets down on one knee. Holds up the ring. "This is the way you imagined it, right? How I look?"

"I'm not going to marry you and your mama."

"Why you bringin' my mama into this?" He gets up. Stands in front of me in his wrinkled suit that needs to be hemmed. I don't think I've ever seen Mustapha in wrinkled clothes and he sleeps in my pantry.

Trey's skinnier too. And Trey doesn't have Mustapha's muscles. I can't help but smile when I think of Mustapha Khan. Trey's getting in the way of my daydream. I had my whole night planned. I was going to go to sleep thinking about Mustapha's arms around me. I gotta get Trey out of my house. He's making my head hurt.

"The honest to God truth is, I let you take advantage of me. I was scared to be alone. I believed you when you said no one would want me. I don't think you're a bad person, not completely. There's good in everybody. Look, you don't want me! I'm not who you want. I'm not even what you want. And God knows, you're not what I want."

"You need to fire mustard greens. He's planting ideas in your head. This ain't my Toni-homie. My tender, Toni-Roni. My heart belongs to a Toni..."

Don't sing. Lord, he's going to ruin the song for me.

"Terrence. You live at home with your mama and you always will. You're selfish and spoiled. You expect women to take care of you. You're childish. Selfish. Yes, I said selfish twice. And you're lazy. You're the laziest man I've ever known. And by the way, I ought to thank you for not marrying me. Whew! I dodged a bullet there. Terrence, and I mean this with all my heart, I am not going to marry you and your mama. She can use the good towels for herself. After 35 years of taking care of you, she deserves them!"

He stands there staring at me. Then he breaks out into the most fool grin. I can't tell if he's mad or happy. He looks demented, and I think about the pepper spray in my bag. I got a good 75 pounds on him. If I had to, I could tackle him and get to my purse.

"I got what you need. You weren't ready to handle all this. I see now. You need The Dick. You done lost your mind waiting on the Vitamin D. You gone crazy. Tonight is the night I make you my woman." All the time he's talking, he's getting naked. He drops his jacket to the floor. Unbuckles his belt and drops his pants. He's standing in front of me in his underwear and t-shirt. If I weren't in shock, I'd burst out laughing. He starts gyrating, slowing pulling down his drawers. "The truth about Toni ... she's a real special girl. Once you've had me Toni you will never get enough…"

Like most neanderthals, he thinks his magical dick will hypnotize me into forgetting the last eight years. Good Lord, eight years of his embarrassing antics. I take a good look at him standing naked with his shriveled up wee-wee hanging limp and dry. It isn't hard. It isn't excited or even curious. His wee-wee is crusty.

"Don't just stand there mesmerized. Come on over here and touch it. Get to know it."

"Terrence, your dick isn't magical. Maybe it is to Pookie but not to me."

"What Pookie got to do with anything? I'm talking about you and me and you're bringing up Pookie."

"Terrence, you're gay. Pookie's your boy and he's your man. I know it. Your mama knows it. Now take your dry, tired limp dick and get the hell out of my house."

He turns red. That's the shame creeping through him.

"I want my cars back." He sneers at me. "You can't just leave me with nothing."

"Sure, just pay me what you owe for the loans I took out for you, $250,000 and you can have them."

I walk over to the door and open it, wide. I turn on the porch light. I turn on all the lights. "Pull up your big boy pants and go home to your mama."

He shuffles out, holding up his pants, carrying his clothes bunched under his arm. I slam the door after him. And release a deep breath. That felt good. My headache is gone. Just as I walk away, he knocks. Do I have to curse him out? I swing the door open, "Look you dumb ass, cheap ass, stupid ass poor excuse for a human being…! Oh, Mustapha. I thought you were…" I look behind him to see if Trey is hanging around.

"He drove off with his friends."

"What are you doing here?"

"You said he comes by to harass you. I wanted to make sure you were all right. But I see you can take care of yourself. You don't need me to protect you," he says, smiling.

"I wouldn't go that far. Come on in."

*****

Sitting in my backyard under the fruit trees, Mustapha and I share the oxtails and peas and rice Terrence so thoughtfully brought over. The warm breeze blows through my potted flowers and herb garden, making the air smell like jasmine and mint. Candlelight and moonlight are all the light we need. Mustapha is easy to talk to and he listens. Not just listens, he hears me. There are no gaps in our conversation. Usually, I'm shy, but with him, I have so much to say. We talk about everything. Religion. His conversion to Islam while in prison. I don't ask why he was in prison. It's none of my business and I don't believe in holding anyone hostage to their past, as Mariah would say. So I leave it alone. But I do get the courage to finally ask him something I've always wondered.

"I'm embarrassed to say, I don't know what Mustapha means."

"It's Arabic for Chosen. And Toni is short for Antoinette?"

I nod, sipping iced tea which tastes like the best-iced tea I've ever had. "What was your name before you changed it?"

"Jefferson Ulysses Washington. I was named after important white men in history. In prison, I decided the first step to rewriting my story was to name myself."

I nod again. I want to ask why he went to prison but like I said, that's none of my business.

"I can see you're curious but you're too polite to ask."

"'Do not judge or you too will be judged.' Whatever you did before, whoever you were before, is in the past. Isn't it?"

"I was married before and I tried to give her everything she wanted. Even if I couldn't afford it, I found a way. When she wanted a bigger house and a better car, I cashed company checks. I worked in the accounting department. I'm actually an accountant by trade. I know what I did was wrong and I'll never do it again."

We sit in silence. I put my hand over his. "No one's perfect."

"You seem perfect to me."

"Me? Ha! Trey can give you a list of reasons why I'm not."

"I thought he was gay, myself. Tell me about your girlfriends. You all went to university together. I bet you were the nice one."

"We all pledged the same sorority, Alpha Delta Zeta. Mariah's the serious, smart one who owns Oyster Music with her husband or ex-husband who kicked her out of her home and now she's staying, you know, I don't know where she's staying. And Vanessa, she's the pretty one, she makes her own lotion because she has way too much time on

293

her hands since her husband left her for an intern and her daughter won't talk to her. There was another girl, Jocelyn. She passed away recently. I think she died of a broken heart. She had everything money could buy but she was empty inside. People like that, people who think if only I had this or that are always looking outward, like an addict."

"An addict? What are they addicted to?"

"Disappointment, maybe. Denial, delusion, maybe even self-deception. No one and no thing holds the key to happiness. Joy comes from within and with God."

He takes my hand and we stare up at the moon. The satellites in the sky shine like stars and that's good enough for me.

"When I saw you, Ms. Toni, I saw a woman with the three Bs. Beauty. Brains. And, her own business."

"No one's ever called me a beauty. Vanessa, she's the beauty queen. And Mariah's the brains. But I do have my own business, that much is true."

"Do me a favor. Stop putting yourself down. It isn't attractive. You are beautiful. You are a queen. You are smart. You are loving and kind and worthy of a good man. You are beautiful."

"You said beautiful twice," I whisper, looking into his eyes. I think I'm leaning closer to him. His eyes are so big.

"Ms. Toni."

"Hmmmm?"

"You. Are. Beautiful," he says leaning in to kiss me. Lord, his lips are soft. he parts my lips and he's going in. A warmth spreads across my mouth and down to my chest. I don't drink but I imagine this is how liquor feels. My mouth is relaxed, and a warm sensation runs down my throat and burns my chest. I'm drunk. My heart is beating so hard my chest might explode.

"Repeat after me," he says, kissing me with each word. "You."

"You." Kissing him back.

"No, you." Kiss.

"No, you." Kiss.

"I." Kiss.

"Me?"

"Yes, you." Smiling. "You." Kiss.

"Toni." Kiss. "Antoinette." Kiss. "Trammell."

"Am."

"Am." Kiss.

"Beautiful."

I pull back and look at him to see if he's making fun of me. He waits. No smirk or anything bad. I lower my eyes 'cause I've never said I was beautiful to a man. And only half-jokingly to myself. He lifts my chin and stares directly into my eyes. "Beautiful?" I ask.

"Yes," he replies. Kiss.

After a few more kisses by candlelight under the moonlight, it is time for the man formerly known as Mr. Jefferson Ulysses Washington AKA Mustapha Khan to say good night. Instead of sleeping at the bakery, he found a place to stay downtown. The evening is going so great I half expect him to ask to stay the night. But he doesn't. He only asks if I feel safe, and when I assure him I do, he kisses me goodnight. I drift off to sleep thinking I am beautiful and I'm worthy of a good man. I have the best sleep of my life.

In the morning, I awake rested and ready to set our Oh-Hell-To-The-No plan in action. Sometimes things do work out. But what I didn't know was that everything would fall apart before falling into place.

TWENTY-ONE

VANESSA

I meet the ladies at The Peterson Auto Museum on Wilshire. The museum became infamous as the spot where Biggie Smalls was gunned down. Heidi's too young to remember the day hip hop music died, but by the time tonight is over, she'll never forget the Peterson Auto Museum. I wanted to bring Breanna into the plan and ask her to encourage Heidi to come out to the auction but Bree's still not talking to me. So I had to ask Leona to reach out to Heidi under the pretense of welcoming her to society and to consider the auction as her coming out debut. I also enlisted the help of her nephew, Eric, a double threat, self-proclaimed rapper and actor. He agreed to help if Mariah agreed to listen to his demo.

"Leona," I say walking up to my co-conspirator. "Toni's cars are in place."

"I never thought I'd say this but for your sake, I hope your husband's girlfriend has access to your money." Leona says.

"That makes two of us."

"My nephew will do his part."

"This is supposed to be a charity auction, what if people find out?" I ask, weighing the repercussions.

"Charity begins at home, honey. And there's nothing to find out. We have real vintage cars mixed in with Toni's relics and what's her name isn't going to know the difference."

"Leona, I can't thank you enough for all you're doing. Arranging this auction and your nephew…"

"I wish I had someone there for me when Bill started acting brand new. Seven years into our marriage, he found a shiny new toy and had no idea I knew about her. He thought he was so clever. Men always tell on themselves."

"What did you do?" I look over at Mr. Ellis, a bald, portly man, chatting with the auctioneer.

"What wives throughout time immemorial have always done. I allowed it. I never said anything. I let him think he was the ruler of the roost. But what he didn't know is that what is good for the goose is better for the gander. While he was taking weekend trips and so-called business meetings, I was home, entertaining. You're not the first wife to be cheated on and unfortunately, you won't be the last."

"That doesn't give me comfort."

"Honey, if you want comfort buy a posturepedic mattress. I'm giving you a reality check." Leona lifts up my chin. "We're wives. We don't have the luxury of living in denial."

I join Mariah, who is inspecting a red sportscar. "How can Trey afford a Lamborghini?"

"It's a kit car. You can build anything with Crazy Glue."

"Could have fooled me."

"It better fool her. Once she writes the check, we'll have Fred's new banking information," I say, praying the plan is going to work. "You think I need a disguise? I brought a wig and sunglasses."

"Is Breanna coming?"

"No. She won't answer my calls."

Just then, Leona's nephew walks in, wearing a slim fitted, expensive suit and a Lakers' hat, just like I instructed.

"Everyone's in place, except for our star." Mariah observes.

"She'll be here. Leona told her that a certain NBA rookie for the Lakers who just signed a $25 million dollar contract loves car auctions. I meant to ask, how's his demo?"

"Let's hope he's a better actor than he is a rapper."

I wave to Toni and Mustapha.

"Look at them. He got her in a little black dress," I say.

"Good for her. I'm so tired of seeing her in those sad house dresses and floured aprons," Mariah adds.

Toni and Mustapha join us.

"Brother, you clean up real nice. I love this suit," I tell him. It's true. He's got the body for a double-breasted pinstripe.

"This is an important night for my lady."

"Your lady, huh. All right," Mariah says smiling at them. Toni blushes.

"We're friends," she replies. But Mustapha squeezes her and she giggles like the Pillsbury Dough Boy.

Heidi walks in with Breanna. I slip behind Mustapha and slide on the wig and sunglasses, rethinking my decision to be brazen. This feels like a low profile situation. More patrons enter until the room is filled with the well-heeled set of Black Los Angeles accompanied by those who love us. As the crowd mingles, admiring the vintage automobiles up for auction, I see Leona chatting with Heidi. She pointed out a few cars, in particular that may interest her. I'm trying to navigate through the crowd so I can overhear them talking when I bump into my daughter. In classic Breanna style, she shows no emotion, just a deadpan stare.

"You're not fooling anyone in that get up."

"I thought I'd try a new look."

"You look ridiculous."

"And to think I miss talking to you."

"I'm not sure how to feel about you and daddy but I'm here to support you."

I hug her. She pulls back. "You don't want to give away your identity," Breanna cautions, still mad at me. "Heidi asked if you were going to be here. I told her you play Bid Whist on Thursdays. Mom, listen. I don't want you to cause a scene but she told daddy she's pregnant." Breanna waits for a reaction. "Did you hear what I said?"

"Yes, I heard you."

"I found tampons in her purse. She's not pregnant at all," Breanna whispers, frustrated.

"Does Dad know?"

"He's not going to hear that from me."

Mariah and Toni sidle up to Breanna. "Sorry to interrupt but you see that guy over there? The tall one with the Lakers' hat? Tell the skank he's been recruited by the Lakers for $25 million. She should hear it from more than one source."

"I'm not comfortable lying," Breanna says.

"Listen, you're going to have to pick a side. You're either Team Parents or you're Team Skank," Mariah tells Bree.

"So you're not trying to hurt daddy?" Breanna asks me.

"I love your father." I didn't realize the depth of that truth until I looked into my daughter's eyes. "Even if he doesn't love me."

Breanna adjusts my wig. "Don't let her see you or she'll know something's up. And keep your cohorts out the way too."

Toni hands Breanna a program. "I marked my cars. Keep pushing her to bid more and more. We want--"

"...her to outbid the Laker. I get it." Breanna cuts her off.

"You looked so lovely at your cotillion. Just gorgeous, Breanna." Toni dabs her eyes. "Now go out there and don't mess this up," Toni warns, pushing Breanna back into the crowd.

From the podium, Leona announces the beginning of the auction, reminding everyone that the proceeds will go to charity and introduces the auctioneer. Instead of a seated auction, the patrons move around the museum bidding on Toni's cars which are mixed in with the authentic vintage cars for sales. Heidi, sipping a martini, stands between Leona and Breanna.

"First item for bid is a midnight blue 1958 Corvette. Collector's edition." The auctioneer says as the car rotates on a dais. "Who will start the bidding at $50,000?"

I make my way through the crowd until I'm standing directly behind Heidi. She doesn't have eyes in the back of her head so I'm perfectly situated to listen and observe.

"Dad's birthday is coming up. He loves corvettes," Breanna suggests to Heidi.

"It's so old," Heidi says.

Eric, dressed in a slim suit and Lakers' hat bumps into Heidi. They make eye contact. He apologizes and smiles at her. As he leaves, he gently touches her butt. Heidi shimmies and winks at him. "Is that the one you told me about, the rookie?"

"$25 million contract over 5 years. Guaranteed," Leona says.

"I didn't read anything about him in the trades. He does look familiar though."

"You've probably seen him out. He looks about your age. How old are you, Heidi?" Leona asks.

"I'll be twenty-four in October. I'm a Libra."

"My father's thirty-seven."

"Yeah, I know," Heidi says with an annoyed tinge. "He gets up like three times a night to go to the bathroom. So annoying."

"My mother never complained."

Heidi shrugs her shoulders. Sips her cocktail.

"Should you be drinking? You're pregnant," Breanna asks.

"Oh, this is a mocktini," Heidi says, swirling it around.

"I have $50,000. Who will bid $100?"

"The car would make him happy. But, if you don't care about his happiness..." Breanna says.

Heidi reluctantly raises her hand.

"Yes, miss. $100,000. Anyone for $125,000?"

No one bids. The auctioneer rings a bell.

"Sold! $100,000 to the lovely young lady in leopard print." The audience claps. Heidi basks in the attention.

"Now you must buy something for yourself," Leona advises Heidi.

"Freezer bought me a Phantom."

"It's a lease. You have to give it back," Breanna says.

I slide away from them and whisper to a waiter. Moments later, he replaces Heidi's martini with a fresh one. "Oh! I didn't order another."

"From the gentleman in the Lakers hat."

Heidi looks around, spots him in the crowd. He raises his glass to her. She smiles, batting her eyes and twirling her hair. When the auctioneer stands before a Shelby. Heidi gasps. "Oh! I love this car. I've always wanted one."

The Shelby isn't marked as one of Toni's cars. I nudge Breanna who flips through her program. "I wouldn't be caught dead in this," she says.

"But it's a collector's item," Heidi whines and bids.

"$200,000 from the little lady," the auctioneer declares.

"It screams nouveau riche," Leona says before walking away.

"Oh. Well, I wouldn't want to look like that," Heidi grumbles, looking confused, following Leona.

A man with a handlebar mustache buys the Shelby. Leona taps Heidi. "See what I mean? No style." Heidi nods. Leona makes a big display of admiration for the Lamborghini.

"Moving onto the prize item of the evening. A fire red Diablo Lamborghini," the auctioneer announces.

Heidi sips her drink, disinterested. "A red car is so ... newer rich."

Breanna consults the program guide. "Red is the new black.".

"Cars are like shoes. You have one for meetings. One for errands. And one that tells the world you arrived," Leona adds.

Heidi notices Eric nearby. She seductively twirls her tongue around the rim of her martini. He bids on the car.

"$100,000 from the young man in the Lakers' hat."

"You know, I've seen his face before. Maybe I did come across him in my research. For work," Heidi says to Breanna.

"You don't have a job. Didn't ESPN fire you?"

"When I did work there, I mean."

"I read he only dates women who are financially sound. He got burned dating a gold digger. You have to have the money of a Kardashian to keep his interest," Leona says.

Heidi smiles wider. Pushes her boobs out.

"$150,000, anyone?" the auctioneer asks.

Heidi raises her paddle.

"$150,000 from the pretty lady. How about $200,000, Baller?

Eric nods. Keeping his eye on Heidi.

"Yes. $200 from the young gent. Miss? $250,000?"

Visibly tipsy, Heidi throws her glass up, sloshing her drink. "What the hell! $250,000! It's not like it's my money."

"Young man? Care to top that?"

Eric bows to Heidi, conceding to her outbidding him.

"Final bid. $250,000 to the car connoisseur on my left."

The crowd applauds. No one's clapping louder than me and my girls.

Mariah and Toni squeeze my hands. I pull Mariah and Toni out of the museum. I can't contain myself. "$350,000!"

"That's more than enough to pay off my loan!" Toni shouts.

"I didn't think we would pull it off but wow! She is stupid," Mariah says.

"Never underestimate someone on the come up," I add.

"What do you think Fred is going to do when he finds out?" Toni asks.

"Hit the roof," I reply, looking in the window at Heidi bidding on another car.

*****

Later that night at Mariah's house in her paisley living room, I pop a bottle of champagne.

"We did it!" I scream. Elated and relieved.

Toni stares at the auction check. Her hands shake. "$350,000. I've never held this much money in my hands before. It's mine. It's all mine?"

"It's all yours. You have more than enough to pay off her bank loan plus you can pay for the bakery's renovations. Or, you can take a vacation," I say, pouring bubbly.

"I suggest you invest it," Mariah says.

"I only needed $250,000. The rest should go to you two," Toni says.

"I only needed Fred's banking information. I got what I want, Toni. The money is yours," I reassure her.

"But it was your idea," Toni objects.

"You supplied the cars and Mariah convinced Leona and the museum to participate," I say, pushing the check back to her.

"We all won tonight," Mariah says.

"Then we should split it. Three ways. And something for Leona," Toni says, her hands still shaking.

I take Toni's hands in mine. "For once in your life, put yourself first. Receive."

Toni looks to Mariah.

"Receive, T. You deserve it," Mariah says, clinking her champagne glass against Toni's.

Toni stares at the check. "$350,000." She exhales.

Mariah turns to the computer. "I found his bank."

"How much is he hiding?" I ask.

"Hold on. I'm using the record company to verify a specific amount. I'll put in $10 million," Mariah says.

Moments pass. DENIED.

"What does that mean?" I ask.

"It means he doesn't have $10 million in this account," Mariah answers.

"Does he have $350,000?" Toni asks.

"The check is certified, Toni. It'll clear," Mariah says.

I sit down and try to figure this out. "He had at least $350,000."

"Maybe he only deposited $500,000 or a million in her account. You know the saying. Don't put all your eggs in one basket," Toni reasons.

"Hold on," Mariah says. She tries another amount. "He has a million in the account."

"Told ya," Toni says. Then she's confused. "What does that mean?"

"It means he could have fifteen separate accounts. A million in each or he could have thirty accounts or offshore accounts. Who knows?" I say, feeling defeated.

"If he hid a million with the skank, where's the rest?" Toni asks.

"That's what we're trying to figure out, Toni," Mariah answers "You know him better than anyone, V. Where would he hide his most valuable possession?"

I'm at a loss.

"In a safe? In a coffee can? The freezer? Hey! Fred, the Freezer, hiding money in the freezer," Toni chuckles.

"No, Fred may be country but he's not ..." I drift off and realize where he's hiding our money.

TWENTY-TWO

VANESSA

Outside of Fred's house, we sit in Mariah's car, peering through binoculars.

"They're home," I announce.

"What are we going to do 'cause I'm getting hungry," Toni asks.

"What's his number? I have an idea." Mariah calls Fred. Heidi answers.

"Yeah, he's here. He's always here. Hold on." Heidi yells, "Freddy! It's for you!!"

Through my binoculars, I watch Fred pick up the phone in the den. "Fred, the Freezer, Jones speaking."

"Hi, Freeze. I'm calling from ESPN. We need you to come in for a last minute football segment. It's a quick radio announcement, no need to put on a suit. Come as you are," Mariah says.

"Now?"

"Can you be here in ten minutes? If not, no worries. You're the first name on my list but I have bunch of other people I can call," Mariah says, playing to Fred's ego. Toni stifles a giggle in the backseat. I'm amazed at how skillfully Mariah can lie. I watch Fred get up out of the recliner, wearing boxers and a University of Alabama t-shirt.

"Yeah, okay. No, no. I'll do it. I'm leaving now." Moments later, Fred drives through the gate. We duck down as he roars past in the 1958 Midnight Blue Corvette, Heidi bought at the auction.

I watch Heidi run a bath. She doesn't have the decency to close the curtains. Skank. Mariah gives Eric the signal and he rings the bell at the gate. A few moments later, the gate opens. Heidi stands in the doorway wrapped in a towel to find Eric, wearing the Lakers cap, holding a bouquet of red roses. Heidi's pleasantly surprised.

"Hey, I remember you. What are you doing here?"

"Let me in and I'll explain it to you."

Heidi backs away from the door. She lets the towel drop.

"We can't talk long. My fiancé will be back soon."

Eric steps in, closes the door, and purposely unlocks it.

We're all disgusted but not surprised. Mariah shakes her head, sucks her teeth.

"You can't turn a ho into a housewife," I say. The ladies nod in agreement.

The security gate's closed. Mariah and I squeeze through the bars. Toni can't fit. "Climb over," I whisper.

Toni steps onto the wrought iron gate, after a few shaky moments she heaves her body over the top where she gets stuck.

"Hurry up!" Mariah orders.

"My skirt's caught."

"Rip it," I tell her.

Toni tears her skirt and falls over the gate, landing on us. We're smashed beneath her. Toni checks herself. No broken bones. "I'm okay."

"Oh, good." I try to untangle myself from Mariah.

"I can't breathe." Mariah gasps.

"My shoe's stuck in the gate," Toni says.

"Will you come on?" I hiss.

Toni reaches up but can't wiggle the shoe free. Two Dobermans round the house. Galloping at top speed. Fangs bared. Barking. Racing toward us. We scramble up and scamper toward the front door. The Dobies leap toward us just as we slam the front door on the dogs. We collapse against the door. I look through the peephole to see the dogs pulling Toni's shoe off the gate.

Soft moans come from somewhere in the house. I motion for Toni and Mariah to be quiet. Toni can't catch her breath. She's wheezing.

We creep across the grand hall, past the living room. Past the study. As we sneak up the stairs, we hear a loud crash and peals of laughter. We bolt up the staircase.

We quietly close the door to the master bedroom. Toni collapses on a love seat while Mariah peeks through the door. I'm transfixed, staring at their bed. I stifle a cry and beat the bed in a rage. Mariah silently pulls me away.

"How about a drink?" Heidi's voice stops us. She and Eric are in the master bathroom. Uh oh. We hear water splashing and the master bathroom door opens. Heidi walks through the empty bedroom, naked.

We're pressed against the other side of the bed. Mariah stuffs a pillow in Toni's face to muffle the wheezing. I get up and peek through the door to see Heidi walking down the stairs.

"She's downstairs," I whisper.

Mariah throws open the bathroom door. Eric, still wearing the Lakers hat, soaks in a tub covered in red rose petals. We stand in the doorway. Eric tips his hat. "How am I doing?"

"Get down there and don't let her come back to the bedroom," I order. Eric does a quick little salute and stands. Soap suds and rose petals slide off his body. My eyes twinkle. I see Mariah smile, and Toni cocks her head to the side, taking in the enormity of the situation.

He twists a towel around his waist. "No problem."

Dazed, I continue staring at the same spot with the same expression when the bedroom door slams shut, snapping me back to reality.

"Toni, watch the door. Mariah, look for something to cut the mattress," I command.

Mariah searches the drawers and the closet as I search the vanity for scissors. In the bathroom, I stop searching, stunned by Heidi's high-end beauty products, complexion enhancers, serums, toners. Clarins. Guerlain. La Mer. "She took my life." Carefully, I open the jar of La

Mer moisturizer. With the utmost reverence, I slowly dab the face cream onto my face and neck, luxuriating in its richness. "No. Nope." I find a cosmetics bag and dump all her face creams and serums into the bag. In addition to breaking and entering, I'm now a moisturizer burglar.

"This might work," Mariah calls out from the bedroom.

Mariah holds up a steel letter opener. "What do you think?"

"Let me see." I strip the bed of its sheets. Feel around the mattress. "No lumps. Feel over there. Anything?" The girls shake their heads. Mariah snaps her finger. "Box spring." We pull off the top mattress. The box spring's been resewn down the middle.

"I got you, Fred." I high five the ladies.

Fred calls out from downstairs. "Babe! I'm home!"

"Uh oh." Toni warns.

We struggle to get the mattress back together. We spread the covers on top. Throw on the pillows. "Wait, wait, wait," Toni cautions. "The sheets were tucked in with hospital corners." Toni starts refolding the sheets.

Rapid footsteps race up the stairs. Mariah peeks through the door. "They're coming! The skank and the Laker." We collide into each other, knocking ourselves to the ground before I pull them into the closet.

Heidi bursts through the bedroom door. She shoves Eric into the closet and races into the bathroom. We hear a loud splash.

The master closet's the size of a studio apartment. Eric peers through the shutters. It's dark. He doesn't see us.

"What's touching me?' Toni whispers.

"My bad. Hey, my clothes are out there."

"Go get them," I whisper.

"I'm not going out there. You go," he says.

"You're still touching me," Toni balks.

"It'll go down."

"Oh, Lord. Fix it Jesus."

"Cover up before somebody steps on you," Mariah says, handing him a suit. "Here."

Fred walks into the bedroom. "Babe, you in here?"

Heidi calls out from the bathroom. "In the bathtub, waiting on you."

We all say, "Skank."

"What do we do?" Toni asks.

Eric slips on the pants. "Wait it out. Turn off your cell phones. Get comfortable."

"I get the feeling you've done this before," Mariah says.

Soft moans and the sound of water splashing come from the bathroom.

I rifle through Fred's drawers. "What are you doing?" Toni whispers.

"Keeping busy," I reply.

"For what?"

"Oh, I don't know, Toni. Maybe because my husband is having sex ten feet away." I find a safe in the back wall and try Breanna's birthdate. The safe doesn't open. "I doubt it." I try our wedding date. Nope. "Wait a minute." I try the date the New Orleans Saints won the Super Bowl. The safe clicks open and I see the holy grail.

Throughout our life together and especially Fred's NFL career, I kept elaborate appointment books of all our day to day chores from Breanna's playdates and artwork to Fred's newspaper clippings and doctor's visits. Everything that mattered to our family is stapled and pasted onto the pages of each year book. Fred's sentimental. I'm not surprised to find our diaries in the safe. 2005 is the year I'm looking for. This is the year his knee needed extensive help. Holding the book close to me, I make my way to the others. "Let's go."

"What about the money?" Mariah asks.

"Forget the money. I found what I need."

We sneak out the closet. Eric picks up his clothes and shoes on the way out.

Quietly, descending the stairs, I think we're going to make it. At the bottom, we bump into Breanna eating a bag of chips. No one says anything. Breanna looks at me holding Heidi's cosmetics bag and a bulging appointment book. Toni's wearing a torn skirt and one shoe. Eric's wearing her father's suit, and Mariah's gripping a letter opener.

Breanna stares at me, shakes her head, crunches a chip and walks on past us. We bolt out the house.

*****

I slide into the leather booth at Mastro's, one of my favorite restaurants. Mastro's is where Fred and I celebrated many milestones. His contract signings. Our anniversaries and birthdays. And now, I'm about to celebrate my self-worth. Never again, will I let a man define me. Yesterday, I was Ms. California, 2001 and today I'm Mrs. Universe of All Womankind 2018. I sip lemon water and wait.

Fred enters. Looking his best. Dressed for war by wearing his finest suit. Our eyes meet. I'm seated in our corner booth. I smile at him. Yes, come to mama. He takes a moment to open his suit coat. I smell the Acqua di Parma cologne. He knows it's my favorite. Nostalgia isn't going to work against me, buddy. He slides across from me, his cologne wafting under my nose.

"Vanessa."

"Fred."

The waiter appears, expertly presents the wine. "The lady ordered a 2007 Domaine Corton 'Clos des Cortons.'" Fred's impressed.

"Sure you can afford that?" The waiter hesitates and looks from Fred to me. I nod for him to continue.

"Positive."

The waiter pours, leaves.

316

"Another desperate attempt to play on my sympathy, V? You're not going to get me drunk and make me forget we've grown apart. Besides you can probably drink me under the table. You're still drinking aren't you? One day, you'll have to admit you have a problem."

"I'm celebrating. You're welcome to join me."

"What have you got to celebrate? A two for one sale on Top Ramen?" Fred chuckles, swirling the burgundy colored wine in his glass.

I raise my glass to him. "You and I reached a fair and just divorce settlement today."

Fred chokes on the wine going down. "Oh! We did? Well hell yeah, I'll raise a glass to that. I knew you'd come around. You've always been sensible. That's what I like about you. You know when to back down." He refills his glass.

I slowly hold up the appointment book. Fred's smile fades into a scowl. He reaches for the book. I hold it just out of reach. "Uh, uh, uh."

"You broke into my house!"

I slowly flip through the pages of 2005. "I know everything about you, Freezer. The good, the bad, the...injections."

Fred leans back, sips the wine, considering the situation.

"You want to ruin me. You can't stand that I've moved on with my life. You women think everybody owes you something. Just plain ole' spiteful."

317

I laugh, genuinely amused by this fool. "You are the father of my only child. I do not want to ruin you, Fred."

"So what do you want?"

"I want what you owe me. I was your wife. I raised our daughter. I kept our home. I made our house into a home. I kept our family together. I nursed you back from injuries and forgave your infidelities."

"No one forced you to stay."

"I loved you, you moron."

Fred shifts. Uncomfortable. "Anyway. I moved on."

I stare at him through the clear eyes of an old acquaintance. Fred is not the Fred I married. "We never needed lawyers to tell us what to do. If you believe I don't deserve anything, then I want to hear it from you." I place the appointment book on the table and push it toward him. He's suspicious.

"You made copies. Boy when you women get bitter…"

"I'm not bitter, Fred. I'm better. Even though you tried your best to make me feel like I was nothing without you, that I was somehow a burden to you. I don't want to be with a man or be beholden to a man who doesn't love me. Don't worry, I didn't make copies. I'm not holding you hostage." I sit upright, feeling regal. And suddenly, I don't feel the need to explain myself to the only man I ever loved. I lightly drum my fingers on the cover of 2005, the year we almost lost everything. "Some secrets should stay between a man and his wife. Don't you agree?"

TWENTY-THREE

MARIAH

Come now. Oyster, top floor. Back door key on rear tire of Cliffie car.

I've been waiting for this text all week. I get the girls and we ride over to Oyster Music. Just as Rose said, the key to the building is on the rear tire of my Bentley. We walk up the seven flights of stairs to the top floor. Toni wheezes a couple of times but she and Mustapha have been hiking lately so she's able to keep up. She rambles on about swearing off eating the unsold pies at night, including her favorite blueberry cobbler. She goes on about Mustapha likes this and Mustapha likes that and he's not a radical Muslim and he got her into meditation and she went to her first yoga class with him.

At the seventh floor landing, I test my pepper spray.

"Oh girl, I'm with you. I got this." Vanessa pulls out a taser from her purse.

I look over to Toni. She opens her purse, takes out a bag of carrot sticks. "You want one?"

I push through the doors and into the master suite, Cliff's renovated office, which takes over the entire floor. We stop and listen. We can barely hear murmuring from the inner office.

"Ready?" I ask. The ladies nod.

"Whatever he's gotten himself into, we're going to deal with it," Vanessa says.

I quietly enter the inner office and see Rose dressed in a French Maid outfit holding a baby bottle and a rattle. She sees me and places a finger to her lips, gesturing to be quiet. I can hear a toy playing a lullaby in the next room. I didn't expect this. Cliff has a baby. I look over at Toni who's already feeling sorry for me. I'm confused. Rose lifts her coat from the coat rack and picks up her purse, and as she passes me I whisper, "Leave my car key." She presses the car FOB it into my hand along with the baby bottle and the rattle.

We enter the inner office and I'm floored. We're all dumb struck. Vanessa's the first to recover. She whips out her phone and starts recording. I nudge Toni, who records back up video on her phone.

Cliff's lying in the middle of an oversized crib. His feet in the air, squealing like a baby. Hanging above the crib is a carousel chandelier twirling and blinking lights while it plays Hush Little Baby. There's an oversized rocking chair next to the changing table where the diapers are folded up next to giant safety pins and talcum powder. He doesn't see us 'cause he's hugging a giant stuffed teddy bear. And then it happens.

"Uh oh, mommy! I went wee-wee." Cliff gurgles.

"What the fuck, Cliff," I say, switching on the lights.

Cliff turns over onto his knees, trying to hide behind his teddy bear. He calls out to his girlfriend/mama, "Rose? Rose!"

Cliff keeps his head behind the bear. "You're trespassing!"

"Come out, Cliff. Come out from behind the big bad teddy bear," I say to him, shaking the rattle. "You can't hide, Cliff."

Vanessa waves the urine stench away. "I've heard of peeing on someone else but I've never heard of peeing on yourself." Vanessa holds her nose and says, "That smarts."

"Make sure you get him from the other side," I tell Toni, who walks around the crib and captures Cliff's face.

"Did you bring my money?" Cliff has the nerve to ask me.

I throw a diaper in the pen. "Change yourself, you stink."

"What's it called when you get pooped on during sex?" Vanessa asks, spritzing perfume in the air to cover the rancid smell.

"Trey once mentioned a dirty Sanchez," Toni answers.

"No, that's when they smear it on your top lip," Vanessa says.

"Cliff, what's it called when you poop during sex?" I ask.

"You think you got something on me? I'm not committing a crime. You're the criminal. Embezzling. That's a crime."

"You don't have any proof of anything, Cliff. I never stole from you. You stole from me. You stole my trust. You stole every chance you could. Years of threatening to leave me out on the street, threatening to take my home away. Kicking me out of the company I built. Humiliating me!"

"Well it worked! I made you better. You're a success because I pushed you. You'd be nothing without me," Cliff says.

"It must be hard having to face your failures. Is that why you're regressing back to your childhood? Because I'm the success you wish you were."

"I'm getting woozy," Vanessa says, opening a window."

"It's not my fault you're not a real woman," Cliff bites back.

"I'm not a real woman?! You wouldn't know a real woman... Cliff, "Rose is a man."

Vanessa's and Toni's mouths drop open.

"Keep taping him," I tell them.

"She's more woman than you could ever be."

"After her next operation, she'll come anatomically close. You never had sex with her have you, Cliff? Not in the traditional, boring, missionary way."

He thinks about it. "All I've ever worked for. My whole life. My legacy. You women take a man's worth like we owe you something."

I hold up the divorce papers. "It's time to let go. I wrote up a fair, even split of our assets. Except for the company. We won't split that."

"Give me a pen. I don't want to be married to you no way."

I give him the papers and a pen, holding it as far away from me as possible, holding my nose. He signs, initials, and gives it back.

I check the signatures.

"You never had respeck for me," he says, squatting in the crib, marinating in a soggy, droopy diaper.

"For the last time, it's respecT with a T. Here. Sign this." I hold out another stack of papers. He rifles through them.

"I'm not signing this. I don't care who sees me in a crib. You can't have my company."

"I'm the one who revamped Oyster's image. Oyster! What does an Oyster have to do with music anyway? Nothing. Not a damn thing until I branded the name and made the business relevant. I did that. What did you do? You peed on yourself for the whole world to see. And they're going to see it, Cliff. They're going to see it on TMZ, YouTube, Facebook Live. I'll email it to every client, every friend and employee. I'll even show it to your mother. Marinate on that."

He scribbles his name on the documents. "I never loved you." He hands the papers back. I check to make sure everything is signed and initialed when the room recedes and I feel light headed. I look at my girls and they're waving the air away from their faces. It smells like someone dropped a watery fart bomb.

The color drains from Cliff's face. He holds his diaper. "I had Jerk Chicken for dinner. You know my stomach is sensitive."

"Take your funky butt and go." I throw his suit in the playpen next to his teddy bear.

"I can't walk out like this."

"Here. Here's a fresh diaper." And I grab his keys. "You won't be needing these. Or the keys to the building."

Vanessa says, holding her nose, still taping, "You nasty, Cliff."

Toni starts covers her nose and mouth, giggling.

"What's so funny?!" Cliff yells, gathering his suit, holding his diaper tight around his legs.

"Poop butt," Toni says.

"Oh crap!" Vanessa wheezes, barely able to stand.

"Shit for brains," I join in.

"Dookie drawers." Toni laughs.

'Brown bagging it," Vanessa's says.

"One pupu platter to go," I laugh, holding the pain in my side.

"Loose bowels is nothing to laugh at. So I'm an asshole. Maybe I wasn't nurtured as a child. You ever think about that? I needed nurturing. I wasn't getting it from you," Cliff says, climbing out of the crib while trying not to fall over.

"Cliff, it is time you face the facts. I run this bitch!"

The ladies lose it again. "I run this bitch!" they yell in unison.

That's it. I lose it. I laugh so hard, I double over. Tears run down my face. We all let loose. Every time I look at Cliff I lose it again. The oversized baby furniture. Rose. The diapers. It is too sad and too funny. The more Cliff tries to hold onto his diaper, the more we howl with laughter. Cliff turns beet red, which isn't easy for a Black man. He stands in front of me. I just shake my head. Oh, how the arrogant have fallen. I point to his leg. Pee is seeping out of his diaper. I've run out words. There's nothing to left to say to this man who is still my husband. He waddles to the door, head low, holding his clothes and his diaper.

"Cliff. Wait a minute." He stops but doesn't turn around. I can tell he's bracing himself for more humiliation. I turn to the girls, "I can take it from here. Don't share anything. I don't want this leaking out. No pun intended."

"You sure?" Vanessa asks, pressing her hand to her nose. Toni tugs Vanessa's shirt to leave.

Cliff had the good sense to renovate a master bathroom with a shower and tub. I guess she used to bathe him here. The bathroom is stocked with baby shampoo, baby oil and yellow rubber duckies. Cliff sits in the tub, diaper off. We don't speak. I soap him up and rinse him down. After he's clean, he steps out of the tub and I towel him dry. In eight years of marriage, I bathed my husband once. We were on honeymoon, soaking in an outdoor heart shaped hot tub with a view of Niagara Falls. The rising steam from the hot tub and descending rain created an otherworldly atmosphere. That was a lifetime ago.

"I knew you were going to take everything from me," he says, staring at the floor. He looks so pitiful. I don't have the heart to go for the kill.

"Cliff. You're bored with your life. That's why you create all this drama. You're not in love with Rose and you don't hate me. I think you're having a midlife crisis, which is not a bad thing. It's time for you to re-evaluate your life and make some changes for who you are now." I mix baby lotion and oil together and gently rub it onto his skin. "I don't want to fight anymore."

"Me either." He looks up at me, his big kind eyes staring at me for answers.

"Do you want to run the company?" I ask. He shakes his head.

"Do you know what you want to do?"

He shakes his head.

"Do you want to stay married?" he asks me.

"No." I hold the suit pants open for him to step into. "And neither do you." I struggle to get through what I have to tell him but he deserves to hear the truth once and for all. "I wasn't the best wife. The truth is, I don't think I can be anyone's wife. You didn't fail me." He looks at me, surprised. "When I was battling cancer and going through chemo, you were there for me. You nurtured me back to health. But I came out of it a different person. I was ashamed of my scars and I blamed you for everything wrong in our marriage. It was just easier to be mad at you than to be honest with myself."

He zips up his pants, feeling a little better than before. He looks at us in the mirror as I help him into his shirt. "I've been an asshole," he admits.

"Amongst other things," I agree, buttoning his shirt. "The first time I met you, you had on that ridiculous shirt. With the crystals, looking like a rock star."

"You said I was corny!" He briefly smiles at me.

"Well, you were kinda fly."

"So what happens now?"

"Clifton Ash, you have two things that people don't have enough of... money and time. You're free to do whatever you want with whomever you want without hurting anyone. And if you need me, I'm here for you." He raises his eyebrow, not believing the last part. "I don't have to be your wife to be your friend." I slip the suit coat on him and I look at us in the mirror and see two people who had good intentions. "We're going to get divorced the same way we got married, with love, care ...

"... and respeck." He says, relaxed, showing signs of my old Cliff.

"Yep. R.E.S.P.E.C.K."

*****

On Monday morning, walking into my building feels so sweet. The receptionist does a double take. She's never seen me casually dressed. I don't have to look uptight to run a tight ship.

"Mrs. Ash?" She stands with an apologetic look on her face, ready to stop me. "I'm so sorry Mrs. Ash but according to company policy, I can't let you onto the premises."

"Mr. Ash is no longer owner and CEO of the Oyster. I am." Please send out a group email to all the employees. Staff meeting, top floor, now."

"I'm sorry, I haven't received a memo."

"Stop saying you're sorry. Women should not apologize for doing their job. Call the HR manager, let Mr. Maldonado know I'm here, and to have everyone meet on the top floor."

"Yes, ma'am." She smiles at me.

"Don't call me ma'am. Call me Mariah."

She smiles even brighter, "Welcome back, Miss Mariah."

My first order of business is to call a company meeting. All the employees from the custodian to the HR manager and the IT guys and girls meet me on the empty top floor. I had the furniture moved out over the weekend and replaced with the latest audio technology. Sound booths. Engineering Studios. It's now a creative space.

With everyone gathered around me, I announce, "We are no longer Oyster Music. We are now…" I unveil the logo of a phoenix rising, "Phoenix Media Group. And like the phoenix, we will rise above the competition through innovation and creativity building on our success as a music company. You have ideas. I want to hear them. You want to explore concepts, I want to see your vision. It doesn't matter what your job title is, if you have an idea, a dream, a side hustle that fits our paradigm, tell me. At Phoenix, there are no ceilings, there are only blue skies."

The employees look at each other, nodding. Scattered applause.

"And in return for your ideas and productivity, I offer profit sharing."

Now the employees break out in real applause.

"Working at Phoenix means playing at Phoenix, so this floor, the top floor will be where we experiment with new ideas. It's where we play the latest games, where we listen to music, watch movies. We'll have a fully staffed kitchen for free healthy lunches every day. We will have a fitness facility attached to the building. Along with a free laundry service. Twenty weeks of maternity and paternity paid leave, plus free child-care on the premises. And Phoenix offers competitive salaries which means everyone gets an eighteen percent bump in pay. There are no salary caps."

"Can we get that in writing?" someone from the back yells out.

"Mr. Maldonado has contracts for each of you to sign a non-disclosure agreement stating the increase in salary plus all the benefits."

Vincent holds up a stack of contracts. The crowd erupts in deafening applause.

"Now what do I require in return? I require your best work. I require your best ideas. Your best efforts. I want results that push our company forward as a media game changer. When people speak of Phoenix, they'll talk about us the same way they speak of Google, Apple and Facebook. Results. No nepotism. No favorites. This is a meritocracy. You rise or fall based on your drive and ambition."

"Mariah! Mariah! Mariah!" As the crowd chants, I finally feel I'm where I'm supposed to be. I'm home.

TWENTY-FOUR

JOCELYN

I hadn't planned on returning so soon after my homegoing but being dead is no excuse to miss Toni's wedding.

The University of Santa Barbara is just like I remember it, sunny, optimistic and populated with students bursting with eagerness and potential. I'm not surprised Ms. Toni is getting married in the little white chapel on the cliff. It's her favorite place on campus. A simple wooden structure, painted white with a steeple top housing a bell. The chapel sits on 'The Point' where you overlook the ocean to watch the sun rise and set. Whenever we couldn't find her, we knew to look for her here.

Leading up to the chapel from the campus are two rows of shady gingko trees. In the autumn, the leaves turn bright gold, but today, in August, the leaves are green and the pledges of ADZ draped stands of pearls from their branches. Our sorority sisters have outdone themselves by decorating the chapel grounds in ADZ colors of pink and yellow. The tree trunks are wrapped in pink and yellow ribbon. The chamber orchestra, playing classical arrangements of modern songs, wears either pink or yellow and there's a wall of pink and yellow peonies for a photo backdrop. There's no mistake, this is an Alpha Delta Zeta wedding.

I'm not the only uninvited guest. While death has its limitations, it also has its privileges, none more beneficial than hearing the thoughts and desires of the living. And right now, Fred wants to kill himself. He's being dramatic. I've never been a fan of "The Freezer" but I do pity the fool. Heidi is demanding he marry her before she gives birth. And she is relentless. He's praying for a way out. Hold on Fred. You're about to be saved.

I find Fred driving through campus on his way to the chapel, remembering his early days with Vanessa. Back when she was the reigning beauty queen and he was a top round draft pick. Heidi's looking in the mirror, checking her face when she notices Fred smiling to himself.

"What are you smiling about?"

"Huh? It's a beautiful day."

"Oh. I thought you were thinking about her. Isn't this where y'all met a million years ago?" Heidi says, applying another layer of lip-gloss. Her lips are so sticky they look like a venus fly trap. "Do they know I'm coming?"

Fred ignores her questions. He's wondering how he's going to get out of this mess. Heidi's complained for the last two hours, why are we going? Is Vanessa going to be there? When are we getting married? I'm nobody's baby mama. You have to marry me, blah blah blah. It's enough to make him veer off the road. Poor guy. He can't believe he got himself in this situation.

Fred pulls the red Lamborghini kit car into the university parking lot. He's has trouble getting out of the car. Heidi looks over at him, rolls her eyes.

"I'm stuck," he grumbles, looking over at her for help.

"Again?" She applies a few angry swipes of mascara. Trying her best not to show her annoyance.

"Do you mind helping me out?"

"Why are we here again?" she asks, jamming the mascara wand back into its case.

"Because my daughter wants me to be. I told you she's a bridesmaid."

Unable to contain her irritation, Heidi brushes her purse off her lap, spilling the contents of her bag onto the floorboard. "I won't always be around to help you get in and out of the car, you know."

Fred looks at the floorboard and sees the tampons from her purse.

"Tampons? You can't be pregnant and be on your period." The smile spreads across his face. "You're not pregnant."

"Ummm... I had a miscarriage!" Heidi scrunches her face up to squeeze out crocodile tears.

"Thank you, Jesus."

"What's that supposed to mean?"

"It means you're lying. You're not pregnant. I'm out. It's over. Keep the toy car you bought with my money. Consider it a parting gift. Goodbye."

"Fred! It was horrible. Don't you care about our baby? Our poor defenseless bundle of joy? How can you be so heartless? I should have known you'd react this way. That's why I didn't say anything. You're so selfish, Fred. I mean, I'm the one who's hurting. What about me?" She pouts. Looking up at him like a petulant little girl.

"Grow up." Fred untangles himself from the car. Twisting his knee. "Damn it."

"Just because you're a million years old doesn't give you the right to talk to me like I'm a child."

He takes her hand and gives her the car keys. "Take the car and go and don't bother coming back."

"Freddie Weddie! I love you!"

"I know how it feels to be loved and this ain't it." Fred hobbles toward the chapel, favoring his trick knee. Heidi leans against the car hood and pouts.

Trey and his boys drive up and park next to Heidi. Trey gets out, shows her a map. "You know where the church is at?"

"Can't help you."

"Nice ride."

"Oh, this old thing. My daddy bought it for me. "

"Where's pops at?"

"He's back with his wife."

Heidi laughs with him. Pookie blows smoke out the window.

You know the phrase water seeks its own level? Heidi and Trey were made for each other. She's going to get pregnant by Trey or Pookie, hard to tell, but the three of them will open a chain of marijuana dispensaries.

Meanwhile, poor Fred limps past the gingko trees and into the chapel right before the ceremony begins. The bridesmaids, Mariah, Vanessa and Breanna are standing at the altar. Mustapha and three groomsmen from the Nation stand across from them. Breanna nudges Vanessa, who watches Fred find a seat in the rear of the chapel. Vanessa scans the audience for Heidi.

"He's alone," Breanna whispers. Vanessa shushes her and smiles to herself and pretends to not pay attention to the man she still loves. Just as Fred sits, the orchestra plays the wedding march and everyone stands. Fred struggles to his feet.

The doors to the chapel open and Toni steps out of a stream of light. The room gasps. She's a vision of heavenly confection. Wearing a full sweeping gown with a beaded bodice and a pleated gathered waist, encased in a chapel veil, Toni looks like an exquisite butterfly. Her body snatched tight in all the right places giving her an hour glass shape. The caterpillar finally emerged from her cocoon. Look at my Toni. Standing on her own.

The men in her family did their best to persuade her to let one of them walk her down the aisle, but the Toni they used to know, Toni the doormat, she's gone along with that doormat. She broke from tradition and decided to walk herself down the aisle. When she told them, she believes her father is with her, if only in spirit, the men fell silent and took their seats in the pew. Here she is, standing at one end of the chapel facing her groom at the other end. Her heart whispers, "Here we go. Are you ready, papa?" And Toni's father appears next to her and takes her by the arm. She feels his presence and knows he's there. That's the power of her faith.

"Will you be my wife?" That's how Mustapha asked Toni to marry him. Just like that. No long-winded promises. She didn't understand what he was asking at first. So she stood there, holding a plate of biscuits.

"Toni." Mustapha dropped down to one knee. "Will you be my wife?" A hush fell over the bakery. Everything seemed to go in slow motion. She glanced up at Vanessa and Mariah sitting by the window, who beam at her waiting for her reply. Breanna stopped taking a customer's order and jumped up and down.

"Woman. I'm asking you to be mine. Forever." And then she looked down at Mustapha, who had the most caring open face she had ever seen. She had imagined this moment for years and replayed it a thousand different ways but seeing Mustapha on his bended knee in the middle of her bakery left her speechless. He opened the Tiffany blue box and someone from the back of the room yelled out, 'If she won't, I will!' And the laughter broke the spell. She didn't know what kind of ring it was, what kind of diamond, what type of metal, Toni only knew the man she fell in love with publicly claimed her as his and she fell into his arms and almost knocked him down. Good thing her man is big and strong so he can handle all her womanhood.

"Is that a yes?" he asked.

"Yes!"

He slipped the princess cut diamond ring in a flawless platinum setting onto Toni's finger. The first thought that came to her mind when Toni finally looked at the ring was, she didn't have to buy it. That was three months ago to the day. Toni didn't need to be engaged for a year. Nah uh. She'd already been down that road. At thirty-eight, there was no time to waste. Why should she? She knew where she wanted to get married, what dress she was going to wear, and the kind of cake they were going to have. So the wedding is precisely ninety days after Jefferson Ulysses Washington also known as Mustapha Khan, depending on which document he's signing, asked our Antoinette Trammell to marry him.

Sometimes the best stories have a few twists and turns before you reach a happy ending. Toni, you never had anything to worry about. You were always wanted and always loved. You just had to let the right man enter your heart. And unlike my wedding day, you are walking toward your husband untarnished and untainted. You're not trying to prove something or become someone else. You have grown into your true self and Mustapha, who is waiting for you at the altar, is your chosen one. And I know from an authority on high that these two will have a long and loving union with six girls, all future Alpha Delta Zetas.

Is that Ms. Mariah Ash crying tears of joy? Well my goodness. I have seen everything. Mariah finds Dr. Simon Davis in the audience and smiles at him. Cliff isn't here… yet. Even though he signed the divorce documents under duress, the divorce proceedings came as a relief to both of them. Mariah has to wait six months until the divorce is final but until then, she and the good doctor have been spending time together. What Mariah doesn't know is that they'll remain devoted to each other and live as husband and wife although she'll never officially marry him. She'll become a second mother to his two kids from a previous marriage and eventually be glam-mama. And the one achievement she's been working towards will be realized next year when her company, Phoenix, is recognized as one of the best workplaces for women in California.

Presiding over the ceremony is Toni's mom, Pastor Cynthia Trammell. "Marriage ain't for sissies," she says. Mariah and Vanessa both solemnly nod. "Amen to that," Vanessa whispers. And the moment we've all been waiting for when the bride and groom kiss, the Pastor says the words her daughter has waited all her life to hear, "Ladies and gentlemen, Kings and Queens, I present my daughter and son-in-law, Mr. and Mrs. Mustapha Khan Jefferson Ulysses Washington! Mustapha scoops up his bride and jumps the broom with her in his arms. "Hallelujah!" Toni shouts.

The tented reception kicks off with a DJ announcing the wedding party. Mariah dances into the reception area doing her jerky version of the nae nae. Lord, she is stiff. The good doctor holds up two champagne glasses and makes his way to her when Cliff steps in-between them. Her face drops. "Cliff?"

He looks healthy and confident. "In the flesh. Give us a minute, my man." He says to Simon. Mariah gestures, it's fine. Cliff forces Mariah to hug him.

"What is it, Cliff?"

"I'm cured of my addictions and demons. And I've had time to reflect and think about what I want to do with the rest of my life." Cliff waits for a reaction but Mariah blinks with disinterest. When Mariah is done with someone, it's as though they never existed. Cliff continues, "I don't want any part of the music business. Too cutthroat and stressful for me. You're more suited for that environment."

"Thanks." Mariah's hoping he's not asking to get back together.

"My future is in yoga. I'm training to be a yogi."

"A yogi."

"Yoga changed my life, Mariah. Look at me. I'm slimmer. Stronger. I can touch my toes." He bends over to demonstrate.

"I'm happy for you, Cliff." Mariah looks past his bent body to see Vanessa and Leona waving her over. Cliff stands up and blocks her view.

"To be a true yogi, I have to go to India and study with real yogi masters."

"Have a good trip." Mariah steps aside. Again, he steps in her way.

"Should I go to India? I've been thinking about vegan farming too. You know, clean body, clean mind. What do you think?" He waits for her input. Mariah patiently smiles.

"Cliff."

"Yes?"

"The world is your oyster. Be the pearl." And with that, Mariah gently squeezes his shoulder and leaves to join the good doctor by the wall of pink and yellow peonies. Mariah passes Toni obsessing over the dessert table. Toni rearranges the pies and tarts as Mustapha tries to pull her away to join the party.

"We're running low on pecan pie and lemon tarts," she fusses.

"You outdid yourself, wife." Mustapha kisses her cheek. Instead of swatting him away, she leans into her husband, ah! Her husband and kisses him. "The girls can do this. Can't you ladies?" Mustapha asks the pledges of ADZ who enthusiastically nod. Toni adjusts the figurines on top of the red velvet wedding cake with lemon icing. She and the pledges baked all night to make sure the wedding cake and all the pies, cookies, cupcakes were fresh for today. Toni has plenty of space to accommodate large catering jobs since she renovated the car dealership into a bakery called Just Desserts. She also has a large doormat of a slice of seven layer cake and she doesn't mind when anyone wipes their feet on it. She sold her old bakery space to Vanessa who sells lotions, face cream and facial treatments. Her shop is called Beauty Queen and her tiara and sash are prominently on display. Beauty Queen is a welcome addition to the neighborhood. Along with products and services, Vanessa gives unofficial poise and etiquette lessons to the young girls. She's thinking about opening another line of business, beauty queen consultation to budding pageant girls. She should. She will.

Toni feeds Mustapha a chocolate cake pop when the University Chancellor, a thin, wiry man who prides himself on being a foodie approaches them holding a half-eaten pecan pie. "Mrs. Khan, I haven't had a pie like this since I was a boy." He praises, "My wife works for the Food Network and I know for a fact, she'd like to meet you."

Toni beams. "You have to try this one. I call it, Shut Your Mouth." She hands him a new plate with a big slice of lemon tart.

"If it lives up to its name, my wife is going to want a lot of these." He digs in. Savoring the first bite, his mouth puckers and his eyes close. "Is this gluten -free? Dairy-free?"

"Guilt free." Toni answers.

The Chancellor openly laughs, showing juicy globes of lemon in his teeth. He looks all of seven years old.

"People are too hard on themselves. They can't enjoy a little ole' tart without beating themselves up. I say, eat your cake and enjoy it. Guilt free."

The Chancellor nods and dives into another bite. He turns to Mustapha. "Congratulations, you married a talented woman."

Mustapha smiles at his wife, "Yes, I did." I hear Toni's heart skip a beat.

The DJ announces the first dance for the couple. Mustapha lovingly twirls his bride onto the dance floor. They are so adorable dancing to Mustapha's favorite singer, Lionel Richie. He softly sings to her about a feeling down deep in his soul. Toni's in heaven. When the song ends, the DJ opens the floor to everyone. That's when Fred makes his move.

He spots Vanessa dancing with Breanna. "Daddy!" Fred wobbles over to his family.

"May I cut in?" Fred asks. Breanna looks to her mom.

"You must be out of your mind." Vanessa says.

Fred's crestfallen. Breanna gives him a consoling hug before joining her friends.

"You can't dance like that." Vanessa bends down, twists his knee back like a seasoned chiropractor. She stands up and fluffs her hair. "Better?" He grabs her and clings to her for dear life.

He finally lets go. "Much better." Although the music is upbeat, he slow dances with her. He stares into her eyes. Appreciating her. Missing her. He deeply inhales her scent. "You smell nice."

"I found something new. "Tokyo Milk, Honey Moon."

"I like it." He inhales her again. "I love you. I don't know what happened to me. I lost my head. I want you back. I miss my family. I love you, Vanessa. You know it's always me and you."

"Fred. I moved on." She watches his face fall into disappointment. "I'm not the little homemaker you left behind. I'm different now. I'm a new woman. And the new Vanessa doesn't allow anyone to take her kindness for weakness."

"I'm different too."

"You look the same to me."

"Maybe we should get to know each other again."

"Maybe? Do you want to get to know me or not?"

"Yes."

"Well, then you can ask me out on a proper date."

"Boy, you're not making this easy."

"If you want easy, you can go…"

"Okay, okay. I can do better than take you on a date."

"I'm listening."

"Mrs. Vanessa Noisette Jones, will you do me the honor of not divorcing me even though I hurt you and I'm not worthy of your forgiveness but I'm begging you please, down on my knees, please be my wife again."

Breanna clamps her hand over her mouth to muffle the squealing. She's nodding yes to her mother. Vanessa looks deep into Fred's eyes. "Let's start with a date and see how you do."

Fred swings her around. "I'm going to date you for the rest of my life!"

The sun is setting and it's time for me to leave. You never want to be the last guest at a party, especially when you weren't invited. At the champagne tower, the ladies watch the sun make its descent into the Pacific Ocean. Vanessa hands Mariah a champagne flute. Toni raises her sparkling cider for a toast. "We did it! Now we all have our just desserts" Toni says.

"Ladies, I'm happy to raise a glass to new beginnings," Mariah adds.

"What about Oh-Hell-To-The-Naw, Naw, Naw club?" Toni asks.

Mariah and Vanessa look at each other, considering the question.

"Who needs a club when we have each other?" Vanessa reasons. The friends raise their glasses. "To each other!"

They are quickly joined by their inner circle: Mustapha, Fred, Breanna and Dr. Davis. The wedding photographer tells them to stand still. The ladies watch as a butterfly lands on Toni's shoulder. FLASH! The photographer snaps our photo, capturing smiling faces of old friends and new loves.

"I wish Jocelyn were here," Vanessa says, watching the sun disappear behind the ocean.

Toni watches the butterfly flutter away from them. "I have a feeling she was." She says a quick prayer for me. She turns to Mariah, "You think she heard me?"

Yes, I heard you, sister.

THANK YOU

I must acknowledge and thank the ladies of Alpha Kappa Alpha Sorority Incorporated, the ladies of Delta Sigma Theta Sorority Incorporated, the ladies of Sigma Gamma Rho Sorority Incorporated, the ladies of Zeta Phi Beta Sorority Incorporated, the ladies of Gamma Phi Delta Sorority Incorporated. Ladies, I appreciate you and am humbled by your generosity of spirit and sisterly support. And to all those who pledged in college or university and used to be active but are now busy with life, family and career; reach out to your sands, attend a graduate chapter meeting and reconnect with your sisters. No one knows you like your sorors.

To my husband, thanks for giving me the space and the time to pursue my ambitions. The nights you read each chapter out loud was the greatest act of love. To my son, thanks for letting me be your mom. You complete our family. To my mom, happy early birthday! See you in June.

Lastly, to my readers, I hope you enjoy the book. If so, leave a review on Amazon and let the world know there's a woman author who writes stories about us and for us.

Thank you!

AUTHOR

MINERVA STEWART

I'm a California, Bay Area girl. Born in Oakland, raised in Vallejo. My father was from Alabama and wanted to see the world. His travels eventually led him to his future wife in the Philippines. They met. They married. And they remained husband and wife for forty-seven years. Together they taught their four kids how to drive pick-up trucks, shoot guns and raise chickens to the background music of Charlie Pride and Johnny Cash and to value family and education. I'm also a product of the public-school system, back when they taught students home economics, drivers' education, typing and music classes, all life skills I still use today. After graduating from Vallejo High School, I attended UC Santa Barbara where I pledged a sorority and met exceptionally ambitious, talented young women. During my junior year, I transferred to CUNY Hunter College in New Year for a one-year program and fell in love with the art, culture and diversity of the city and New York became my home.

New York is where I launched my professional career as an advertising copywriter at UniWorld, where I met more amazingly creative women. After thirteen years in New York, I returned to California to attend the American Film Institute. I graduated with an MFA in Screenwriting. I sold a screenplay, optioned several others and pitched television pilots.

This story, My Awfully Wedded Husband, is an adaptation from one of my scripts. I have several other works that I am adapting and I'm currently writing an instructional guide to help screenwriters adapt their scripts to novels.

I currently live in Las Vegas with my husband, son and Italian Mastiff. Please contact me for book signings, book clubs, speaking engagements and panel discussions. Or, if you just want to drop me a line to say, "Hey, girl. Hey."

For upcoming book information and all inquiries:

www.minervastewart.com

Upcoming books

Can We Still Be Friends?

How to Adapt your Screenplay into a Novel